MAR -- 2018

IRVIN L. YOUNG MEMORIAL LIBRARY

P9-BZG-855

Tilly scrambled to her feet, but twisted her ankle in the process and fell back down.

Damn it.

Her heart pounded and she was having difficulty breathing. If she couldn't stand, she'd crawl. Sobbing, she all but clawed her way toward the butler's pantry. She only made it a few feet before she heard the metallic click of a gun.

ALSO BY TARA THOMAS

E-NOVELLAS
SHATTERED FEAR
HIDDEN FATE
TWISTED END

AVAILABLE FROM ST. MARTIN'S PRESS

DARKEST NIGHT

TARA THOMAS

St. Martin's Paperbacks

NOTE: If you purchased this book without a cover you should be aware that this book is stolen property. It was reported as "unsold and destroyed" to the publisher, and neither the author nor the publisher has received any payment for this "stripped book."

This is a work of fiction. All of the characters, organizations, and events portrayed in this novel are either products of the author's imagination or are used fictitiously.

DARKEST NIGHT

Copyright © 2018 by Tara Thomas.
Novella *Shattered Fear* Copyright © 2018 by Tara Thomas.
Excerpt from *Deadly Secret* Copyright © 2018 by Tara Thomas.

All rights reserved.

For information address St. Martin's Press, 175 Fifth Avenue, New York, NY 10010.

ISBN: 978-1-250-13800-2

Our books may be purchased in bulk for promotional, educational, or business use. Please contact your local bookseller or the Macmillan Corporate and Premium Sales Department at 1-800-221-7945, ext. 5442, or by e-mail at MacmillanSpecialMarkets@macmillan.com.

Printed in the United States of America

St. Martin's Paperbacks edition / March 2018

St. Martin's Paperbacks are published by St. Martin's Press, 175 Fifth Avenue, New York, NY 10010.

10 9 8 7 6 5 4 3 2 1

TO MY HUSBAND,
FOR HIS UNCONDITIONAL SUPPORT.

ACKNOWLEDGMENTS

A few years ago, I was on a research trip in Portland with my crit partner, Elle Mason. After a productive weekend, we had lunch on Sunday with author Tiffany Riesz. The conversation we had at lunch gave me the encouragement to go in a direction I wanted, but was uncertain and hesitant to travel. Elle and Tiffany, thank you both. You have no idea what an impact you've both had on me.

Not long after, I was looking for a new agent. I made a game plan, complete with timelines and spreadsheets. My first call was with Emily Sylvan Kim and it was as if we'd known each other forever. The call lasted for over an hour and when we hung up, I deleted my plan. Emily, thank you for being more than my agent, but also my sounding board, my safe place, and my friend.

Everyone I've spoken to at St Martin's Press about this series has been so supportive and excited, and no one more so than my editor, Alex Sehulster. Alex, working with you on this series has been an incredible experience, and I feel so fortunate to have the opportunity to do so. Thank you for making my stories look so good and taking it all in stride whenever I say, "I had this idea . . . ."

To every reader and book blogger who has offered encouragement while I worked on this new endeavor, and for understanding why I dropped off social media and was so bad at returning e-mails: You're the reason I have my dream job, and I couldn't do it without you.

To those new readers who have never read me before, it's so good to meet you. I hope you enjoy reading this series and would love to hear from you.

CHAPTER 1

As the youngest of three boys, Keaton Benedict was familiar with his older siblings using whatever means necessary to beat him at target practice. But as he stood and observed the target he'd missed completely on his last shot, he decided his oldest brother, Kipling, had hit a new low.

"Damn," Kipling said. "I don't think I've ever seen you miss something that bad. You do know you're supposed to hit the circle in the middle, right?"

"Like you didn't time your announcement to coincide perfectly with my shot." Keaton unloaded his gun and watched while Kipling lined up his own shot and hit the exact center of the target. Keaton shook his head. "You know I'm a better shot than you. The only way you ever win is by cheating."

Kipling grinned and started the process of unloading and cleaning his own weapon. "Now, that's where you're wrong. It wasn't cheating. It was strategy. Cheating would have been if what I'd told you was a lie."

Keaton had purposely focused on his brother's actions as opposed to his words because part of him hoped he had been lying. Unfortunately, not only had he lost to Kipling but it appeared that the news he'd shared while Keaton was taking his shot was true.

"Elise is really coming to stay with us this summer?" Keaton asked.

Kipling ran his hand through his dirty blond hair that was just a touch lighter than Keaton's own. All three of the Benedict brothers had the same coloring. Right down to the light brown eyes that looked almost golden in the right light. Keaton remembered when they were growing up how he wanted colored contacts because he got tired of people commenting on them all the time. Now he appreciated their eyes' uniqueness.

"Yes," Kipling said. "Her father asked if she could stay with us while she worked as an intern at a local law office. They sold their Charleston place when he retired and they moved to Pennsylvania."

Keaton bit his tongue so he wouldn't say what he wanted to. There was no way he could ever see Elise practicing law. For her entire life, she'd been groomed by her mother to be the perfect Southern lady and, in her mother's eyes, perfect Southern ladies did not work. Especially as a lawyer. Odds were, the Germain family was simply using the internship as a way to get Elise to stay at Benedict House for the summer in the hopes that Keaton would see her potential as a wife and be unable to keep himself from proposing.

There was a zero-to-none chance of that happening, but the Germains were old family friends and he wouldn't disrespect his brothers or his parents' memory by being anything other than polite to Elise.

With their weapons unloaded and cleaned, they headed out of the shooting range at their country club and walked toward the bar. It was tradition for the losing brother to buy drinks. They snagged a few stools and Kipling ordered for both of them.

"It's good to have you home," Kipling said, and looked up when the bartender brought their drinks over. "Thank you."

"You mean, it's good that I can finally join the family business."

"That, too." Kipling didn't try to hide his smile as he took a sip of his scotch.

As the oldest, Kipling ran the family shipping business, Benedict Industries. Though Kipling would beat Keaton's ass for calling it a business. He always referred to it as an empire. The middle Benedict brother, Knox, also worked there and it was assumed Keaton would as well.

Keaton didn't plan to buck the plan, so to say, but he didn't relish joining the company the way it was assumed he would. However, now was not the time to bring it up.

"I've only been out of college for a week," Keaton reminded him. "I'm still considering the possibilities."

Kipling didn't reply, but gave him that *I know what you're doing* look that every older brother had down to an art. Keaton was almost ready to ask him when they could talk about his new potential role when a country club employee approached them.

As he drew near, Kipling frowned at the slender white box the man held.

"Mr. Kipling Benedict?" the employee asked.

"Yes," Kipling replied, still eyeing the box.

"This was left at the reception desk for you." The man held the box out, but Kipling didn't take it.

"By whom?"

"No one saw them, sir." He placed the box on the

bar beside Kipling. "The employee working the desk had turned away and when she turned back, it was there." He raised an eyebrow. "Is there a problem, sir?"

Kipling sighed. "No. No problem. Thank you."

Keaton waited until the employee left. "What was that about?"

Kipling still hadn't opened the box; he twisted the pale blue ribbon that sat on top. "It's nothing, I'm sure. More of a nuisance than anything."

Keaton wasn't sure what he was talking about. "Have you gotten other white boxes with blue ribbon?"

"Yes." Kipling untied the ribbon. "And if this one is like the others, it'll contain a single rose."

Sure enough, once he took the top off, a long-stem rose set nestled in white tissue paper. Keaton didn't see a note. "Looks like someone has an admirer."

Kipling reached under the tissue and pulled out a typed note. Wordlessly, he passed it Keaton.

There were only a few words typed on the thick card stock.

THE TIME HAS COME.

Keaton flipped it over but there was nothing on the other side. He looked up at Kipling. "What the hell does that mean?"

Kipling shrugged. "I don't know, but they've all said the same thing."

"How many have there been?"

"Half a dozen." Kipling picked up the card. "They've always come to the office before. This is the first one that I've gotten outside."

"I don't like it."

"Me neither, but it's pretty harmless, all things considered." Kipling gathered the rose and the wrappings, and asked the bartender to throw them away.

"Are you going to tell the police?" Keaton asked.

Kipling actually laughed. "What? That someone's sending me roses? Yes, I'm sure that would go over really well."

Keaton had to admit that on the surface, it would seem rather minor, but as they walked out of the club, he couldn't help but notice Kipling looking around the parking lot. He had the uneasy feeling there was something bigger going on.

There were times The Gentleman was slightly irritated and times when he was mad as hell. But very rarely did he feel like he did today. Like he could skin someone alive with only a look.

His men gathered in the room behind him and he waited until he heard the door close before talking.

"Men, we have a problem and its name is Benedict. We are going to have to step up our plan. Take no prisoners. Show no mercy. As of today there is a new plan. The roses have laid the groundwork and they're showing some concern, but the threat the family poses is growing bigger.

"The first step is to eliminate a problem I should have taken care of years ago. Unfortunately, this person isn't a Benedict."

There was a slight murmur behind him.

"Quiet," he said, and the chatter stopped. "The people overseeing her removal have already been notified. If you all do your jobs, she won't know what hit her and we can deal with the Benedicts once and for all."

The end of the night was always Tilly Brock's favorite time of day and not just because it meant she could go home. She loved how quiet the outside world was. She would step outside of what had been bustling chaos of the nightclub and into the quiet stillness of a sleeping world.

She also enjoyed the short moments she had while everybody was preparing to leave when she could chat with other employees. She was closest to the bartender, Raven. They were the same age, attended the same school, and planned to graduate at the same time. With the spring semester over, they both only had summer school to get through.

"Have you started the countdown yet?" Tilly asked Raven as the petite bartender wiped the countertops down.

"Are you kidding?" she replied with a grin. "I've been counting down since last August. Two more months and I walk out of this place forever. Maybe sooner."

"How's that?"

The introvert bartender's eyes danced. "I have an interview coming up the day after tomorrow at Bergman and Biddle."

Tilly recognized the name of the prestigious advertising agency. "That's fabulous! How exciting. I bet you won't miss this place at all." Two blond dancers Tilly had dubbed the Wonder Twins sashayed their way past them. They had been working in the club for six months and they hated the fact that Tilly routinely got better tips and was able to keep her clothes on. Perhaps if they were better dancers, they could earn more. Club gossip alluded that they were only able to keep their positions because they provided "special services" for the managers.

"Good night, bar wenches," Twin One said, and Twin Two laughed like it was the funniest joke she'd ever heard.

Raven rolled her eyes as the duo made their way out the door. "I definitely won't miss them."

"Right?" Tilly shook her head. "But then I tell myself every job will have difficult people and you never know what pain someone is hiding that makes them the way they are."

"That's why they hate you, you know. Because you're a good person and everyone likes you."

Tilly eyed the manager as he walked out of the office. "Not everyone."

Raven lowered her voice as he approached. "He likes you. He just hates that he can't get you to preform special favors for him." She added air quotes around favors.

"The very thought makes me throw up in my mouth." Tilly forced a smile as the manager stopped at the bar. "Good night, Mr. Granger."

He grunted at Tilly and looked at Raven. "I've already locked the back. Make sure you lock the front door when you leave. It was unlocked when I got here this afternoon."

"I don't know how, sir," Raven said. "I know I locked it last night."

"Then why was it unlocked this afternoon?"

"Raven isn't the only employee with a key," Tilly said. She hadn't worked the night before, but she knew Raven and there was no way her friend had forgotten to lock up.

"I wasn't talking to you, girl." He nodded toward Raven. "If it happens again, you're fired."

"But—" Raven started.

"No buts." And with that, he turned and walked out.

"I know I locked that door," Raven said when he'd left. "I know I did."

"I'm sure you did."

Raven bit her lip, looking like she wanted to say something, but shook her head.

"What?" Tilly asked.

"I'm sure it's nothing, but when I left last night, there was a man standing outside. I didn't see him until I'd locked up and turned around and nearly ran into him. He was all nice and everything. Kept apologizing. But that's how I know I locked the door because he walked away and I double-checked."

"That sounds creepy. He was just standing there?"

"But it wasn't, really. Not after I got over the initial shock. He was nice. Wore a suit and everything. He was like someone's dad."

"I don't care. I still don't like it. You don't need to be walking out after work by yourself." She started to add that just because someone wore a suit didn't mean they could be trusted, but didn't. Raven was an adult. Tilly grabbed her purse from the barstool. "Ready?"

Neither one of them had a car, so they both took the bus to and from work. Tilly typically didn't mind taking public transportation by herself, but tonight she was thankful for the company. Raven said she was glad to have Tilly as a witness that she had locked the door, but there was an underlying hint of worry in her tone that led Tilly to believe she was a bit more unsettled than she let on.

Tilly was unsettled as well. Part of her hated the job, but the upside of it was graduating at the end of the summer debt free. She'd get her diploma and then thank her lucky stars that she would never have to wait tables or serve drinks in a micromini and crop top again. Even better, when she held that diploma in her hands, she wouldn't owe anyone anything. Years ago when her father had been accused, wrongly, she always thought, of siphoning funds from Benedict Industries, and her mother was diagnosed with breast cancer, she'd feared the only way to graduate was with a mountain of debt.

She'd been working at this club for just over three years. It hadn't always been easy juggling her school-work with the late nights and early mornings the club required. But the tips were great and the club had a strongly enforced no-touching-in-public-rooms rule.

In a perfect world she wouldn't have to work at a gentlemen's club to pay her way through college. No, in a perfect world, her parents would still be alive and her dad's reputation wouldn't be tarnished by those false allegations of embezzlement.

And since she was naming everything that would be in her perfect world, Keaton Benedict would still be in her life.

But over eight years ago, her father *had* been fired from Benedict Industries when Keaton's father accused him of stealing from the company. It made no sense at the time and the following years had done nothing to lend credibility to the claim.

Be that as it may, the elder Benedict believed the worst of her father and he'd left the company disgraced. It was something her dad never got over and was, she believed, the main factor in the heart attack that took his life a short six months later.

Her mother did her best, often working three jobs at a time, but it wasn't enough. In the blink of an eye they had gone from well-off to welfare. Worse, she lost her two closest friends, Elise Germain, whose father actually replaced Tilly's dad, and Keaton Benedict, who had been her first kiss the week before her life changed forever.

CHAPTER 2

"To strong booze and hot women!"

Keaton Benedict raised his glass at his friend Brian's less-than-sober toast and shook his head. One would have thought the guy would be better able to hold his liquor.

"Hell," Michael, another friend, grumbled from the barstool beside him. "Someone take him home to sleep it off before he starts to sing."

Keaton shook his head. "Let him have his fun." He smiled. "Besides, I want to see if his Céline Dion has improved."

Michael tapped his bottle to Keaton's glass. "You're a mean bastard, Benedict."

"Never claimed to be anything else."

Michael chuckled, but didn't say anything further. Keaton took a sip of his gin and tonic and looked around the smoke-filled bar of the upscale Charleston gentlemen's club they had picked for their post college graduation celebration.

One last night of debauchery. That was what his friends wanted. When they had arranged this party,

Keaton had gone along with them, but as a Benedict, he knew the truth. The debauchery never had to end. Not if you knew how to play your cards right, and as the youngest Benedict, he'd never had that problem.

"There we go. Finally," Michael said, as the lights around them dimmed and everyone's attention turned to the stage at the front of the club. "Time for dancing."

Two scantily clad women strutted out onto the stage. Keaton was too far away to see details. All he could make out were tiny bikini tops and even tinier thongs. Blondes. And pretty enough to make any red-blooded man fantasize about ripping the scraps of fabric off them. A movement to the side of the stage caught his eye. A server. He only saw her profile, but there was something about her.

He slid off the barstool to get a closer look.

"Hey, man," Michael called after him. "Where are you going?"

Keaton didn't reply.

"Where's Benedict going?" he heard someone ask.

"He's interested in a *dancer? Here?*" someone else asked.

Keaton shook his head; it wasn't a dancer that captured his attention. He wasn't a stranger to the numerous clubs around the city that catered to wealthy men and their carnal needs. However, he'd never singled out any particular woman while at one. After all, he'd always said, one half-naked woman was just as good as another. As made evident by the number of times his picture was in the society pages, but never with the same woman twice.

And yet, here he was, eyes fixed on the petite waitress at the side of the stage, currently trying to blend into the background and not take away from the duo on the stage. It was a horrible failure. He wasn't sure why the management even felt the need to put anyone onstage with her working here. How could anyone look at those two with *her* in the room?

She moved with a grace that made the two blondes look like ducks swimming alongside a swan. She stretched out her hand to pass a glass to a man sitting on the far inside of a booth. Everyone in her vicinity turned to watch her lithe body.

"Drooling over a topless dancer?" Michael asked, coming up behind him. "I have to say, I'm a bit surprised. They look a bit rough."

"Not a dancer," Keaton let slip before he could stop himself.

Michael moved to stand beside him and followed his line of sight. His low whistle signaled he saw the woman in question. "Hot damn. Wait until a certain blonde hears about this. I'm sure Miss Elise Germain will love the fact that her intended is drooling over a half-naked barmaid."

"Shut the fuck up." Keaton didn't shift his attention from the goddess taking drink orders. "I'm not engaged."

"Please," Michael's voice dripped with sarcasm. "You two have been promised to each since you were what? Fifteen?"

Keaton mumbled a curse under his breath, but right now, he couldn't focus on anything other than the serving siren. It sounded so crazy, he couldn't even verbalize it, but he thought he knew her from somewhere. Something about the way she moved called to him. Pulled him forward for a better look.

He took another step toward her.

She was magnificent. And the way she moved con-

tinued to captivate the audience near her. Keaton's eyes
traveled over her body, taking in as many details as
possible: her light brown skin, the curve of her hips, and
the slope of her breasts covered by a tight cropped shirt.
He knew they would be oh-so-soft to touch. His eyes
drifted higher at the same time she turned her head his
way and he froze.

Tilly.

He couldn't breathe. It couldn't be.

What was she doing in Charleston? The last he'd
heard, her family had moved to Texas. Granted, they'd
both been fourteen at the time, but he'd never forgotten the day he'd got home from school, walked into the
eerily quiet kitchen, and discovered his life had changed
forever.

Tilly always came over to his house after school to
help him with his homework. Usually her mother would
come over with her and gossip with his mom. But there
was nothing that day. He'd looked out the back door to
get a peek of their house and gasped. There were men
all over the yard, carrying furniture.

He'd run back inside and up the stairs to his mother's
room and, with a stomach filled with dread, asked
where Mama Ann and Tilly were. His mother arched
a perfectly shaped eyebrow. She didn't like that her
children called their neighbor Mama Ann, but everyone called her that. It was just her personality. She was
so kind and loving, the name came naturally.

"They're moving to Texas," she said, and his world
shifted out of focus.

"Why?" he managed to croak out. Texas was so far
away. It made no sense why they would move away
from their family like that and so suddenly.

"It's been discovered that Mr. Brock has been embezzling money from your father."

"What?" He couldn't believe it. Not Tilly's dad. He was stealing from them? Something didn't sound right.

His mother gave him a sad smile. "I'm afraid he was caught red-handed. The Brock family's basically ruined now. Best they move and try to start over."

His parents had always joked that he and Tilly would get married one day. Everyone talked about it and he didn't even care because Tilly was smart and pretty. The week before, he'd kissed her for the first time. Her lips had been soft and sweet, and he'd looked forward to kissing them over and over. How could he kiss her if she were in Texas?

"Your father's going to promote Howard Germain. Isn't his daughter in your class, too?"

Elise. Tilly's best friend. Or was. He felt sick. He mumbled a half-intelligible answer to his mom and ran down the stairs to the living room. He had to call Tilly. Had to talk to her, even if it was only to say good-bye.

But their phone had already been disconnected and when he went to their house, the men moving all the furniture told him they'd already left.

Tilly Brock put on her best plastic smile and muttered a soft, "Excuse me, please," to the man blocking her path to her customer. She recognized the move for what it was: an attempt to make her reach across him. *Two more months. Two more months.* She grit her teeth and made sure the men saw just enough of her cleavage as she handed the drink to the waiting customer.

"Thank you, darling," he said, eyes firmly planted on her chest, never once looking her in the eyes. "Why ain't someone as pretty as you up onstage?"

Like she didn't hear that ten times a night. Her mother might not roll over in her grave at the thought of her daughter serving drinks at a gentlemen's club, but Tilly knew she'd come back from the dead for the sole purpose of telling her how disappointed she was if she even thought about dancing topless.

"Two left feet," she told the guy instead.

"Trust me." His laugh gave her chills. "It ain't your feet we're interested in."

Two more months. I can do two more months.

Onstage, the dance was almost over. One of the blond twins glared at her and in doing so, tripped and almost fell. Several men booed. The other twin shot her a look that told Tilly they were blaming everything on her. Oh well, what else was new. It wasn't a day that ended in "y" if she didn't piss off the Wonder Twins.

She gathered several empty glasses and nodded as a few drink orders were given. Her tray was heavy, but she thought she could make it back to the bar. She turned that way and suddenly felt someone's eyes drilling holes into her from the back of the room. Out of habit, she lifted her head to try and find who was watching her so intensely.

She scanned the crowd, but no one looked out of place. Then she saw him, standing slightly off to the side, watching her with an easy confidence, but with a tilt of his head that somehow seemed familiar. He recognized her at the same instant she recognized him.

Keaton Benedict.

Her tray and glasses fell to the floor.

CHAPTER 3

Tilly blinked and he was gone. Just that quickly. She scanned the crowd, but Keaton had disappeared. She wondered if it'd really been him or if she'd only imagined him standing there.

"Damn klutz."

"I think I stepped on some glass."

"These are two-hundred-dollar shoes."

Unfortunately, she did not imagine the mess she'd made, the angry customers, or Mr. Granger, standing near the bar with his arms crossed. The twins, wearing matching see-through wraps, stood beside him, both with evil grins.

Shit.

Not only had she made a god-awful mess, but she knew the Wonder Twins would somehow make it out that the trip and resulting boos were Tilly's fault. They never got in trouble, of course. Tilly supposed she could provide her own special service for Mr. Granger, but in all honesty she'd much rather put up with his anger than to have his dick in her mouth.

She held her hand up before he could talk. "I take full responsibility. It won't happen again."

He snorted. "Clean it up and then come to my office." Then to the blondes, he said, "Good job as always, girls."

Twin One and Twin Two sashayed past her with their noses stuck in the air.

"Our dancing's a gift," Twin One said.

"I'd like to exchange it for a gift card," Tilly mumbled under her breath.

She bent down and started picking up the larger pieces of glass. Not for the first time, she missed Janie, who used to work the bar, but had moved to Washington, DC, with her fiancé. If Janie had still been working at the club, not only would she have come over to help, but she'd crack a joke or two and make Tilly laugh as well.

"Need some help?" a voice from her past asked.

Her heart skipped a beat, causing her hand to slip, cutting her thumb on the broken glass. "Damn it." She shook her finger, trying not to let the threatening tears escape.

In a swift move, Keaton knelt beside her, took the tray from her other hand and started picking up fragments of glass.

"I somehow feel as if I should apologize." He never stopped what he was doing as he continued to talk while clearing the floor. "I don't believed you would have dropped anything if it hadn't been for me."

She had no idea what to say to him. What do you say to someone you'd spoken with every day for eight years and then didn't see for another eight? Not that it mattered. The shock of seeing him seemed to strip her of her ability to speak because when she opened her mouth, nothing came out.

Instead, she rocked back and sat on her heels, while doing her best not to flash the entire club with her underwear. She took a deep breath and tried again.

"No, it's not," she said, taking a few seconds to study him. He hadn't changed all that much. He'd always been a ridiculously handsome boy and had matured into a devilishly handsome man. His hair was the same dirty blond and his eyes were the strange light brown that looked almost golden at times. All three of the Benedict brothers had that odd eye color. The lanky frame of a teenaged boy had been replaced by solid muscle.

Out of the corner of her eye she saw Granger watching her. He really wouldn't like the fact that a customer was helping. She reached for a large chunk of glass the same time Keaton did and their hands brushed. She jerked away.

He held her gaze. "Tilly . . ."

He hesitated and before he could finish, a silver stiletto stepped between them. "Hey there, handsome," Wonder Twin One said. "Why don't you come with me?"

"What are you doing here?" Tilly asked, when what she wanted to ask was, *Just what the hell do you think you're doing?*

"Mr. Granger sent me," she said with a shake of her head that made her blond waves bounce around her shoulders.

"Why?" Keaton asked in a hard voice Tilly didn't recognize. She glanced at him, surprised at how angry he looked.

Apparently, his tone of voice shocked the other

woman as well. She shrugged. "I don't know. I guess he thought you needed more than what she could provide," she said with a pointed look at Tilly. "He wants me to give you a private dance."

Tilly was used to the barely concealed barbs, but seriously? She acted like she wasn't even listening to the conversation, afraid if she did, she'd blurt out something that would get her in more trouble than she was already in.

Keaton picked up the last big shard of glass and put it on the tray. "I would think it's very clear to anyone who looks that I'm busy helping his employee. I'd also like to point out that no one else is."

"It's okay. Really," Tilly said.

"It is not okay." Keaton was still watching the blonde as he took his wallet out of his pocket and peeled off several bills. Tilly couldn't see the amount from where she stood, but she could see the other woman's eyes grow large. "I assume this will cover the cost of a dance?"

Tilly eyed him in disgust while trying to avoid what she knew would be a seething look of victory from the blonde. As it was, she couldn't miss the "Oh yes, more than enough," given in reply.

Damn, but this shift sucked. Tilly turned to take her tray back to the bar, but Keaton put a hand on her arm to stop her.

"Good," Keaton said. "Then take it to your manager and tell him the dance isn't wanted or needed."

"What?" Tilly heard the blonde say and she couldn't help but smile. "We can't take your money and not give you anything in return."

Tilly watched in satisfaction as the twin handed the money back to Keaton. He caught her staring and winked. Wanting to talk to him just a few moments more, she turned her attention to the twins, and played on their gullibility, since Twin Two had just walked up. "That new dancer Granger hired walked in about thirty minutes ago. She asked for you. I think she wants advice or something?"

The twins looked at each other and then with almost synchronized movements, tossed their heads and walked toward the employees lounge.

Keaton waited for them to disappear from sight before speaking. "I'm sorry we got interrupted, but I don't think this is the best time to chat. When do you get off?" He hesitated. "That is, if you want to chat with me."

Tilly couldn't believe it: After all these years daydreaming about Keaton walking into the club, he'd actually done it.

"Two hours," Tilly said.

Keaton flashed her a smile. One that was so familiar yet seemed even sexier now. "See you then."

Once he left, Tilly carried her tray to the bar, where Raven was working.

"Wonder Twins are in a rare mood tonight," Tilly said while cleaning the tray.

Raven shook her head and gave a soft, "I saw," in reply.

They worked side by side for a few minutes. Tilly kept playing the encounter with Keaton over and over in her head. She still had a hard time believing he had been here. In this bar.

She loaded her tray up and was getting ready to head back to the area near the dance floor when one of the Wonder Twins blocked her path.

She turned to Tilly. "Where are you going, klutz?"

Tilly rolled her eyes. Either they hadn't found the new girl or else the twins decided they didn't want to share advice. "I'm trying to get these drinks to customers up front. Maybe they'll drink enough to forget that dance you did."

"Ha ha. Very cute."

"It's funny you think I'm joking." Tilly kept walking while the Wonder Twin trotted along behind. Tilly finally turned. "You know, if you want to do something useful, you could mop where the tray dropped."

"It's funny you think I mop," the twin said, obviously pleased with herself at using a similar line Tilly had just used.

Tilly spoke soft enough so only the Wonder Twin would hear her. "I'd rather mop than have to suck old-man dick. How long did it take Granger to come? Sore mouth?"

"You bitch!" The Wonder Twin took a swing and Tilly, without thinking, threw the tray up as a shield. The twin couldn't stop in time and her hand crashed down on the tray. For the second time that night, Tilly stood in a mess of glass and booze.

Of course, by that time, a security guard finally decided to see what was happening. Not surprising since they'd also captured the attention of the entire crowd.

The guard stood over the blond woman sprawled out on the floor. "What's going on?"

"She pushed me," the twin said pointing at Tilly, sitting up. "And when I told her to leave me alone and tried to leave, she dropped the tray on me."

"You lying . . ." Tilly told herself to remain calm. She looked up at the guard. "You know she's lying, right? I mean, you were standing right there. You saw everything."

"I didn't see nothing," he said, and the blonde's eyes flashed in victory.

"Ohhh, I think I have glass in my foot. Help me?" the twin asked, holding out her hand and fluttering her eyelashes.

Tilly sighed. She should have known better than to deliberately piss off either of the twins. It never ended well for her and since the Wonder Twins had management eating out of their hands, it wasn't hard to know which side they'd pick.

She didn't even make it back to the mess with a mop in hand when she heard Granger yell, "Tilly! Office!" The twins stood behind him with matching expressions of glee.

Keaton walked to the historic district where his brothers had offices. He'd decided to park his car at their office building, thinking it would be safer there than on one of the bar's side streets. He stepped over a pile of clothes and various stuffed bags and frowned because there was no one anywhere nearby. It wasn't usual for the homeless to leave their stuff unattended. Or at least that had been his experience while doing charity work. He looked around for a few minutes, but didn't see anyone.

Keaton checked the time, noting when he needed to be back to meet Tilly, and started the walk to his car. Once inside, he decided to drive the long way home because that would take him back past the club. He'd just driven past the entrance when he saw a familiar figure dart across the road. *Tilly?*

He pulled up, got out of his car, and went to where the woman stood at the bus stop, and was surprised to see it was her. Her arms were crossed and she tapped her foot while waiting. The two men who were also waiting for the bus nearby watched her with wary eyes. He didn't blame them; she looked mad enough to bend the bus stop sign in half.

"Tilly?" he asked, not really sure if he should try to touch her or not. "What happened? Are you okay?"

She nodded. "I was sent home early."

His chest felt hollow. "Was it because I walked out? If I need to go explain or talk to someone, I'll do it."

"It wasn't you." She straightened her back. "It was on account of me dropping another tray. I'd blame it on the Wonder Twin taking a swing at me, but I probably brought it on myself when I told her to enjoy sucking Granger's dick."

"The same blond ones from earlier?" *The evil little scumbags.*

She nodded. "You know, they aren't natural blondes."

"There weren't much of them that were natural, if you know what I mean." He waggled his eyebrows to lighten the mood and smiled when that got a laugh out of her.

"True. I remember one of them saying they got boobs for graduating high school."

"Jesus. Are you serious?"

"Right?"

"Want me to take care of them?" He was joking. Of course he was, he thought. But again, it got a laugh out of her. "I'm sure Kipling knows a few people."

"No, it's okay."

"So, the upside is that you're free now." He waved to his car. "I have wheels . . ."

He needed to get away from the club before he went

inside and did something he'd regret. Like give that manager a nice talking-to. And by talking-to, he actually meant threaten. But doing something like that would only make him feel better. It really wouldn't be in Tilly's best interest. His heart felt lighter as he remembered the way he looked out for her when they were kids. No one picked on her twice or else they'd find themselves dealing with him.

She held out her hand. "Lead the way."

He opened the door for her and as they drove away from the club, he felt better with each passing mile. Unfortunately, he couldn't say the same for Tilly. As they drew deeper into the downtown district, her hands tightened in her lap and her eyes darted around the area.

"Tilly?" he finally asked. "Are you okay?"

"Are we going to your house?" she asked, and he knew he didn't imagine the distress in her voice.

"I was planning on it." Where else would they go? Home was the best place to go.

"Can we go somewhere else?"

He frowned, but didn't want to push her. Later, when they had talked more, he'd find out why she didn't want to be at his house. "Like a hotel?"

It was the only other place he could think of and he hesitated even bringing it up because it made him sound like he wanted to sleep with her. He glanced over at her to make sure she didn't take his suggestion to mean he was a creeper, but she'd visibly relaxed.

"Yes, that would be fine."

It wasn't anything for a Benedict to be seen getting a hotel room for the night, even as late as it currently was. Hell, he himself had done it a time or two. But this was different. Tilly wasn't a one-night stand he didn't want in his home and, in addition, he didn't want the fact that she was checking into a hotel late at night—with him—to reflect badly on her. More than one of his dates had been photographed leaving a hotel after spending a night with him.

He turned the car around. "Let's go to Kiawah Island. I don't want your reputation to be tarnished."

"Umm," she said. "You do realize I work at a gentlemen's club, right?"

"There's a big difference between that and renting a room for the night with a guy you left the club with."

She didn't say anything, but a soft smile covered her face and he knew he'd said the right words. The miles passed quickly. It was after midnight, so traffic was light and it wasn't long before they arrived.

"I'm only working at the club to put myself through school," she said with a sigh, out of the blue. "I have two more months left."

"You don't have to justify anything to me."

"I didn't want you to think less of me."

"Never." How could he possibly pass judgment when it had been his family that was probably the cause of her having to work there in the first place?

He'd never completely bought his parents' story that Mr. Brock embezzled money. Not Mr. Brock, with his easygoing nature and a sense of compassion, whose kindness was surpassed only by his wife's. And quite possibly, his daughter's.

Tilly was still as gorgeous as ever and it didn't surprise him that she was in school. She'd always been smart. Smarter than he'd ever been. She used to sit at the big table in the Benedict House kitchen and patiently go over his homework with him.

He pulled into the parking lot of an upscale hotel. "Stay in the car while I check us in."

It only took him a few minutes to secure a room and order food and toiletries to be delivered. Tilly was waiting for him in the car and they entered the hotel together. He felt a bit awkward. Normally when he met a woman at a hotel, they'd be all over each other. But this, this was Tilly, and she was different.

With Tilly, he wanted to sit down and talk, find out what she'd been up to, and see how the teenaged girl he'd had a crush on had turned into the intriguing woman he saw today. Sure, she was hot as hell, but that was secondary to everything else.

He unlocked the door and let her enter first. He'd decided to get a suite, if for no other reason than the bed wouldn't be the focus of the room. This way they could talk. And eat. He wondered when she last ate.

Tilly took in the room with a wary look before sinking into the love seat in the living room and taking off her heels. "Hope you don't mind," she said. "My feet are killing me."

Keaton shook his head. "Make yourself at home."

She patted the spot beside her. "Why don't you sit down?"

"I will in a minute. I'm waiting for a delivery."

She tilted her head, but right at that moment someone knocked to the door.

"Delivery for Mr. Benedict," a voice said from the hallway.

He smiled. "And there it is. I hope you're hungry. I ordered us dinner when I checked in."

"Famished."

Keaton opened the door and took the offered paper

bag and pointed to the coffee table when asked where he'd like the tray. After giving the deliveryman a tip and showing him the door, he took a seat beside Tilly.

She leaned forward toward the silver-domed plates. "What's for dinner?"

"I went simple." He lifted one of the lids. "Cheeseburger and fries. Hope you haven't gone vegetarian."

She took the plate he offered her. "No way. This is perfect." She took a bite with closed eyes and moaned. "Oh my God. This is the best. Thank you."

"You're welcome." Pleased that she was happy with dinner, he took a bite of his own burger. "When did you move back from Texas?"

She opened her eyes and swallowed the bite she had in her mouth. "What?"

"When did you move back from Texas?" he repeated, not understanding why she looked so confused.

She slowly shook her head and a strange sense of dread filled him.

"Oh, fuck," he said. "You didn't move to Texas."

At her whispered "No," he set the burger down, no longer hungry.

"Did your mom tell you we moved to Texas?" she guessed.

"Yes, but it never made sense that you would leave so fast and go so far." And whenever he'd bring the Brocks up to either of his parents, they would refuse to talk about them.

"I always guessed your mom would say something like that." Tilly frowned at her burger. "That's why I didn't want to go to your house tonight. I'm not ready to see her yet."

"Mom died," he said simply. "About five years ago.

She and Dad were on a trip to Europe on a private jet. It crashed."

She grew pale. "Keaton, I'm sorry. I didn't know."

"It's okay. But I'd rather not talk about it."

She nodded in agreement and he vowed to himself that one day he'd find out what really happened between his parents and the Brock family, but not tonight. Tonight he didn't want to think about the past. He especially didn't want to talk about his mother.

But he did want to know one thing. "How's Mama Ann?"

He couldn't help but smile when he thought about her. She'd been so full of life, so carefree and joyous. It was one of the reasons why he loved being around her. She was one of those people who just naturally drew people toward her.

"Breast cancer," Tilly said, tears filling her eyes.

His chest ached as the truth hit him and he realized he'd never see her again. That he never got to say goodbye. "When?" he asked in a tight voice.

"Two years ago. You really didn't know?"

She was looking at him strangely, as if she thought he should have known. But why would she think that? Especially when he'd just told her he'd thought she'd been in Texas all these years.

She must have seen the questions in his eyes because she continued, "Kipling sent Mama checks to cover the chemo treatments. She tried to send them back, but he wouldn't take them. He said she was family and he always took care of family."

There was little she could have said that would have surprised him more than the statement that his oldest brother not only knew about Tilly and Mama Ann, but called them family and was also sending them money.

Why would he be doing that if Tilly's dad had been embezzling money? It didn't make any sense. Though, truth be told, little of his conversation with Tilly had made any sense. But she was unexpectedly back in his life and damn it all, he was going to figure every detail out.

CHAPTER 4

One look at Keaton's face told Tilly all she needed to know. He hadn't been avoiding her for years. Hadn't ignored her mother's passing. He hadn't known.

"We need something stronger to drink," she said.

"What would you like?"

"Gin and tonic?"

Without a word, Keaton stood up and walked to the minibar. When he returned, he handed her a glass. She took the drink, enjoying the burn as it made its way down her throat. Beside her, Keaton watched her with careful eyes.

"What are you in school for?" he asked.

She took another sip. "You won't believe me."

"Try me."

"Education. I'm going to be a teacher."

He nodded. "Yeah, I totally see that."

"Right. The elementary teacher who works at a gentlemen's club." That was another reason she was looking forward to quitting in two months.

"Hey." Keaton set his glass on the table and turned

to face her. "Don't sell yourself short like that. I think you'll be a wonderful teacher."

"Based on what?"

"I wouldn't have made it through the ninth grade without you by my side." He scooted closer to her, so close their legs almost touched. "Remember?"

She remembered it had been so easy to talk to him back then. When there were no grown-up worries to weigh on her mind. When they weren't defined by status and were friends because they liked hanging out together.

Actually, it was still easy to talk to him. Either that or the gin was affecting her already. Come to think of it, she did feel a bit weightless and warm.

"I remember," she said, looking at his lips. They had only kissed once and they had both been fourteen, but, oh, she remembered that kiss. Back then, she'd thought he was a great kisser. She had a feeling he'd only grown better with time.

He lifted his hand and played with a piece of her hair. "I used to think you were pretty."

Used to think?

His head drifted oh so near. "But now, you're downright beautiful."

She knew they were more than sweet words spoken by a player. She only had to look in his eyes to see the truth of that. And no matter what happened after tonight, for the moment she had her childhood friend and first kiss back. Damned if she was ready to give them back.

So instead of pulling back like she knew she should, she moved closer and placed her hand on his thigh. "You're not too bad-looking yourself, stranger."

He dropped the piece of hair he'd been playing with and traced her lips with his thumb. "Remember our kiss?"

She bit the fleshy part of his thumb, surprising herself with her aggressiveness. "Every day."

His sucked-in breath and low moan might have meant he was surprised as well, but also showed he liked it. His voice was husky when he spoke again. "I think I need a reminder."

"Yes," she managed to whisper before his lips brushed over hers. Softly. Almost a tease. In fact, it would have been a tease if they hadn't touched hers again. Stronger this time as if he'd been testing her, making sure she wasn't going to pull away.

There was no force on earth that could pull her away from him tonight.

She woke before he did the next morning. Even though they hadn't done anything other than kiss and cuddle and talk, she'd feared things would be awkward between them in the morning light. Sure, he'd been happy to see her last night, but how would that translate to the real world?

Though she'd never been his equal economically, she was very much aware of just how far apart they were on that particular scale. The Keaton she used to know wouldn't care and the man she'd talked with last night didn't appear to, either, so why was she so worried about it?

"Hey."

She looked down to find him watching her. "Hey."

"What's up with the frown?"

"I don't want to step outside this room. I like what I found in here."

He smiled and reached up to wrap his arms around her and brought her to rest where she was almost on top of him. "I like it, too. Let's stay here forever."

Her giggles were silenced by his kiss. Soft and gentle, his lips brushed over hers. Her heart sighed and she forgot what she'd been so worried about.

He pulled back slightly. "Of course, they'll probably want to clean the room eventually."

"Right. And I do have to go to class if I want to graduate."

"There is that." He entwined their fingers. "How about this? We agree to leave the room, but only because I'm taking you to dinner tonight."

"I have to work tonight."

"Damn."

"How about we do breakfast tomorrow?" she asked. "There's a little biscuit place by the waterfront. Their biscuits remind me of Mama's." She normally preferred to go there alone, but Keaton had loved her mom, too. She wanted him with her.

"It's a date, then," he said, with a smile on his lips and understanding in his eyes.

She had a feeling they would handle the real world just fine.

Her happy mood continued after Keaton dropped her off at her apartment with another kiss and promises of breakfast the next morning. She breezed through the homework she had planned for the day and before she knew it, it was already time to head back into work.

Raven had arrived before her and she let out a sigh of relief. Apparently, all had been well when Granger arrived. Tilly stepped inside, still smiling. However, seeing Granger standing at the bar with one of the Wonder Twins put a bit of a damper on her mood. The club didn't open for another hour and the twins wouldn't dance for at least another two. Why was she here?

"Tilly," Granger said. "Mindy wanted to come in early to talk with you. I don't know what went on last night, but you two work it out because if it happens again, you're both out."

Tilly nodded and hated that she felt like Mindy was trying to pull one over on her. Even so, she knew she wasn't able to hide her suspicion when Mindy waved toward a barstool.

"I wanted to apologize for last night," the twin gushed out before Tilly's butt hit the stool. "I was way out of line and it won't happen again."

Tilly didn't say anything. Surely, she hadn't shown up at work hours earlier than she needed to just to say that?

Mindy dabbed an eye. "The thing is, you're so perfect. I mean, you're pretty, and smart, and you're going to school and will be out of here and Mandy and I will still be taking our clothes off and dancing for money." She took a deep breath and gave a weak smile. "When that hottie showed up last night and only had eyes for you? I kinda lost it. I'm sorry."

There was little Mindy could have said that would have surprised her more. She reached her hand out and put it on top of Mindy's. "Apology accepted. I said some hateful things as well and I'm sorry for that."

"There's one more thing."

Tilly bit back the moan threatening to escape. She should have known better. "Yes?"

"I told Mandy I wanted to enroll at the community college. And I heard you tell Raven," she looked back at the bartender who was doing a horrible job at pretending she wasn't listening, "that you want to be a teacher. If I take a few classes, will you help me study?"

Tilly broke out into a huge grin. "Of course!"

Typically, The Gentleman wouldn't allow for his lunch to be disturbed, but his admin assured him that Jade said it was important. Since he trusted Jade more than the admin, he told her to send Jade in.

He could almost see the excitement radiating from her. "Don't just stand there. Tell me what you have that's so important, it couldn't wait until I finished eating."

"Keaton Benedict was at the club last night," she said in a rush.

He blinked and carefully wiped his mouth in an attempt to project the image that he was calm and unaffected by her news. The truth was, that he felt the exact opposite. "Oh?" he asked, sounding bored to his own ears.

"There's more," Jade said. He lifted an eyebrow and she continued, "Tilly Brock left with him."

This time he couldn't hide his delight and he smiled and templed his fingers. "This is excellent news. Of course, it also means we have to be precise with our plans."

Jade nodded. "Make Tilly's death look random?"

"Yes," he said. "And when she's finally gone, the Benedict's grief will be a happy bonus."

Keaton was waiting for Kipling in his office when his oldest brother got home that night. It was always his first stop and Keaton was glad some things never changed. He left the door open so his brother would see him before he entered the room.

"Keaton," Kipling said, putting down the mail he'd been holding. "Is something wrong?"

"Just wanted to talk with you."

Kipling stepped inside and sat down at the massive wooden desk that had been their father's. "Sure, what's up?"

"I ran into someone last night," Keaton said. "Tilly Brock."

Kipling cleared his throat and steepled his fingers. "How did you and Tilly happen to hook up last night?"

Keaton flinched at his choice of words. Hook up. Like she was a bimbo or something. "We didn't *hook up*. The guys and I went to the club and I saw her serving drinks." He leaned forward. His brother might run the family business, but Keaton was still a Benedict and knew a thing or two about getting what he wanted. "The real question is, why didn't you tell me you kept in contact with the Brocks?"

Kipling weighed his response before answering. "I really only dealt with Ann. After Mom and Dad died and I took over the company, one of the things I did was perform an audit. I went back twenty years. In the middle of doing this, I received a call from Ann. She'd recently been diagnosed with breast cancer and was needing information on a life insurance policy her husband had taken out years before."

Keaton could only imagine the courage it must have taken for Mama Ann to call Kipling. There was only one reason he could think of. "She wanted it for Tilly."

Kipling nodded. "That would be my guess. We didn't speak long, I had a meeting and she had an appointment, but later that day when I was looking for the life insurance, I found some of the records from that time period were missing. Not only business records, financials and invoices. Which is troubling enough. But large sections of the data-based backup files are also gone, including calendars and emails."

Keaton had always suspected Mr. Brock had been set up. The fact that records from that period of time were missing only seemed to confirm that suspicion.

"When I called her back to give her the insurance info, we talked some more and while I can't prove it, I'm almost positive Dad was wrong about Mr. Brock." Kipling shook his head. "It just never made sense, you know? I mean, I was away at college when it all went down, but I remember then thinking how strange it all seemed."

Keaton nodded in agreement. "What would have been his motive? Aside from the fact that he was a Benedict employee, he and Dad were friends. Remember how they played golf every Saturday?"

"And Ann and Mom were always doing something for that garden club they loved so much." Kipling tapped his fingers on his desk. "And where did the money go if he did take it? From all appearances, the Brocks were basically destitute after."

"I know Tilly doesn't have it. She's working to put herself through college."

Kipling sighed. "With those records missing, though, it's all just speculation and I can't prove anything."

"But you found the insurance information?" Keaton asked.

"Yes, and it was a hefty policy, too."

Then why the hell was Tilly working in a gentlemen's club? Unless she had already spent all the money. But he dismissed that thought as quickly as it came to his mind. There was no way the woman he'd talked with into the early hours of the morning could have done that.

Kipling knew exactly what he was thinking and answered his question before he could ask it. "Tilly never cashed in the policy." He reached into his desk and pulled out an envelope. "She signed it over to me."

Keaton opened it, at once recognizing Tilly's neat script.

> Mr. Benedict,
> Thank you very much for finding this and passing it along. You've already done so much, and with the history between our families, I can't do anything with this. There's no way I'll ever be able to repay you for what you've done in providing for Mama over the last year. Please accept this note as a humble "thank you."
>
> Yours,
> Tilly

"I didn't cash it, obviously." Kipling took the note back. "I called her a few times, offering it again." He grinned. "That is until she told me if I called her again, she'd file harassment charges."

Keaton couldn't help but laugh. *That* sounded like the Tilly he talked with last night.

Kipling ran the fingers of one hand through his hair. "I had no idea she was working at that dive, though. If I had, I'd have risked the harassment charges. That is legally her money. Her father paid for the policy, no questions asked."

Keaton decided to let the comment about the club being a dive slide. He didn't like her working there, either, but it wasn't his place to tell her what she could and couldn't do. He couldn't do the same for Kipling, however, for keeping Tilly from him. "One of these days I'll kick your ass for not telling me you were in contact with her."

Kipling raised his eyebrow and studied him. "The two of you were close back then, weren't you?"

"Yes," Keaton replied. "And it pisses me off you didn't tell me about your business with her."

"It wasn't done on purpose. I guess I didn't realize how much she meant to you."

"She was also best friends with Elise," he said.

"Was she now? That's interesting." Kipling appeared to be thinking that through. It didn't surprise Keaton that Kipling was unaware of Tilly and Elise's past. After all, when the whole fiasco happened, Kipling was already in college.

"Yes, and just so you know, I have no intention of marrying Elise, so if that's the only reason she's staying here this summer, she can room somewhere else for her internship. I find it hard to believe she wants to be a lawyer anyway."

Kipling's look softened for a minute. "And just so you know, I would never want you to marry somebody you didn't love."

Keaton threw his hand over his heart in mock outrage. "Do my ears deceive me? Does Kipling Benedict actually have a heart?"

Kipling laughed. "It's small and dark but yes, I have one."

"Don't worry," said Keaton. "I won't tell anybody. It'll be our little secret."

"Thanks. I appreciate that." Kipling sighed heavily.

"As much as I know you don't want talk about it, and as much as I don't want talk about it, we need to discuss your future with Benedict Industries."

Keaton cringed inwardly. It wasn't that he didn't want to work for the family business, he just didn't want to do it in the manner expected of him. What Keaton wanted to do was create a division of Benedict Industries solely focused on charitable endeavors. He had traveled out of the country several times in college as part of humanitarian relief and whenever he thought about all the people in the world that desperately needed help, it almost overwhelmed him.

He knew, though, that you had to step lightly around Kipling. He worked a certain way and one had to play their cards right in order to have a chance of succeeding with him. And because Keaton was aware of that, he also knew that now was not the right time to have the necessary conversation with him.

"I actually have a few ideas I want to look into," Keaton said. "I'm not ready to share any details, but I think you'll like what I've come up with. How about I write up a proposal and give it to you?"

"That sounds great. I look forward to reading it." Kipling looked down at his watch. "Lena probably has my dinner reheated. She gets mad when I'm not home by six and I don't want to piss her off further, so I'm going to make it to the dining room before she comes looking for me."

Keaton smiled at the mention of the housekeeper who'd worked for the family since before he was born. "Sounds like her."

"It gets better." He rolled his eyes. "This morning she sighed and said it sure would be nice to have guests for a change. A not-so-subtle implication that it's time for me to settle down or at least bring someone over for dinner. I told her she could cook all the fancy dishes she wanted while Elise was here."

Keaton groaned at the reminder that his unwanted houseguest would be arriving in less than forty-eight hours.

"That's about the same response Lena had. Said that girl wasn't worth the effort." Kipling had a faint smile. "She never did like Elise."

"I knew she was a smart woman."

Kipling looked as if he was getting ready to lecture him, so to stop him before he started, Keaton held his hand up. "No need to say it. I'll behave while she's here."

He looked at his watch, wondering what time Tilly got off and counted the hours until he could see her again.

Tilly hopped out of bed the next morning, excited and eager to have breakfast with Keaton. They had texted a few times the night before. Tilly had shared with him the conversation she had with Mindy. He'd been surprised, too, but said he knew she'd be an awesome teacher.

To hear him say that made her realize just how infrequently she received compliments since her mom died. To have them come from Keaton meant even more. She puttered around her apartment while waiting for him to show up. She really needed to spend a day cleaning up her apartment. She shoved some old papers into a pile and her glance fell on a book she'd read for school on adult education.

She picked it up and flipped through it, remembering the class. Mindy might find the book useful. The club was on the way to the biscuit shop; she'd have Keaton stop by there on the way and she'd leave it for Mindy. It was her night off and, if all went according to plan, she would be spending the majority of it with Keaton.

He arrived at her apartment five minutes early. "Good morning, gorgeous."

"Hey yourself, handsome." She moved aside to let him by. "Let me grab one thing and I'll be ready to leave."

He waited in her small entryway, casually looking around. She grabbed the book and found him studying her pictures. "Ready?"

"Yes." He eyed the book in her hand. "You planning to study while we eat?"

"No, it's for Mindy. Mind if we stop by the club on the way to breakfast?"

"Sure, no problem."

They hopped in his car. She loved how he insisted on opening her car door before she got in and out. It was so nice to be with a gentleman. Keaton was completely different from anyone she'd dated before. It was so easy to be with him. At times, it felt as if they'd only been apart for days as opposed to years.

They didn't speak much on the way to the club, but Keaton held her hand, letting go only when he parked. He reached for it again as they made their way to the front door.

"Someone's here," he said.

"Cleaning crew," she said, taking note of the van currently parked in front. "I forgot they came by in the mornings. Let's go around the back. The dressing room's back there and I can leave the book for her."

Keaton seemed to be up for anything. "Lead the way."

She sensed something wasn't right the moment they rounded the corner. The feeling was so strong, she halted for a second. It started as a slight queasy feeling, but soon escalated to where she had to force herself to move forward.

"Tilly?" Keaton asked. "Is everything okay?"

"Yes," she said, but then stopped again, as the queasy sensation grew three hundred times worse. "Is that door open?"

She tried telling herself that it was simply the cleaning crew. That they had opened it. But for some reason, she kept hearing Raven telling her about the friendly man in the suit.

"I think so," Keaton said. "Must be the people inside working. Looks like they left some laundry outside."

"We don't have laundry," Tilly said.

"I'm not sure what else it could be."

Tilly made it to the laundry bundle in question before he did. She had been correct, it wasn't laundry. It was Raven. And her throat had been cut.

Tilly screamed.

CHAPTER 5

Keaton sat with his arms around Tilly, trying to shield her from the sight of her coworker, and letting her sob in disbelief.

"I just saw her last night. She was fine. She told me she was expecting to hear about a potential job today."

He didn't have any comforting words to offer, so he simply held her. The police should be arriving soon; he'd called them as soon as Tilly had been able to tell him who the dead woman was. The cleaning crew stood away from them, but close enough to see what was going on. They'd come running as soon as they heard Tilly scream and now just watched in shock.

An unmarked car with flashing lights pulled up.

"Police are here," he whispered to Tilly. She sniffled once more and took a step back and out of his arms.

A woman got out of the car first. She was petite and had her hair pulled back in a ponytail. But what primarily caught his attention was the confidence in her step and the way her eyes took in her surroundings. Her male partner glanced around the area quickly, but his

steps were hesitant. The woman walked toward them
and flashed her badge.

"I'm Officer Alyssa Adams. This is my partner, Officer Drake. We had a call about a body."

Tilly pointed to Raven. "It's Raven. Raven Todd. We
work together."

"And you are?" Alyssa asked.

"Tilly Brock."

A flash of something flickered in Alyssa's eyes, but
she didn't address it. Turning to him, she asked, "And
you?"

"Keaton Benedict."

Alyssa nodded to her partner, who started making
calls, and turned back to the couple. "Tell me what happened."

Keaton let Tilly give a rundown of the day's events.
By the time she'd finished, more law enforcement
agents had arrived to process the scene.

"Did Raven mention anything about someone threatening her?" Alyssa asked.

"No." Tilly's forehead wrinkled. "But she did mention that two nights ago. No, three. She told me about
it two nights ago. She said she was locking up after
closing and she ran into a man who was just standing
there. Said he was friendly and wore a suit."

Alyssa frowned. "Has anyone mentioned this man
other than Raven?"

"Not to me."

"I'll ask around." Alyssa looked toward where someone was taking pictures. "Okay. Thank you. Those are
all the questions I have for the moment."

"Can I go?" Tilly asked with a look of longing
toward Keaton.

"Yes, of course. Be sure to let me know if you remember anything."

Tilly thanked her after they all exchanged information and walked to Keaton. He opened his arms and she went into them silently. He held her close, feeling that she was only just holding it together. "Let's go," he whispered, and she nodded.

He didn't want to let her go long enough to drive back to her place. She looked so vulnerable as she huddled in his front seat. So many questions ran through his head. He never saw her with a car, so did that mean she rode the bus to work and back? He didn't like that one bit. Obviously, there wasn't much he could do, short of buying her a car and she wouldn't allow him to do that. But he would think of something. He had to. The voice in the back of his head kept whispering that she was in danger. As much as he'd like to ignore it, he couldn't, because it was usually right.

Jade stood at the side of the massive stone mansion, thankful for the multitude of trees that hid her from the road. She had wanted to do this at night, but no, *he* had said it had to be done during the day and it had to be done today. Once, just once, she'd like to tell him no. But since people who did that typically wound up dead, she wasn't going to chance it.

"Look for an old ivy-covered arbor," she muttered to herself, repeating his words. "Once you move it out of the way, you'll see a wooden door." She eyed the only ivy-covered arbor in the garden. It looked like it hadn't been moved since the Revolutionary War. "Yeah, right."

But since the only people who didn't do what The Gentleman told them to do were those with a death wish, she looked over her shoulder and moved the arbor. It was surprisingly light and easily moved, and, just like he said, revealed a wooden door.

Knowing she didn't have a choice, she checked to make sure her knife was easily accessible and picked up the rose she'd been told to plant on the desk in the home office of the house she was unworthy to enter by the front door.

Keaton stayed with Tilly all day, rarely leaving her side. Since she hadn't been to the grocery store in over a week, he ordered delivery from her favorite Italian place for lunch and sushi for dinner. Tilly didn't have much of an appetite, but she ate anyway, knowing she had to.

Throughout the day, Raven's death would hit her suddenly and she'd find herself crying. It didn't seem possible her friend was gone forever and she didn't know how she'd face going back to work knowing Raven would never be there again.

By late afternoon, she'd finally stopped crying so often and sat cuddled in Keaton's arms on the couch. He'd found an old romantic comedy playing on the TV, but neither one of them was paying very much attention to what was happening on screen.

"I don't know what I'd have done today without you." She turned in his arms to get a better look at him. "Thank you for staying."

He tightened his arm around her. "I would never leave you alone after what you've been through. And besides," he added with a grin, "I like your company."

"Now I know you're lying. I've been the worst company today. I haven't done anything other than cry."

"I've missed you for eight years, you think a few tears are going to chase me away?"

She dropped her head and placed her hand on his thigh. "I missed you, too. In fact, I used to have this daydream of you walking into the club."

"You did?"

"Mmm." She still didn't look up. "And then you did."

He covered her hand with his. "Hey, look at me." He waited until she did. "If I'd known you were in town, I'd have been there a lot sooner."

Her heart ached thinking of all that lost time. "I wish I knew you'd felt that way. I'd have called you."

His forehead wrinkled. "Why didn't you?"

"After what everyone thought Dad did? And then when Mom got sick and she talked to Kipling? I never heard from you, I figured you didn't want anything to do with me. It never occurred to me that Kipling never mentioned it."

"I owe Kipling a kick in the ass for not telling me."

She sighed and they were silent for a few minutes. It wasn't an awkward silence, rather it was peaceful. Until Keaton cleared his throat.

"Tilly?"

She didn't like the way he said her name, but she looked up anyway. "Yes?"

He must have seen the worry in her expression because he smiled and kissed her forehead. "Don't look like that, it's nothing bad."

"Tell me."

"I don't like the thought of you riding a bus to and from the club when there's a killer on the loose."

If he thought she was going to argue with him, he was mistaken. She didn't like the idea, either. Unfortunately, there was no other option. She had two months until graduation and there was no way she could afford a car. "I don't have a choice."

"What if I drove you?"

"I can't ask you to do that." But the fact that he offered was amazing.

"I don't think you did ask me," he said. "I believe I volunteered."

"It's too much." She shook her head, but when she looked in his eyes, she could tell he wasn't going to back down.

"Nothing is too much to keep you safe." He ran his fingers through her hair. "I know you have to work. I know how important it is for you to get your degree, and I want that for you. Let me take care of your transportation these last few months. It would make me feel so much better. Plus, I get to see you a lot more."

Her eyes filled with tears for what felt like the two hundredth time that day, but this time they weren't in sadness. She lifted her head and kissed him gently. "I would like that very much. Thank you."

Tilly slowly became aware of the bed shifting—*Keaton*—and she smiled before opening her eyes.

"Hey," Keaton said, holding something that looked a lot like a note in his hand. "I didn't mean to wake you up."

It was a note. She swallowed her disappointment. "Were you leaving?"

"No. I wouldn't do that without telling you. I was going to run out and pick up a few things for breakfast."

She could have smacked herself for thinking he'd leave without saying good-bye. He just wanted more to eat than the two eggs and stale cereal she had on hand.

Her stomach rumbled at the thought of food. "Let me get dressed and I'll go with you."

"I'd like that." He kissed her cheek. "I'll go wait in the living room."

She didn't spend too much time getting ready. They were just going out to pick up a few things and she'd take a shower when she got back. As she was trying to tame her hair, it hit her that Raven's interview was supposed to be today and a fresh wave of grief washed over her.

Keaton smiled when she made it to the living room a few minutes later and she knew her return smile wasn't as bright as his.

He reached for her hand and she let his warmth and strength comfort her. She felt better as he opened the door and she knew with time, she'd one day feel normal again. A flash of red caught her eye and she looked down. One of the twin's lifeless body blocked her way.

Like Raven, her throat had been cut and Tilly's free hand flew of its own accord to her own neck. This wasn't a coincidence. This was a warning.

"This is twice in as many days that you've called in to report a body," Officer Adams said, as if somehow both Raven and Mindy were dead because of them.

Tilly started to say something, but Keaton stopped her by answering first. "We're not saying anything without a lawyer present."

Officer Adams cocked one eyebrow. "Noted."

"Doesn't that make us look guilty?" Tilly asked Keaton.

"No, it makes us look smart."

Tilly sighed and stood up from her couch. She wanted

to go outside, but the crime scene team she recognized from the day before was blocking her doorway, processing Mindy's body. She thought she would have felt something over the death of another coworker, but all she felt was numb.

From outside a commotion began to stir. Keaton stood up and put his arm around her.

"Let me in," a familiar voice said from outside. Tilly looked at Keaton in question.

He nodded. "Kipling."

Sure enough, a few minutes longer and Kipling stood in her apartment, Officer Adams and her partner nearby.

"Tilly?" Kipling asked.

"Hi, Kipling," she answered. "Long time no see."

"Mind if I come in and sit down?" he asked, and at the shake of her head, he added, "I guess you two should come, too," over his shoulder to the cops. To Keaton, he shot a *watch yourself* look, which translated to: Don't say anything until the lawyer arrives.

When they'd all sat back down, Alyssa asked, "Who are you?"

Kipling shot her a smile. "Kipling Benedict."

"I'm Alyssa Adams and this is Officer Drake. We're looking into the death of Mindy Jackson," Alyssa said. "I'm glad you're here. Now, Keaton, we've heard there was an altercation between you, Tilly, and Mindy a few nights ago at the club."

Keaton's mouth dropped open. He hastily closed it and said, "I, uh, don't know if *altercation* is the right word."

"Keaton," Kipling said in the low, but dangerous voice he had. "Shut your fucking mouth and keep it closed until Derrick gets here."

"Or he could answer a few questions and we'll get out of your hair," Alyssa said.

"No one says anything, damn it."

They all turned to see who had spoken.

"Derrick, our attorney," Keaton explained as the man in question entered Tilly's apartment. He was short and overweight and though it was early in the day, already sweating.

"Officers," he said. "I'm here representing the Benedict family and we're not answering anything."

Derrick made it into the living room and stood with his arms crossed. His gaze landed on Tilly. "Who are you?"

"Tilly Brock. I live here."

Derrick looked from her to Keaton and back again. He snapped his head back to the two officers standing. "She's my client, too."

Alyssa's lips tightened into a thin line. She didn't like that at all and if Keaton wasn't mistaken, it appeared Kipling was hiding a smile.

The male officer, who had been silent since the moment Keaton and Tilly arrived, stood. "Come on," he said to Alyssa. "We're not going to get anything here."

Alyssa wasn't happy to be leaving, that much was clear. "I suggest you don't leave town," she told Keaton and then looked at Tilly. "You, either." To Kipling, she simply said, "I'll be in touch."

Kipling saluted her and appeared to be watching her ass as she left.

Everyone held his or her breath until the two officers left. Derrick then looked at Keaton. "Want to tell me what's been going on?"

Keaton took a deep breath and told him everything he knew, everything he remembered, and everything that happened after they left the club, up until this morning. Derrick made a couple of notes in his phone and then turned to Tilly for her story. When they both finished, he put his phone aside and clasped his hands. "We'll get statements from everyone and that should be it."

He stayed at the apartment for a little while longer, mostly making small talk. Keaton whispered to her that the small man was more intelligent than he appeared. He said he was always looking, always taking in the details.

It wasn't until the attorney left that there was a noticeable change in Kipling's demeanor. Keaton's oldest brother took a deep breath and rolled his shoulders. He closed his eyes and sighed, but when he opened them, he was all smiles.

Tilly wanted to smile back, but she found she couldn't. How could she smile when Raven and Mindy never would smile again?

Keaton seemed to pick up on her mood, because he was frowning, too. "You okay, Tilly?"

She shook her head. "It's just sinking in that Mindy's gone. I mean, I didn't like her, but I didn't want her dead." She dropped her head into her hand. "Who could do this?"

Keaton put his arm around her. "I don't know, but I'll do anything I can to help, because it makes me sick to my stomach, too. How could someone I talked with less than forty-eight hours ago be dead? Even more upsetting is the thought that maybe there was something that happened, something I saw or heard, that might be a clue."

"Right?" she agreed. "What if there was something and I'm not able to remember it? Even more sickening is the thought that it happened outside my door." She tightened her hands into fists. "I told her to come by and get that book I'd planned to leave at the club the morning we found Raven dead. And I can't help thinking, was it Mindy or me the killer was after?"

Keaton's lips tightened into a thin line. "Why would you be a target?"

"I don't know, but I have to think about it, don't I?"

He didn't look too happy with her statement and she expected him to argue with her. Which is why his next question confused her.

"Do you know if any homeless people stay near the club on a regular basis?"

Tears filled her eyes. "There used to be one. His name was Charlie. Janie, a bartender who used to work there, and I would take him food when we saw him."

"Was?" Keaton asked, picking up on her use of past tense.

"He was murdered in the homeless shelter Janie took him to." Her shoulders slumped. "He was such a sweet old man."

He took her hand and she knew he was trying to offer her comfort, but she also knew he couldn't take the pain away. "I'm sorry," he said.

She squeezed his hand and gave him a small smile. "Thank you. But no, since Charlie, I haven't seen very many homeless around and none on a regular basis." Her forehead wrinkled. "Why do you ask?"

"There was a pile of clothes and some other items near the club last night, but I didn't see anyone near them."

"That's odd," she said. "I wonder what it could mean?"

Kipling's phone rang and he cursed as he looked at the display. "Hello, Mr. Germain," he said, answering while at the same time keeping his gaze locked on Keaton. "Yes, I understand. No, there's nothing to worry about. Yes, he has an alibi. Of course. No offense taken. I'd have done the same. Yes, sir. We're looking forward to her coming back home and staying here."

"The hell we are," Keaton mumbled under his breath.

Tilly sucked in a breath and Keaton turned his attention back to her.

"Are you okay?"

Tilly hadn't meant to be so loud, but hearing Kipling talk to Mr. Germain brought home the fact that there were relationships at play she didn't know about.

"I was wondering, you and Elise . . . ?" She didn't ask the question, hoping that he would see what she wanted to know. Though she'd like to think that Keaton wouldn't be kissing her if he was engaged, the truth was, they had been separated for years and his circumstances and character may have changed.

He shook his head. "There's nothing between me and Elise. She would like for there to be. Her parents would like for there to be. But it's not going to happen. Elise is a beautiful woman and I'm sure she'll make some guy a wonderful wife, but it won't be me."

"Did your parents want you two together?" she asked.

"It was mostly the Germains. They thought our business portfolios would match up. Mom and Dad would have never wanted me to marry someone for business gain." He grimaced. "That memo hasn't made it to the

Germain house, though. Her parents have selected me in much the same way you would a horse to breed. Good bloodlines. Sturdy stock. Not too bad to look at. Loaded. Yup, I'll do for a husband."

The whole thing sounded clinical and cold. "Kinda makes me glad my parents didn't have much money." *After,* she could have added, but didn't.

"The bad part is, her parents still don't see the fruitlessness of it." He hesitated a second before adding, "She's actually spending the summer with us at Benedict House."

"Elise? Here? I thought she went to Yale or Harvard or something."

"Harvard."

"When's she arriving?"

He shot Kipling a look. "Monday."

"Day after tomorrow? This Monday?"

"Unfortunately."

"How long is she staying?" she asked, even though she had a bad feeling she knew.

"The whole damn summer. She'll be interning at a law office."

She tilted her head. "Something about the way you said that makes me think you don't believe it."

"I can't picture Elise as an attorney. She's been groomed from the crib to be a trophy wife."

It sounded awful coming from Keaton's lips, but Tilly knew he was telling the truth. Years ago, whenever she'd spend the night at the Germains' house, her mother was always on Elise to do this and act that way and to stop doing that, because no lady would act that way. To Tilly, it sounded like a bunch of worthless rules her friend had to follow.

She'd told Elise that once, but her friend had denied it and said that her mother was just making sure she grew up to be a proper Southern lady. Tilly had snorted and said that sounded boring as hell. She remembered Elise hadn't taken that very well.

Looking back, they probably wouldn't have been friends if it weren't for their fathers both working for the Benedicts, but they had. Tilly and Elise met in kindergarten and were inseparable until that fateful day when they weren't anymore.

"She probably went to Harvard for her MRS degree," Tilly said.

"Without question," Keaton agreed.

There was a lull in the conversation and with it Tilly realized how quiet it had grown outside. She stood up to walk to the front window, right as someone knocked on the front door.

She opened it to find Officer Adams. "Can I help you, Officer?"

Alyssa shook her head. "No, Ms. Brock. I just wanted to let you know we were finished and will be leaving. I'll let you know if I have further questions for you."

Tilly nodded. "Thank you."

Once Alyssa left and Tilly closed the door, Kipling stood. "I'll get out of your hair, too. Keaton, are you staying here or coming home?"

Keaton turned to her. "Why don't you come stay at Benedict House?"

As much as she would like to, she didn't want to be around Elise. Though they had been close at one point, they hadn't talked in years. From what she understood from Keaton, Elise was not the same person she'd been then and he'd hinted that she'd become quite the snob. Add on top of that the fact that she wanted Keaton, and Tilly just wasn't ready to see her yet.

"I'll stay here," she said. "I need to study and I'll probably take a nap."

"I'll stay, too," Keaton said.

"No, I'm sure you have other things to do. You haven't been home in days."

He looked like he was going to argue, but she stopped him by walking to him and slipping her arms around him. She was vaguely aware of Kipling leaving. "This way you can take me to dinner tonight and I won't feel bad about monopolizing your time."

"You call me if you need anything," Keaton whispered against her cheek. "Anything at all."

"Okay," she said, and turned her head so their lips met.

He groaned low in his throat and took her lips in a kiss that started out gentle, but soon grew in intensity. She clutched the fabric of his shirt and wondered if telling him not to stay was the stupidest thing she'd ever done.

Jade looked up as the Gentleman walked into his room. She frowned. It wasn't often he sought her out. She put the knife down she'd been sharpening.

"Something wrong, Sir?"

He didn't smile, he rarely did, and nothing about his expression set her mind at ease.

"No," he finally said and she could breathe easier. "Just wanted to let you know I appreciate your work at the club. You did well not being seen."

His praise was rarer than his smile and a flicker of warmth started to fill the dark and empty places inside her.

"You aren't totally worthless after all," he said and the warmth died and she was once more cold to her very soul.

"Thank you, Sir," she whispered, not able to look at him. She had the feeling he wanted to say more, but his phone rang.

"Tom," he said. "Phase two is a go. Bea Jacobs has been busy looking into things she has no business looking at. You know what to do."

He ended the call and put the phone in his pocket, his gaze falling on her knives. He nodded toward them. "Bring them and come with me. You need more practice."

Her stomach flipped in revolt, but she did as she was told.

Tilly unplugged the landline after Keaton left. She wasn't even sure why she still had one; no one ever called it. That was, until today, when it stated to ring nonstop as soon as everyone had left her apartment. She turned off her cell, too. She was going off grid. If someone needed her, too damn bad.

Her current plan was to stay sequestered inside her apartment for at least the next eight hours. Maybe by then the reporters would be tired and would leave her alone.

She plopped into her couch and hugged a pillow to her chest. When had everything gone so crazy? In just a few days, so much had changed. Starting with Keaton.

Oh yes, she thought. She could definitely start and end with Keaton. It had to have been fate that brought them together again. She still couldn't believe both of his parents died. That's what she got for refusing to watch or read anything mentioning the Benedict family.

It had probably been selfish, but after what his father had accused her father of doing, she saw it as self-preservation.

For the longest time, she'd felt lost. When her father had to leave Benedict Industries and they moved, she no longer went to the same school as Keaton and Elise. Ashamed about the stigma on her family and fearful they both believed Keaton's dad, she hadn't reached out to either of them.

Though the fact that neither one of them ever tried to contact her hurt a bit as well. Keaton she understood, at least a little bit, especially if he believed her father had stolen from his family and he had been unaware she still lived in Charleston. Elise, though, had been her best girlfriend since kindergarten. Elise was the one she'd giggle over boys with, do makeovers with, and have sleepovers with. Boys came and went, but girlfriends were supposed to be forever.

Eventually, she made new friends, but the pain of leaving behind those she knew so well and never got in contact with followed her. It had actually been a surprise when she realized Keaton had grown up. Of course, in her mind, she'd known they were the same age, but still. Seeing the man he'd grown into was beyond the beyond.

Restless, she got up from the couch and paced to the window, surprised to see a few reporters lurking in the parking lot. With a sigh, she turned on her computer and opened the spreadsheet she kept her budget on. She did the math three times. It would be a stretch, but if she only ate beans and rice, she might be okay not working until graduation. She really didn't want to go back to the club, but she doubted she could find another waitressing job. Unfortunately, with her name and picture all over the news, she didn't think it was probable that anyone would hire her.

The only thing to do was to focus on school so she could graduate. She tried for an hour to concentrate on the paper that was due in a few days, but her mind was spinning in too many circles to focus on anything. She tapped her fingers on her desk, wondering why Keaton hadn't called.

She reached for her phone and remembered she'd turned it off. Chuckling to herself for losing it, she turned it back on. Almost immediately, her screen was filled with missed calls. Two were from Keaton, one was from her friend Janie, and, as expected, numerous numbers she didn't recognize and a few simply listed as *unknown*. Interestingly enough, there was only one voicemail.

She hit Play, expecting to hear Keaton, but it wasn't his voice that filled her ear. It was a robotic sounding, maniacal rough voice.

"You got lucky this time, bitch. Your luck won't last forever."

She deleted it with a shiver, telling herself it was to be expected. Damn media spreading her name all over the news. Field day for perverts and other creepers. The phone rang again and flashed UNKNOWN. Best to let it go to voice mail. If it was important enough, they'd leave a message. At the moment there was only one person she wanted to talk to.

Keaton tried calling Tilly for the second time after he got out of the shower, but it once again went to her voice mail. More than likely, she was being bombarded and had turned her phone off. He didn't bother to leave a message, since it wouldn't be too long before he took her to dinner.

He stood in the hallway and looked at his watch, wondering how long was an acceptable period of time to wait before heading back to Tilly's.

Kipling walked by him and chuckled. "Come eat lunch with me. Then you can go see her."

"That transparent, am I?"

"Slightly."

Keaton's phone buzzed with an incoming text. *Tilly. Finally.* But when he pulled the phone out of his pocket, it was an unfamiliar number and his blood ran cold at what had been sent.

Do you know where your girlfriend is?

Twenty minutes later, Keaton stood at the doorway of Tilly's apartment. There were a few reporters in the parking lot and they all said they hadn't seen anyone leave or enter her place. But that didn't erase the fact that Tilly still hadn't answered her phone. Even if she'd turned it off to avoid reporters, surely she would have turned it back on to check for voice mails.

A tiny trickle of fear twisted in his chest, even as he knocked on her door. He told himself he was being ridiculous, that she would open the door and he'd feel foolish. She'd welcome him inside and they'd share a laugh over his overreaction.

Except she wasn't opening the door.

"Tilly!" He banged harder. "Tilly, it's Keaton. Open up and let me know you're okay."

Still nothing from within.

He looked under the welcome mat, but of course, there was no key to be found. There were no potted plants and the mailboxes were located across the parking lot. Frustrated, he tried calling her again.

Nothing.

Damn it.

He ran his fingers through his hair, telling himself to calm down and think about the situation rationally. No one had entered or exited the front door. His head shot up.

The front door.

Was there a back door?

Seconds later, he made it to the backside of the apartments and his worst fear was confirmed. On the backside of Tilly's second-story apartment, there was a deck and the back door was open.

CHAPTER 6

He stood, frozen in place for several seconds while fear held him tightly. He couldn't lose her. Not after they'd finally found each other after so many years. He couldn't begin to describe his terror, but he refused to give into it.

He had to find her. She had to be okay. There was no other option.

He took his phone and right as he hit the nine for 911, the back door on the apartment next to Tilly's opened and Tilly herself stepped outside onto the deck and then, graceful as a cat, hopped over the divider and landed on her own deck.

Keaton shoved the phone in his pocket. What the fuck? "Tilly?" he called out.

She spun around and her face broke into a huge smile when she saw him, but quickly faded. "What? What's wrong?"

"I was scared out of my mind. I thought someone had broken in." She was fine. He took a deep breath and went back up the front steps to Tilly's apartment. She opened the door before he could knock and, without thinking, he took her in his arms, and crushed his lips to hers, while at the same time, shutting the door with his foot.

It wasn't a gentle kiss. It was raw and rough and he didn't care. All he cared about was that she was in his arms and she was safe and alive and for the moment, his. For her part, Tilly didn't seem to mind his less-than-gentlemanly behavior. She wrapped her arms around him and gave back to him as much as he gave her.

They were both breathing heavily when they pulled back.

He ran his hands over her hair, looking deep into her eyes. "Oh my God, I thought I'd lost you. That you were gone."

She wrinkled her nose. "Why would you think that?"

"You aren't answering your phone and I got a text asking if I knew where you were. I got scared and came over here. You don't answer your door and when I go to the back, I see your door wide open. What else am I supposed to think?"

He hadn't planned to tell her about the text he received because he didn't want to worry her unnecessarily. Though not worrying didn't seem to be working at the moment, Tilly looked several shades paler.

"What?" he asked. "What's wrong?"

"I got a threatening voice mail."

"Do you still have it?"

"No, I deleted it. It said something like, 'You won't always be so lucky, bitch.'"

Keaton was so stunned, he couldn't say anything and Tilly paled even further.

"Oh my God," she whispered. "They're after me, aren't they? The person who killed Raven and Mindy."

"I think we have to assume that's the case." It pained him to even think it, much less confirm out loud.

"Oh my God," she repeated.

"Tilly," he said, to get her attention. "Please think about staying at Benedict House so I can protect you better. Please. I've only just found you. I couldn't stand it if anything happened to you."

"Okay, I'll think about it," she said in a tight voice. She sniffled and added, "I didn't know you called. I had no idea. I turned my phone off because of all of the media calling me. And I went to my neighbor's because I stress bake and I didn't want to go out the front because then I might run into the reporters."

He cocked an eyebrow a her. "Two people you work with are murdered. You get a threatening phone call. And you go next door to bake?"

"I had to do something. The only other option was to sit here and drive myself crazy over every little sound I heard." She led him into the kitchen. "I haven't been to the store lately and I didn't feel like going today. When that happens, Ms. O'Donald next door lets me use her kitchen and supplies. She's seventy-eight and is good company. Plus, I like to keep an eye on her."

When that happens, she'd said. He had a feeling she couldn't afford to buy groceries, especially based on what he remembered from her kitchen. Plus, from the sound of it, this wasn't the first time she'd been in that position. Damn it, why wouldn't she take the insurance money? She was seriously going to let pride keep her from eating?

"What did you bake today?" he asked to change the subject.

Even as she started rattling off the things she had

baking in the oven next door, he couldn't stop thinking about her not being able to afford groceries. It was
grossly unfair—he had all the money he'd ever need
and she had to scrimp pennies to buy food.

"How about I take you to the store to buy groceries?" he asked.

"No, that's okay." She glanced at the clock on her
empty oven. "Besides, I need to check on the muffins
in five minutes. Want to go with me?"

After thinking he'd almost lost her, there wasn't a
force on earth strong enough to keep him away from her.

"As long as we go out and come back in the front
doors."

"Deal."

"And you promise me you have something to eat
other than sweets."

"I promise."

Thirty minutes later, Tilly and Keaton sat at her small
kitchen table, eating muffins and drinking ice tea.

"Forget teaching," Keaton said, reaching for his
third muffin. "You should open a bakery."

She laughed and refilled his tea. "I only stress bake,
I don't think I have it in me to do it as an occupation."

"Shame," he said, mouth full of muffin.

It was amazing how easy it was to be around him.
She'd have thought it would be awkward, given not only
their history, but that of their fathers as well. But it
wasn't. It was almost as if the years they were apart
melted away, but then she'd catch a glimpse of him
watching her and his eyes were so intense, she swore
she felt it all the way to her toes.

And the way he kissed her when she opened the

door? Uh, yeah. That certainly hadn't happened when they were kids.

"What about you?" she asked. "Now that you've graduated, are you going to take your place at the helm of Benedict Industries?"

"Not if I can help it."

"Really? Why? I thought it was like a Benedict rule or something."

"I'm going to talk to Kip or Knox about it soon. I don't mind working for Benedict Industries, but not in the capacity they want me to."

She tilted her head. "What do you want to do?"

He looked slightly uneasy, as if he didn't want to answer the question. "My sophomore and junior summers during college I spent in India, working to bring water to remote villages."

There was little else he could have said that would have surprised her more. To hear that this wealthy man the world wrote off as a playboy spent summers in India helping the impoverished endeared him to her all the more. "Wow, had no idea."

"I don't talk about it a lot."

She nodded. Not only did he spend his time doing that work, he didn't go around boasting about it. Matter of fact, it sounded like he didn't want anyone to know about it. "How does water in India fit in with Benedict Industries?"

"I want to open up a division within the company, one that deals with giving back. First of all to Charleston, and then South Carolina, and to keep spreading outward like that. It just seems so wrong, you know, to have all that money and not to give back to the community. There are so many people in need . . . I can't help them all, but hopefully I can make a small effort.

Can you believe how much of the world doesn't have safe water to drink?

"You're amazing," she whispered, in awe at the man he'd become.

"You flatter me. I'm sure all you have to do is pick up the society page and you'll get an eyeful of how not amazing I am."

Yes. She'd read those. And he was right, there were plenty of them. He was one of the Benedict brothers, after all. All three of them were regarded as prime picking and the media loved them.

"But those don't represent the entirety of you," she said gently.

"They represent enough."

"You'll never do great things until you believe you can do them."

His face broke into a calming smile. "You're going to be such a great teacher. Any student would be lucky to have you."

Her face heated at his compliment. "Thank you."

"I made you blush," he teased. "I don't think I've made anyone blush in years."

"I'm pretty sure that means you've been hanging out with the wrong people."

"I'm pretty sure you're right. This one girl I know, she likes to hang off the side of buildings."

"Really?" Tilly laughed. "Now *she* sounds like a winner. You should definitely hang out with her more."

His eyes grew serious and his expression made her belly tighten with the awareness of just how close he was sitting to her. She'd never been more thankful for such a small table.

"Oh, trust me. I plan to," he said, and his voice was several octaves lower than it had been. It made shivers run down her back and her skin break out in goose bumps. "You see, I lost track of her several years ago and now that I have her back in my life, I plan to hold on tight."

"You better."

CHAPTER 7

Hours later, he took her hand and they walked to his car. "Where are we going for dinner?" she asked.

"There's a new seafood place near the office. I can't remember the name, but Kipling went on and on about how good it was and he's a seafood snob."

She knew of the place. It was upscale, supposedly ridiculously delicious, and nothing she could normally afford.

"What?" he asked, catching her side eye at him. He opened the car door for her. "I want to take you somewhere nice."

"You know you don't have to."

"I've bought you cheeseburgers and takeout. Let me do this."

She knew he was wealthy, just as she knew he wasn't trying to impress her with his wealth. In his mind, he was taking her to a nice seafood restaurant. It was her hang-up that it cost so much. If it didn't bother him, it shouldn't bother her.

"Okay," she said, as he pulled out of the parking lot. "But next date, I'm in charge."

"There's going to be a next date? We haven't even finished this one yet," he teased. "Damn, I'm good."

"Don't let it go to your head," she said with a laugh.

Instead of answering, he picked up her hand and kissed it.

If it had been another man of Keaton's means taking her out, she'd be worried that he was taking her to such an expensive place to try to get in her pants. But she trusted Keaton and knew he wasn't like that. He simply wanted to do nice things for her. Like when he'd stayed with her and brought up taking her out for groceries. It was rather nice to be taken care of in such a way. She hadn't experienced anything similar since her mom died.

He didn't let go of her hand until they had reached the restaurant and he turned the car over to the valet. And though he didn't hold her hand on the way to check in, he kept his hand on the small of her back. It felt oddly reassuring.

The hostess led them to a relatively private table that had an oceanfront view. Keaton ordered them a bottle of wine and she tried not to be too obvious as she took in her surroundings. The restaurant was made from an old fish market, but had been redone with rich woods and new brick. She didn't even want to look at the menu, afraid that if she did, she wouldn't be able to keep the cost from bothering her.

Keaton, however, had no such issues. He looked up at her over the top of his menu. "Know what you want already?"

"No," she said. " I'll let you order for me."

"You sure you trust me that much?"

She knew he asked it as a joke, but her reply was completely serious. "And more."

He held her gaze for a long minute. "I'm going to beat Kipling's ass for not telling me he had been in contact with you. All that wasted time."

"We have a lot of making up to do."

Whatever he was going to say was interrupted by the waitress coming to take their order. He ordered them both a cup of she-crab soup and the catch of the day.

"I'm on a mission to find the best she-crab soup in the city," he said. "I haven't tried here yet."

"That makes sense. I was wondering why anyone would order soup when it's so hot outside."

He cocked his head to the side. "It does sound a bit absurd, doesn't it?"

"Absurd is how unreal it is this is really real." She laughed. "And how many *reals* were in that sentence."

When they were young, she'd been captivated by his good looks and kind personality. But as the date progressed, she saw that the older Keaton was so much more. He was easy to talk to, intelligent, and compassionate. Most guys she dated only wanted to talk about themselves, but Keaton always wanted to know how she felt and what she thought. It made her feel cherished and important. By the time they'd finished the delicious dinner, she feared her heart wasn't at all safe around the youngest Benedict.

The ride back to her apartment was passed in a comfortable silence. She'd expected the date to go well, but Keaton was simply amazing. It didn't even bother her too much that Elise was spending the summer in his house. It was obvious in the way he looked at her and how he talked about her that he was not interested in her at all. Tilly was willing to bet that would piss Elise off something horrible.

But she didn't want to think about Elise tonight. She wanted to think about Keaton and how she was going to invite him inside for a little dessert. She hid her smile. The upside to being stuck in the house all day was she got plenty of baking done.

When they were kids, Keaton's favorite cake had been a ten-layer chocolate. She didn't start baking to relieve stress until she was in college, but when she started, the first cake she taught herself to make was a ten-layer chocolate.

And there was a freshly baked one sitting right on top of her kitchen island.

"Come inside?" she asked when he'd parked in front of her building. "I have cake. One I didn't tell you about before."

He reached over and brushed her cheek. "I'd have come inside without the secret cake, you know."

She nodded, suddenly feeling very nervous.

"Don't touch that door," he said, hopping out of his side. "I'll get it."

She sat back in her seat, happy to be taken care of. Even though she believed his parents had been tricked by someone into thinking her dad had stolen from them, and even though it'd hurt her that they never questioned it and believed it so easily, the one thing she could say was they did a fine job instilling manners into their boys.

She knew the reputation of the Benedict boys—she wasn't a fool—but that was only on the surface. She had a feeling not many people knew the real men underneath the playboy façades.

Keaton took her hand and they walked up the flight of stairs to her apartment. She couldn't describe why or how, but she felt like something was off. When they made it to the landing halfway there, the skin on the back of her neck prickled. She stopped and looked over her shoulder.

"You okay?" Keaton asked, his gaze following hers. "Did you see something?"

"No, I just feel odd. It's probably nothing." She strained her ears. Were those footsteps on the stairs? And were they coming closer or further away?

"How so?"

How could she explain it to him if she couldn't understand it herself? "Something feels off."

Once more he looked over the parking lot. He was frowning. "Do you see anything that looks out of place? A strange car? Anything?"

She walked closer to him. "No, but I feel like I'm being watched."

They didn't say anything else as they continued the walk up the stairs and the feeling only grew worse. In fact, by the time they reached her door, her hands were trembling so hard, she dropped her keys.

Keaton reached down to get them. "Are you sure you didn't see anything?"

He didn't give the keys back to her, but took them in hand to unlock the door himself. He turned the key to unlock the door and his frown deepened. "It's not locked?"

Fear spiked through her chest. "What? Are you sure? I know I locked it."

"I know you did, too; I watched you." He twisted the handle. "It's definitely unlocked. Does anyone else have a key?"

Relief washed over her body. "Yes, my neighbor Ms. O'Donald. She probably needed her cake pans back."

He nodded. "Okay, but you seriously need to consider

taking the key back if she can't remember to lock up when she leaves. I'm slightly paranoid after that voice mail you got."

"Me, too." Tilly nodded, but wasn't sure what she was going to do. Ms. O'Donald was seventy-eight. Sometimes, she forgot things. But what if it wasn't Ms. O'Donald?

Keaton pushed the door open and stopped. "Oh, fuck."

CHAPTER 8

Tilly's apartment was a total wreck.

Furniture was overturned and slashed through. Mirrors and picture frames were broken, with shards of glass littering the floor. Worst of all was the WHORE written in red along the far wall of her living room.

Behind him, Tilly whimpered. He turned and took her in his arms, right as her legs buckled. He held her and as he did, he felt her resolve return. She took a deep breath and pushed back, her eyes darting around the room. "How? Who?"

"We need to call the police and then wait downstairs." Keaton was leading her out of the apartment as he talked. "I don't think whoever did this is still around, but we can't be too sure."

She didn't argue with him and by the time they'd made it back to his car, he'd already called the police. As they waited, he thought about asking her again to move in with him. Surely now she'd understand the danger she was in and would agree to come to Benedict House. He looked up as flashing lights signaled the arrival of the police department. Once again it was Alyssa and her partner, Officer Drake.

"Mr. Benedict. Ms. Brock," Alyssa said, coming toward them.

Keaton and Tilly spoke to Alyssa and told her what they'd found in the apartment. Alyssa sent her partner up to check everything out. It wasn't too long until he came back down. He spoke briefly with Alyssa and then walked to the car to make a phone call.

"No one's in there now," Alyssa said. "You'll need to go through and see if anything has been stolen, but it looks like the place was just trashed."

"Why would anyone do that?" Tilly asked.

"I don't know," Alyssa said. "If it's the guy who killed Raven and Mindy, he broke pattern. He didn't do this to either of their places. Of course, that doesn't rule him out. We also have to consider the possibility that the two previous victims were warnings."

Which wasn't what Keaton wanted to hear. He'd wanted Alyssa to say that, of course, this wasn't the work of the killer. And since she couldn't say that, it was even more imperative that Tilly move in with him.

Tilly thought for a few seconds, before saying, "I had a prank call yesterday. Whoever it was said I was lucky, but my luck wouldn't last."

"I received a text message yesterday asking if I knew where she was," he added.

"I meant what I told you before," Alyssa said. "If either of you get another message, I want you to let me know."

They both agreed and Alyssa told them they were free to go back into the apartment, but to let her know if anything was missing.

Keaton waited until the two cops left before taking Tilly's hand. "Ready?"

"No," she answered, looking toward her door. "But I don't think I'll ever be completely ready, so I might as well go now."

Her grit and determination amazed him and he leaned over to give her a quick kiss. "Let's go see if anything's missing, and then I'd like you to pack a bit and come with me to Benedict House."

"I can't do that. No."

"I don't like the idea of you staying here."

"Then I'll get a. . . ." She didn't finish her sentence and he winced as he realized she probably didn't have the funds for a hotel room.

"Tilly, please." He'd beg if he had to, knowing that he wouldn't feel comfortable with her anywhere other than Benedict House.

It was on her lips to say no, he could see it in her eyes, but then her expression softened. "Keaton."

"Please." he repeated, softer. "I need you safe. I've only just found you again." He lowered his head so his lips almost brushed her ear and he delighted at her shiver. "Please."

Some part of him knew he was playing unfairly. She was vulnerable and he was pulling at her emotions, but he didn't care. He'd meant every word of it and he'd do far more to keep her safe. No matter what, she was staying with him tonight.

She sighed deeply, but tilted her head up and whispered, "Yes."

He gave her a quick kiss, promising himself he'd make up for it with a longer one as soon as everything got settled, and took her hand so they could face her apartment together. She squeezed his hand in a silent thank you.

Even though they'd seen the mess earlier, it wasn't any easier the second time. As heart-wrenching as it was for him to see all her things scattered and broken, he could only imagine how it made her feel.

One glance at her told him she was putting on a brave front. She walked stoically through the tattered living room, seeming to note each item with a nod of her head. He followed quietly, aghast at how much damage had been done. Hell, there wasn't one picture unbroken or one unslashed cushion. Even her clothing had been pulled from her bedroom and was scattered throughout her hallway. He wasn't even sure there was enough untouched clothing for her to pack in an over-night bag. Heaven alone knew what kind of damage they'd find in the bathroom.

A muffled sob from the kitchen caught his attention and he hurried to catch up with her. He hadn't realized she'd moved ahead of him that far. She stood by the kitchen island, her face in her hands, sobbing.

"Tilly?" He came to a halt behind her and placed a hand on her shoulder.

She turned around and her red, wet eyes hurt his heart. When he found out who did this, and he would, they were going to pay. He'd see to it himself.

"They ruined your cake," she said, pointing to the floor, which he now noticed was covered with yellow cake pieces and smears of light chocolate icing. "Your ten-layer chocolate cake."

She buried her head in his chest and cried. Not knowing what else to do, he simply held her, stroking her back and murmuring that it would be okay. The entire time, he hoped and prayed that he was right, but was very afraid he was telling her lies.

Tilly decided Keaton must think she was idiot. Her entire apartment was trashed and she fell apart because of a *cake*. Though to be honest, she'd been pretty close to losing it since the first step into her apartment. It was just seeing the cake all over the floor that finally pushed her over the edge. The cake she'd baked because once upon a time it had been his favorite and she wanted to do something special for him.

And now, it was smashed all over her floor.

She pushed back from him and wiped her eyes. "I'm sorry. I'm okay now."

"What in the world are you apologizing for?" he asked. "I believe coming home to find your apartment ransacked is a perfectly acceptable reason to be upset."

She straightened her back. "I need to clean this up."

"No." He held out an arm to stop her. "Do a quick look around to see if anything's missing, grab an overnight bag, and we're going to Benedict House."

"I can't just leave this like it is."

"Yes, you can."

"No. I can't."

"You can and you are." His voice had changed. He probably wasn't even aware of it, but he'd taken on the *You'll do as I say because I said so* tone she'd heard Kipling use before. Most likely it was embedded in the Benedict DNA. "I'll send over a cleaning crew tomorrow."

"A cleaning crew? Keaton—"

He put a finger to her lips. "Check to see if anything's missing. Pack an overnight bag. We can argue about cleanup later. I don't feel comfortable with you being here any longer than you have to be."

His words had the desired effect and she looked over her shoulder. No one was here now, but did that mean they were really gone or they were just hiding and couldn't be seen? Without another word, she checked on the few valuables she had.

Her laptop screen had been smashed as well as her TV, but the secret hiding place she kept her mother's few pieces of jewelry was undisturbed. She lifted the small velvet bag from between her boxsprings and mattress and looked around for an overnight bag.

She found one in the hall and forced herself to turn off her emotions while she packed. She could do this, just put clothes in a bag. She didn't even look to see if they were messed up; rather, she shoved anything nearby into the bag.

"I don't think you'll need the puffer jacket," Keaton said, gently removing it from the bag. "How about you go gather what you need from the bathroom and I'll finish up in here?"

With a nod, she was off, doing her best to shut herself off from what she was actually doing and instead focused on what she needed. Toothbrush. In the toilet. Surely the Benedicts had a spare. Makeup. Dumped out across the countertop. With a sound that wasn't quite a laugh, she decided she didn't need anything in the bathroom after all.

"I need to borrow a toothbrush," she told Keaton as she walked back into her bedroom.

He looked up from zipping up her bag. "We can handle that. You ready?"

She took one last look around what a few hours ago had been her safe haven, her home, and sighed. "Yes."

She was not going to cry again. She was not.

"Hey," Keaton tugged the strap of the bag over his shoulder and pulled her to his chest. "It's going to be okay. I promise."

It took everything she had, but she managed to control her tears. "How do you know? Look at this." The wide sweep of her arm encompassed the whole of the apartment.

With one finger, he lifted her chin so she had no choice but to look into his eyes. "Because there are two of us now. And together we can handle it."

She wanted so desperately to believe him. Truly she did. And she believed that he thought he would be right there through it all with her. But they had only reconnected two days ago and had spent years apart. Emotionally, she couldn't afford to put all her eggs in his basket; it was too risky. Her heart couldn't handle losing him twice.

But as she looked into his strange brown eyes, she knew she'd offend him if she spoke her doubts, so instead she swallowed them, smiled, and said, "Okay."

"Good," he said even though he probably knew she wouldn't argue with him. "It's settled then. We'll get you to Benedict House, have a good night's rest, and the cleaning crew will come by in the morning." He took her hand and led her to the door.

"What's it like?" she couldn't help but ask.

"What's what like?"

She waited while he locked the door. "To speak a word and have the whole world do your bidding?"

He looked momentarily stunned as if he hadn't heard right or maybe it was just that he never realized that was what happened. She feared it was the first and she'd gone and offended him anyway.

But he flashed that easy smile that always seemed to make her heart flutter *just so* and said, "Pretty damn good, actually."

His answer was so unexpected, she broke out into laughter. Still smiling, he took her hand and said, "Let's get out of here."

She couldn't agree more. And even though the apartment was a wreck and she was moving temporarily into a house she wasn't completely comfortable living in, his hand felt perfect and right wrapped around hers. It didn't escape her attention that he was once more protecting her in that caring way of his. Even with all that had gone on and even with all the questions surrounding her apartment and who had trashed it, her heart still felt light because she knew Keaton would keep her safe.

Their levity was shorter than expected, however, because when they reached his car, all four tires had been slashed.

It had been dangerous for Jade to stick around once she'd finished trashing Tilly's apartment. But she had wanted to slash Keaton's tires because she knew The Gentleman would like it. She waited behind a bush on the outskirts of the parking lot. Enough out of the way so that no one would see her, but close enough that she could see and hear what was happening.

She'd heard them talking with the policewoman and was able to confirm that the local police department had nothing figured out. Just the thought of it made her smile. She couldn't wait to share that tidbit with The Gentleman.

Keaton Benedict didn't look scared yet and that was the only downside to the night. His girlfriend, though, looked scared enough for both of them. If everything went according to plan, it wouldn't be long before she saw that look on Keaton's face.

"Are you calling the police?" Tilly asked him as he pulled out his phone.

"Yes," he said. "Part of me believes it won't do any good, but in this case, I think it's best to err on the side of caution." He cocked an eyebrow. "Do you feel the same?"

"I trust Officer Adams," she told him. "I'm not sure I feel the same about her partner yet. But there's something different about her."

Keaton nodded and started dialing. "I saw it, too."

They didn't have to wait long for Alyssa to show up again. This time she arrived without her partner. She explained that he was writing the report from earlier in the evening. Something in her tone of voice and the look in her eye gave Tilly the impression she was relieved he'd stayed behind.

Tilly and Keaton stood off to the side while she looked over the car and made a phone call. It seemed to Tilly that she took her time and was surprised when the officer waved them over to her instead of coming to them.

"Did you find something, Officer?" Keaton asked, slipping his hand into Tilly's.

It was such a simple gesture, but one that had an instant calming effect on her. She squeezed his in a silent thank you.

Alyssa's gaze followed the movement. "I'm going to be honest with you both, because I think it's the right thing to do and because this could potentially be a dangerous situation."

What the hell? Beside her, she felt Keaton tense and she knew he hadn't liked Alyssa's response, either.

"Officially," Alyssa said. "It is the position of the Charleston PD that the break-in and the tires are not related to the recent kidnappings and murders."

"And unofficially?" Tilly asked while giving a sideways glance to Keaton. He looked seconds away from exploding.

"Unofficially," Alyssa said, "I find everything to be too coincidental. I don't believe in coincidence. Come here." She walked to the back tires and waited for them to join her. She pointed to the slash. "See this? It's not the sort of slash we normally see. Based on my experience, it looks more like it was made with an elite type service knife."

"What are you saying?" Keaton asked.

"I think we're seeing a break in pattern because there is more than one person involved: the mastermind and his minions. I'm also saying that you should be extremely vigilant about your safety. Don't take unneeded risks. Be on the lookout for anything suspicious. That sort of thing."

Alyssa waited until they'd called a cab and it picked them up before she left. On the way to Benedict House, Keaton sent Kipling a text telling him he'd be home in ten minutes, that Tilly was coming to stay, and that he'd explain everything when he got there. Kipling sent back a simple **Okay**.

His older brother was waiting outside as they pulled up. "Lena is putting some things for Tilly in your room," Kipling said to Keaton after greeting Tilly. "I trust that's acceptable?"

"Perfect," Keaton said.

"Come in and sit down." He led them into the living room and motioned toward the couch. Keaton took a seat and pulled Tilly into his lap. "You look like you need a drink. Tell me what's going on while I pour."

Keaton knew he'd given his oldest brother hell while they were growing up. Heck, he still liked to push his buttons on occasion, but it was times like this when he wondered what he'd do without him. Kipling was often viewed as cold and ruthless, but that was only if you didn't know him. To family, he was loyal and fiercely protective.

For all appearances, his family now included Tilly. As Keaton and Tilly drank the scotch Kipling poured them, they gave him the rundown of what happened at Tilly's apartment. When they finished, Kipling didn't say anything, but stood up and poured his own drink. He didn't speak again until he sat down.

"I don't like it," Kipling said. "Not one bit. You did the right thing, though." He sighed. "I'm not sure what's gotten into the Charleston PD. It's utter bullshit they didn't do more than they did. Though it does sound like Alyssa has a brain in her head, unlike the other so-called police officers."

"That's what I told Tilly." Keaton stroked her arm. She smiled sweetly at him and yawned. He kissed her cheek. "I think it's time we turned in. Looks like the scotch made her sleepy."

Kipling nodded. "Go get her settled. I'll have your car taken care of."

"Thank you." Keaton stood to his feet, holding Tilly close to him. "Come on," he told her. "Let me show you where my room is, just in case you've forgotten."

"Tilly," Kipling called out and the couple turned to face him. "It goes without saying, but you're welcome to stay here for as long as you need."

"Thank you," she whispered, and she sounded so fragile, Keaton tugged her closer. He couldn't help but think how perfect she felt in his arms.

He'd dropped her overnight bag in the foyer when they came in and Lena—bless her heart, that woman needed a raise—had already taken it upstairs to his room.

Though she'd been yawning in the living room, the walk to the bedroom seemed to have woken Tilly up a bit. Her eyes darted around the hallways and he wondered how much had changed since she'd last been inside.

"It's so strange being back here," she said. "It all looks so familiar, yet different."

He knew exactly what she was talking about, but he didn't want to think about the past. Too much wasted time stayed there. He wanted to focus on the future, because the more time he spent with her, the more he saw Tilly being a part of it.

"I hope you don't mind sharing a room with me. If you do, I'll have Lena set up a guest room."

"I don't mind a bit."

Keaton smiled and pointed. "There's a full bath through that door and Lena should have set you out a toothbrush."

Tilly nodded, wrapping her arms around her body. "Where will Elise be staying?"

"She'll be at the opposite end of the hall." At her nod, he added. "Simply because Kipling wouldn't let me stick her in the pool house."

That got a smile out of her, but it quickly faded. "Is

it stupid that I'm not looking forward to seeing her tomorrow?"

Keaton closed the bedroom door. "No. I'm not overly pleased about her being here, either."

"It's just, she went to college and graduated and now she's interning . . . and me? I wait tables at a gentlemen's club."

She was playing with her nails. Keaton took her hand, forcing her to stop. "And you are sweet and beautiful and determined and strong and smart."

She held her hand up. "Okay. I get it."

"Are you sure? Because I'll keep saying it over and over." He didn't like her insinuation that she wasn't as good as Elise or that she wasn't good enough for him. Especially since the exact opposite was true.

"I think we better stop before my head gets inflated."

His plan had been to leave her alone so she could get some rest, but he realized he needed to make sure she knew exactly how he felt. He strolled over to her and lightly placed his hands on her shoulders so she had no choice but to face him.

"You see, that's where you're wrong," he said. "I don't think your head is inflated enough. Because if you saw what I see, you'd understand just how wonderful you are."

He knew Mama Ann had been proud of her and he remembered her as being a nurturing and kind woman. But who had been there for Tilly after her mother's death? Who had supported her, been her cheerleader, made sure she knew how accomplished she was?

He had a feeling it was no one. Especially if that ass of a manager was any indication of the people she'd been around the last few years.

"It's been so long," she said and her eyes grew wet.

"What's been so long?"

"Since there's been anyone other than me. I'm so used to doing it all on my own, starting when Mama got sick, it's hard to believe all this." She waved her hand to indicate the room.

"You better get used to it because I'm not going anywhere and I'm not letting you go."

She smiled for what had to be the first time since they'd found her apartment in shambles. "That's good to hear."

Her fingers brushed up and down his arm and he knew he had to get out of the room and fast before they went too far. He took a step back and she frowned.

"As much as I'd like to stay here and prove to you just how wonderful I think you are, I think I'd better let you get some rest," he said.

"Rest?" she asked. "Who needs to rest? Not me." She took a step forward and placed a hand on his shoulder. "Tell me you're tired and I won't say another word."

He had the strength to walk away before, but not now. Not with her touching him. One touch of her hand and he was done for. "You're making it difficult for me to remember why not doing this is a good idea."

"Excellent." She kept her eyes on him as she moved closer when he was within reach, she wrapped her arms around him, pulling his head down and whispering, "Take me to bed, Keaton." Before he could say anything, her lips were on his and leaving no doubt that she didn't mean to sleep.

Any further thoughts of resting flew out the window with her soft-spoken request and the brush of her lips against his. "Are you sure this is what you want?" he asked. After all, it'd been an emotionally intense day and he never wanted her to look back and feel that he'd taken advantage of her.

Her lips grazed his cheek and she whispered in his ear, "I'm very, very sure."

"Because we don't have to do anything."

She pulled back and he couldn't help but relax at the playfulness of her expression. Her hands drifted to the waist of his pants. "I think this calls for an alternate plan."

"You don't have to . . ." he started, but let the protest die because she already had his pants undone and was licking her lips even though he still had his boxer briefs on.

She palmed him through the thin material. "What was that?"

"Nothing, absolutely nothing."

He didn't miss her look of triumph when she replied, "That's what I thought."

She eased his underwear down, licking her lips again, and he thought he might lose it at the sight of her tongue. Fortunately, he was able to hold on to some sort of control, because the sweet haven of her mouth was unlike anything he'd ever experienced.

"Tilly!" he panted out as her hands came up to his upper thighs and held him in place.

He wasn't going to last long. That was the only thought in his head other than the one acknowledging how perfect her mouth was.

Only when his climax approached did he pull her head back, or at least tried to. But she wouldn't budge.

"I'm going to—" he tried to warn her.

She responded by pulling him deeper into her mouth and holding on to his thighs tighter. He groaned as he realized what she was doing and allowed his release to overtake him.

Tilly rocked back to sit on her heels and gazed up at him with an expression of such satisfaction, he couldn't help but grin at her. Whenever he looked at her, his heart threatened to overflow with emotions. How was it possible she'd been back in his life for such a short time? And how was it possible he already felt as if he couldn't live without her? But at the moment, her expression was still playful and he wanted to be playful back.

"Oh, now you've done it," he warned her. "Now it's time."

"Time for what?"

Instead of answering he swooped down and picked her up, startling her so much she squealed. In one quick move he had her on top of the bed beneath him. "Payback."

But instead of doing what she thought he'd do, he pushed himself up on his hands and lowered his mouth to hers. She gave a whimper of surprise before kissing him back. For several long minutes, he got lost in her kiss. Her lips were soft and her body responsive.

He was going to give her as much pleasure as possible.

After a few minutes of kissing, he slowly pulled himself away from her sweet lips, ignoring her soft protests. Ever so gently, he kissed his way down her stomach, giving her skin a tiny nibble every so often.

When he made it between her legs, she sucked in a breath and fisted his hair in her hands. She had the sweetest-tasting skin and he swore he got lost in the sensations that were Tilly: her taste, the sounds she made as he used his mouth to drive her toward her own climax, the feel of her as she came around him, and how right it felt when he gathered her to his side and gave her lips one more kiss before her rhythmic breathing indicated sleep had overtaken her.

He tightened his arms around her and whispered to her, "Sleep well, my Tilly. I have you and I'll keep you safe."

Keaton jerked wide awake the next morning at the sound of someone walking down the hall. It took a few seconds for him to realize it was Knox. Surprised, he rolled over to look at the time. Almost five thirty. That didn't sound like Knox. He'd never known the middle Benedict brother to get less than eight hours of sleep a night. In fact, Kipling and Keaton had often joked that they weren't sure how the Benedict DNA managed to create such a straitlaced member.

Tilly was still sleeping and though his body balked, he knew he needed to go for a quick jog before showering and eating breakfast. The last few days had been hell on his workout schedule and if he was going to jog, he needed to get it done before it got so humid outside, he felt like he was breathing water.

He kissed Tilly's shoulder, and smiled as her eyes fluttered open. "Good morning, beautiful."

"Morning," she said, still half asleep.

"I'm going for a quick jog. Want to join me?"

She snorted and rolled over. "It's like you don't know me at all."

He laughed and got out of bed to get dressed. On his way out of the house, he passed Lena in the hallway, turning down her offer of coffee and promising he'd be back in time for breakfast. He started with a slow, but steady pace, warming his muscles before settling into the brisk pace he enjoyed.

He loved Charleston. Many of the kids he'd gone to high school with had given him a hard time for enrolling at an in-state university nearby. They didn't understand why he'd decide to stay in the city he grew up in when he had the grades and money to go anywhere he wanted.

He didn't even try to explain. Most of them had grown up here, just like he had. Many of them were also from old Charleston families. Frankly, he thought if they didn't experience the same feeling of just *being* that he did, there was no point in even trying to explain.

He loved the history, the charm, and the strength of the city. He loved the diversity of the people and the taste of its cuisine. He was proud of his heritage and the role his family had played.

He looked out toward the water as he ran. The water that was life to his family's shipping empire. He often wondered why, if he was so proud of what his family had accomplished, why he didn't want a more active role in the business?

That question had bothered him until he went on his first international relief trip. Then he knew the answer immediately.

Deep in his soul, he knew it wasn't enough to simply make the most money and wield the most power. In order to be fulfilled he needed more. For as much as he loved his city, he wasn't blind to her problems.

His city was also filled with poverty and abuse and had history that couldn't be washed away or overlooked. There were still inequalities and perceptions that had to be dealt with. And as much as he'd enjoyed his work overseas, he felt he needed to straighten out the needs of his own home before he tackled someone else's.

That was what he wanted to do with Benedict Industries. It wasn't enough that they were shipping giants. He wanted them to be giants of charity, too. But it went beyond charity. There had to be a way, with a business as large and diverse as his family's, to not only help the people of Charleston but to set them on an upward path.

Sometimes, it felt like a burden too heavy for him to carry by himself.

He should ask Knox. He was the heart of the three brothers. The true do-gooder. If he wasn't able to help, Keaton was willing to bet he knew someone who would.

He turned and started back toward the house. Maybe Knox would be at breakfast and he'd be able to set up a time to talk with him then.

More people were out and about as he headed home. Several of them looked his way. They probably recognized him from the recent news. Not only had his name been spoken and written by the media, but at its core, Charleston was a small town and everyone knew everyone else's business. It was always the same, someone's cousin was on the rescue squad, and so and so heard about it on the prayer chain and it wasn't gossip if it was on the prayer chain. He could almost hear the sure-to-follow "bless his heart" the conversation would end with.

As he approached Benedict House, he slowed down a bit. He'd have to take a shower before breakfast and he really wanted to talk to Tilly, too. If he managed his time right, he should be able to fit everything in without irritating Lena too much, he decided with a smile.

But as he turned the final corner to the long drive, his heart sank. He dropped his speed from a jog to a walk and then from a walk to a stroll, cursing under his breath the entire time.

There was only one reason for a black limo to be parked in his driveway.

Elise had arrived early.

He considered turning around and heading back out, but before he could get his feet to move, the front door opened and Elise stepped out. She spotted him almost immediately, of course. She lifted her arm in a wave.

Damn it. No way could he pretend he didn't see her, not with her eyes locked on his the way they were. With a sigh, he continued walking up the drive. By the time he made it to where she was, her father had joined her.

"Keaton," he said with a nod and a handshake. "Congratulations on your graduation."

"Thank you, sir. Nice to see you again."

Mr. Germain nodded toward his daughter. "Look after my girl this summer."

"We all will, sir." Keaton didn't think he'd imagined the look of spite Elise gave her dad before her features settled once more into nothing.

"Oh, I know that. But I was meaning you especially." He ended his sentence with a wink.

Keaton was glad he hadn't yet eaten breakfast. He was sure if he had, he would have lost it right there on top of Mr. Germain's ridiculously expensive Italian leather shoes. As it was, he decided to remain silent.

"Hello, Keaton," Elise said and he turned to her.

She was so perfectly good-looking, she looked fake. From her perfectly styled blond hair, to her perfect body hidden by her perfectly tailored summer suit. Her perfection did nothing for him.

"Hello, Elise. You look well."

Elise wrinkled her nose. "You can welcome me after you shower."

Just as well, he didn't want to touch her anyway. "Have you had breakfast yet?" Keaton asked. "I was going to get a shower and then eat a quick bite."

"Yes," Mr. Germain said. "We ate before we headed out."

"I'll sit with you while you eat," Elise said to him.

"No need for you to do that," Keaton said. "I'm sure you need to unpack and get settled in."

"It can wait," she said in a perfectly sweet voice that make him feel sick. "I'd much rather hear what you've been up to since we last saw each other."

Of course she would.

"And I can put some stuff away while you shower," she said as if it were the most brilliant idea ever.

"I have to go," Mr. Germain said. He gave Keaton a slap on the shoulder before turning to his daughter and pointing at her. "Be good."

"Aren't I always?"

"I'm not answering that."

Keaton stood in front of the house with her while she watched her father get into the limo and leave the property. No sooner had the car disappeared, then Elise turned to him.

"I heard about what happened at that club," Elise said. "Thank goodness you're okay. I hope they find the person who did it. Scary to think they're just walking around."

"You'll be safe here." He shot her a fake smile. "I have to shower, so I'll see you later." He walked inside, grumbling under his breath, still irritated that she'd shown up so early, and ran into Kipling and Knox.

"Whoa," his middle brother said. "Where are you stomping off to?"

"To shower." From the looks of it, they were both ready for the day. "By the way, I need to speak with you about something. Do you have time to get together later?"

"Sure," Knox said. "Why don't you meet me at my office at five? We'll go have a drink and talk."

Ordinarily, he'd agree, but not tonight. "Can't do it tonight. I have a dinner date."

"You're not going to be here on my first night back in Charleston?" Elise asked from the doorway. Kipling shot him a look of sympathy, before leaving.

"No, I'm not. I made plans and I'm not cancelling." He felt like a petulant four-year-old, but he didn't care. Damned if he was not going to be with Tilly just because Elise had arrived.

"You don't have to be rude about it; I was only asking a question." Elise looped her arm through Knox's. "Besides it's no big deal. I'll have dinner with Knox."

"I'm afraid I'll have to take a raincheck." Knox looked completely ill at ease. "I have dinner plans as well."

"You do?" Keaton asked. That was interesting. Knox typically wasn't one to go out of an evening for business and wasn't seeing anyone that Keaton knew of.

"It's business," Knox quickly added. "Just business."

Keaton got the impression it was a lot more than business, not that he would question him about it in front of Elise. Nope. Anything having to do with either charities or Knox's love life would have to wait until later.

"But you were going to meet Keaton," Elise countered.

"Only for drinks," Knox reiterated.

"You can always have dinner with Kipling," Keaton suggested, which was somewhat of an asshole move. It wasn't fair to pawn her off on his brother.

"That's okay," Elise was quick to counter. "I'll probably turn in early tonight. I'm sure I'll be tired." Lifting her head, she pulled her arm away from Knox. "If you gentlemen will excuse me."

As she disappeared up the stairs, Keaton looked at his older brother. "I know I should probably feel bad, but I really don't care. I don't even know what she's doing here."

"She's interning," he said, his eyes filled with amusement.

"I'm glad this is so funny to you."

Knox clapped him around the shoulders. "There's no way you're going to marry that girl. I forbid it. Let's just get through the summer, okay?"

"Easy for you to say. You didn't have your life partner picked out for you in the cradle."

"Thank the heavens above."

"Although, come to think of it, it probably should be you. I mean, you aren't seeing anyone, you might as well marry her." Keaton shrugged. "Bet it wouldn't bother you at all."

"You don't know everything, little bro." Knox looked at his watch. "I have to head into the office. Want to talk later this morning? I mean, I assume you aren't a useful member of society yet?"

"No, but I have an idea and I want your opinion."

They decided to meet for breakfast at eight. With that settled and Elise out of his hair for the moment, Keaton decided to take a shower and then see if Tilly was awake yet.

It irritated him that Elise had shown up and assumed he had nothing better to do than to hang out with her. Elise felt as if she was *entitled* to his company. She expected to snap her fingers and he'd do whatever she wanted.

Which was totally at odds with how he remembered her being. How her passiveness came out when it came time to give her opinion on anything that mattered. Then she'd go along with whatever Keaton wanted. It was infuriating as hell.

By anyone's standards she was stunning. The sundress she'd had on this morning showed off her figure perfectly. Her skin was so pale, he guessed she probably kept the sunblock industry in business single-handedly. He remembered when they were in high school, she always wore her long blond hair in a ponytail. Today, it fell to her shoulders. And her eyes were just as blue as they'd always been.

Yet, even as stunning as she was, she did nothing for him. No, it was a sultry waitress who worked her ass off and refused to take anything from anyone who captured his attention.

Tilly stretched out in Keaton's bed, thinking about the night before with a smile. It had been prefect. Keaton had been perfect. And his mouth? Oh yeah, more perfection. But even as perfect as the night had been, the truth about the danger she was in, stood nearby, waiting.

She slipped her hand between her legs as if she could conjure him up with her thoughts. Too bad he went for a jog; she could definitely go for an encore.

"Oh my God," a familiar voice said. "Who are you and what are you doing in that bed?"

Tilly propped herself up on an elbow and looked

toward the doorway that suddenly flew open. Elise stood there with a look of shock on her face and a see-through robe on. Damn, she was a bold one.

"Tilly?" Elise asked. "Tilly Brock?"

"Hello, Elise."

"You and Keaton?" Her once-upon-a-time best friend asked the question as if it were the most ridiculous thing she'd ever heard.

Tilly looked her up and down. "Well, it's not like I just showed up half naked to see what would happen."

Elise gasped and her eyes grew icy cold.

"I mean," Tilly continued, "you couldn't have been in the house longer than what . . . half an hour?"

Elise didn't say anything and turned and left the room, but not before shooting Tilly a look that left her with the impression that the blond hadn't surrendered yet.

"Oh my God, Tilly!"

Tilly nearly jumped out of her seat thirty minutes later at breakfast at Elise's shrill good morning. Apparently, her plan was to pretend the conversation in Keaton's room never happened. Tilly only regretted she hadn't told Keaton, but there hadn't been time. After Elise left, Tilly had taken a shower and when she got out, Keaton was waiting at the top of the stairs to walk her to the dining room for breakfast. His hair was still slightly damp. He'd mentioned he sometimes took a shower after jogging in the pool house.

"Elise," Tilly said dryly.

Across the table, Keaton glared at his other houseguest. "Damn, Elise. Take it down a few notches."

Elise sat down beside Tilly. "Tell me everything you've done since the last time I saw you."

Was she serious? "Nothing much, you know. Shower. Get dressed." She shrugged.

"What?" Keaton asked, as Elise's fake smile faltered.

"Good morning, everyone," Kipling said, strolling into the dining room and unfortunately saving Elise. He sat down and poured a cup of coffee. "Keaton, your car will be here in half an hour, and Tilly, your apartment will be cleaned by noon."

The long-reaching, all-powerful arm of the Benedicts never failed to amaze her. Though before, that power had been used against her family. It was an odd comfort to be on the safe side.

And no matter what Keaton or Kipling said, she was going to pay them back for the cleaning service.

"Thank you," she said. "I guess I can go back later today."

Kipling looked to Keaton, who only answered with, "The hell you will." She tried to say something, but he cut her off. "We don't know who it was or if they'll come back. You're staying here."

"You can't force her, you know," Elise said.

"We aren't forcing anyone to do anything," Kipling said. "Keaton, calm down. Tilly, until we have additional information, I think it would be best for you to remain here."

"I don't want to be an imposition." She looked at Elise. "You already have one houseguest."

"And Lena is thrilled to have a house full again. Trust me, if you leave now, she'll mope for days." Kipling gave her a rare smile. "Don't break her heart, Tilly."

He was being overdramatic, which really wasn't like the Kipling she remembered, but it was a nice change to Keaton's overprotectiveness. Though, that was nice, too. It felt good to be wanted. She knew Keaton wanted her to stay, but she wasn't sure she'd have considered it if Kipling didn't feel the same way.

Keaton pushed back from the table. "I have to meet Knox for breakfast. Walk with me outside, Tilly?"

"Sure." She'd wondered why he was only drinking coffee.

He waited until they were out of earshot before talking. "I'll be back in about two hours. Please tell me you'll still be here when I get back."

He looked so worried. She pushed his hair back from his face. "I promise. I'm not going anywhere. I'll stay here with Elise and Kipling."

"Just Elise. Kipling's probably going into the office."

Ugh. Suddenly she remembered one of the reasons why she wanted to leave. "In that case, I promise nothing," she teased.

He brought his head down low and whispered in her ear, "If you're still here when I get back, I promise to make it up to you."

"Oh? And just how do you plan on doing that?" She shivered as his breath brushed over her skin.

"If you have to know, I was up most of the night, thinking of all the reasons why your staying here is a good idea." He kissed her neck. "Or rather, I tried to think of all the reasons. To be honest, I never got past you in my bed."

The rumble deep in his throat may have been the sexiest sound she'd ever heard. "Hold those thoughts and we'll discuss them in greater detail when I get back."

"Two hours, right?"

He nodded.

"Don't suppose there's anything you can do to keep Elise in her room while you're gone, is there?"

"Nothing that won't get me arrested."

"Don't even joke. I've had enough of police officers to last me for just about forever."

"I'll be back as soon as I can." He gave her a quick kiss and then he was off.

She didn't want to go back into the dining room, but she refused to let Elise get the best of her. So instead of hiding out in Keaton's room, she squared her shoulders and went to face the woman who used to be her best friend.

It was quiet when she returned to the dining room, but then she remembered Keaton saying that Kipling was Elise's least favorite brother. Unfortunately, Kipling appeared to finishing up his breakfast and she knew he'd soon be on his way to the office. Her fear was confirmed when he stood and left right as she sat down.

Elise, strangely, didn't say a word until he'd pulled out of the driveway and when she turned to face Tilly, gone was the debutante and in her place was a calculating shrew.

"How long have you been fucking Keaton?" Elise asked.

Even though Tilly had half expected the change in demeanor, it still came as a shock. That was the only explanation she could come up with as to why she actually answered the question.

"Ages," she lied, just to see the look on Elise's face.

"I don't believe you."

"I don't care." Tilly ate a bite of egg. She wondered when Elise started her internship and hoped it was soon.

"I can't say that I blame you for not wanting to stay here," Elise said, changing the subject. "I certainly wouldn't want to hang out with people who were only putting up with me out of respect for my mother."

"What?" Tilly asked even though she knew that was exactly what Elise wanted.

"Everyone loved your mother, Tilly. Mama Ann was the sweetest and dearest woman anyone ever met. But your dad was a rat. You know he was running around on your mom."

Tilly couldn't believe the lies spewing from Elise's mouth. How was it lightning hadn't struck her dead yet? "He did not." It was paltry, but they were the only words she could manage to get out at the moment.

"Please. Grow up. Everyone knew about it. Why do you think you and Mama Ann spent so much time over here?" Elise asked.

Because before the scandal that ruined her family, her mother and Keaton's mother had been best friends. They were always doing things together. Shopping, volunteering, hosting parties.

"Oh my God," Elise said. "You really didn't know?"

She sounded surprised, but Tilly had a feeling she'd been planning what to say since the second she heard Tilly would be hanging around.

"Of course I don't know, because it's completely made up." It had to be, her father had been one of the kindest men she'd even known. And he'd adored his wife.

Elise stood with a look of pity that made Tilly's stomach turn. She had to be lying. She had to be.

"I guess for some people, reality is just too hard to live with. That's okay, you can live in your make-believe land." Elise stood up and smoothed her skirt down. "I'm going to go shopping. Alone."

Tilly tried not to snort as her ex–best friend walked away. Did Elise actually think that Tilly was going to ask if she could go? Seriously?

"And another thing."

Tilly hated Elise's voice. The very sound of it made her blood boil.

"You may have Keaton in your make-believe land," Elise said from the doorway, and there was no hiding the satisfaction she obviously felt. "But here in reality, he's mine. You'd do well to remember that."

Tilly bit her tongue so she wouldn't spout out the *Now who's living in make-believe land* line she wanted to say so badly. No, she would sit right here and not move. She would not let that meddlesome bitch know how much her words hurt her.

"Come on in, Keaton," Knox said. "Just let me grab my jacket and we'll go get some breakfast."

Knox gave a friendly "hello" and "how are you" to the two admins already at their desks. Both ladies looked up at him and smiled.

"Can I bring either one of you something back to eat?" Knox asked. "Barbara? Joy?"

Barbara was in her late fifties and had been working for Benedict Industries for as long as Keaton could remember. "Nothing for me. You boys go have a nice breakfast."

Joy, however, was only a few years older than Knox. "You know if I even look at bakery food, I gain ten pounds."

They both thanked him and told Keaton to stop by again soon. Keaton noticed that Joy's eyes followed Knox out.

"I think Joy likes you," Keaton said when the door closed behind them.

Knox rolled his eyes. "I don't get involved with our employees."

"I wasn't suggesting that. It was a simple statement."

As they walked to their favorite breakfast spot, Keaton counted no less than five women who said hello to Knox in passing. All that attention and, to Knox, it was no big deal. Keaton shook his head. A few weeks ago, it might have bothered him, but now? The only woman he had eyes for was Tilly. The only woman . . . Knox not paying attention . . .

"Damn." Keaton stopped. "I can't believe I didn't see it before."

"See what?" Knox asked, pulling him out of the middle of the sidewalk.

"Who is she and why haven't you introduced her to the family?"

Keaton didn't know it was possible for his brother to look that deathly pale and not pass out. For all that he might try to deny it, Keaton knew he'd guessed right.

Knox had a girlfriend.

A secret one.

Keaton smiled and started walking again. "That's okay. You don't have to tell me. Obviously, you're keeping it a secret for some reason."

Nope. He didn't have to know who she was or why they didn't tell anyone about their relationship. Not yet anyway. For now, it was enough to know she existed. And if Knox felt for her anything like what Keaton felt for Tilly? He was glad his saintly older brother had found someone.

Knox didn't say anything, but soon caught up to him.

Keaton refrained from glancing his way and it wasn't until they made it to the restaurant that Knox spoke.

"It's not for the reason you think," he said. "It's . . . well . . . we're complicated."

Knox looked troubled. Because he didn't like keeping his relationship hidden or because Keaton had figured it out?

"I don't *think* anything," Keaton said. "It's not my business. Just don't go getting married without telling me, okay?"

This time, Knox turned positively green. Keaton punched his older brother on the shoulder. "You need to loosen up some. Seriously, you'll tell us when you're ready."

They stood at the counter to order. Even though it was early, the place was packed. Knox ordered his usual: a breakfast sandwich with scrambled eggs mixed with sausage and cheese and topped with bacon. Keaton didn't think that was best choice, seeing how green he looked moments before, but Knox was an adult.

Keaton took his order of French toast and slid into the booth across from Knox. His brother's color looked better. Apparently, the greasy sandwich didn't make his stomach worse.

"What did you want to talk with me about?" Knox asked.

"It's an idea I had for Benedict Industries," he said.

"You have an idea for the business?" Knox leaned back in his seat. "That will make Kip very happy."

"Yeah, he's been on my ass about working for the company."

"He means well. Just doesn't always come across that way." Knox sipped his coffee. "But tell me about this idea you have."

"It struck me during my summers overseas."

"The ones in India with the water project?"

Knox would know about his not-so-public summers just as Keaton knew about his middle sibling's own summers overseas. Except Knox spent his time learning about computer hacking as a military consultant in Afghanistan.

"Yes. It occurred to me that I'm in a position—well, *we* are in a position—to give back. In a way that few people are because of how successful the businesses have been."

While he talked, Knox was listening very intently and nodding with what he said.

"I'd like to create a division within Benedict Industries to give back tangibly to our community. It's not only in India that people need help. It's right here in our backyard."

"Damn," Knox said.

"What?"

"People call me the saint and look at you." Knox waved toward him. "Creating a charitable division of Benedict Industries."

"Do you think Kip will go for it?"

"It'll create a lot of good PR. He'll care about that and he'd like to help people, too. Do you plan to do this all on your own?"

"Probably. To start with, at least. I was going to put a proposal together for Kip. Will you look at it before I give it to him?"

Knox nodded. "I think it's a great idea and you definitely have my support. After you write the proposal, we'll approach Kip together."

It was the outcome Keaton had hoped for and he felt as if a huge burden had been lifted off him. He could work for the family business and do something he felt passionate about.

After Elise left to go shopping, Tilly ventured out of the bedroom. Benedict House was so familiar and yet, oddly different at the same time. She strolled through the hallways, remembering snatches of her childhood she hadn't thought of in ages.

Eventually, she found herself in the kitchen where Lena was preparing lunch. Tilly remembered her from years past. "Can I help?"

Lena turned around with her hand over her heart. "Tilly. Lord, it does these old bones good to see you in my kitchen again." She held out her arms. "Come here."

Tilly walked into her embrace and held back tears as Lena whispered how much she'd missed her. And even though she'd known Elise had lied about no one really wanting her at the Benedict House, it felt good to have that assumption proven wrong. Being held by Lena wasn't the exact same as being held by her mother, but it was a second and the closest she would be able to find on earth.

"I know you've had some trouble the last few days," Lena said. "But it's so good to see you again. This place was never the same without you and your mama."

"It's so good to see you."

Lena took a step back and looked Tilly up and down. "Look at you. Beautiful."

Tilly's cheeks heated. "Lena."

"I mean it and you can tell you're just as beautiful on the inside. Unlike that high-and-mighty Elise." Lena shook her head. "That girl is nothing but bad news and trouble, mark my words. Mrs. Benedict would never stand for Mr. Keaton to marry such a ball of fluff."

"Keaton told me he had no intention of marrying Elise."

"Good, he needs someone like you."

Tilly shook her head. "I don't know, Lena. We've only just met again."

"When something's right, it's just right. Time won't change that." She turned back to the stove. "Now enough of that jabbering, you said you wanted to help?"

"Yes, ma'am."

"How about you make a nice salad for lunch? All three of my boys will be here and Mr. Knox likes salads. Mr. Kipling needs more greens in his diet. Mr. Knox says it's lack of nutrients that makes his brother so ornery. I told Mr. Knox, it had nothing to do with diet and greens, but that Mr. Kipling needs to get laid."

"Lena!" Tilly laughed. "I can't believe you said that."

"Why? Because old people don't know about getting laid? Please, child. How the hell do you think you got here?"

Being in the Benedicts' kitchen was the closest to feeling as if she was at home than anything she'd experienced in years. She stayed with Lena, making lunch, talking, and laughing until she heard Keaton return.

Lena laughed at the way she dropped her knife when the side door of the house opened.

"Sorry," Tilly said. "Let me finish."

"What? And risk you chopping off a finger or getting blood all over lunch? No way. You go see what Mr. Keaton is up to. And don't you worry about rushing back for lunch. It'll be at least two more hours on this bread."

"Thank you," Tilly called over her shoulder as she hurried up the stairs to the bedroom.

She paused outside Keaton's half-closed door, unsure if she should knock or not. She'd done her best not to think about what he'd said before he left. It had been easy when she was in the kitchen with Lena, but now that she was alone with her thoughts, she remembered his whispered promise.

"There you are," Keaton said, pushing the door all the way open. "I was getting ready to come hunt you down."

"I was in the kitchen helping Lena with lunch."

He dragged her into the room and closed the door behind them. "I bet she loved that."

"Yes, she did."

He grabbed her hand and tugged her to sit down beside him on the small loveseat at the end of bed. "What else did you talk about?"

She picked at imaginary lint on his shirt. "Oh you know . . . this and that."

"This and that?"

"Yes," she said, knowing he wanted her to admit they talked about him, but wanting to tease him. "Did you know she has seven grandchildren?"

"I did."

"And she still calls you and her brothers *her boys?*"

"She's as much a Benedict as we are."

She was suddenly very nervous, which she told herself was stupid. This was Keaton. She'd known him forever, even if she hadn't seen him in years. She knew him.

Maybe that's why she was nervous, because she somehow knew this moment would change everything.

He pushed a piece of hair out of her face. "Hey,

where did you go? You're thinking about something awfully hard."

His eyes were so sincere and calm, she felt she could dive into them and stay forever. She had the oddest thought that this building they were in, this house, was not home. Rather, this man in front of her was.

And that made her even more nervous.

"I feel as nervous as a teenager on her first date," she admitted.

"Why?"

Why? He asked her why? When he was sitting there, all handsome and good and smart and perfect, and she was just Tilly? She shook her head. "It seems as if the last few days have been a dream. Is this really happening? For real?"

He scooted closer, but instead of answering, he put his hand behind her head and leaned in for a kiss.

Heavens above, what the feel of his lips on her did to her insides. One touch and she was a quivering pile of goo. She took hold of his shirt and fisted it in her hands, holding him close and not allowing him to get away.

He pulled his head back and whispered against her lips. "Real enough for you now?"

"Not in the least," she said. "I think I need more reassurance."

"Mmm, do you? Let's see what I can do."

He reached down and gently pried her hands away from his shirt. "What would be more real to you? Your shirt off or mine?"

He wanted to play, did he? Well, two could do that. Instead of answering, she drew her shirt off over her head and dropped it on the floor. Her eyes never left his, so she didn't miss the seductive grin that covered his face when he realized what she was doing.

"Is that the way it is?" he asked, and within seconds his shirt was on the floor beside hers.

Her eyes bulged out at the sight of his chest. Holy shit. He obviously did more than jog. There was no way jogging alone would result in a chest that looked as if it belonged on the cover of a magazine. She had to resist the urge to reach out and touch it.

Soon, she told herself. She would touch it soon. Not only that, but soon she'd be pulled in close to it. Just the thought of her body being pressed against that hard plane of muscle was about enough to make her body tremble with need.

It was damn scary what he could do to her without even laying a finger on her.

His head tilted. "What are you thinking?"

She saw no reason to lie or be coy. "How much I'm looking forward to feeling you against me."

He didn't say anything, but rather held out his arms and drew her into his embrace. She sighed at the sensation of feeling him skin on skin. But it wasn't enough. She ran her fingers down his back, learning the feel of the muscles there.

He hummed in pleasure. "Your hands feel so good. So right."

Everything about the moment felt right. His hands, his touch, his smell. He slowly stood to his feet and she followed, not wanting to go a second without touching him. He walked her backward, until the back of her legs hit the edge of the bed.

"I want to see you," he whispered. "All of you. Will you show me?"

With anyone else she would be self-conscious, but for some reason it felt completely natural to lay down on the bed, move to her back, and lift her hips so he could take off her pants. His touch was electric as he tugged her jeans down her legs until all she wore was a tiny pair of panties.

Keaton looked appreciative over her body. "My God, you're beautiful."

She didn't argue with him because under his gaze, she felt beautiful. When he dropped his head and lightly brushed his lips across her belly and called her sexy, she felt that way. It was beyond any fantasy she'd ever had. She dug her fingers into his hair as he dipped lower and lower.

He placed kisses over the silk fabric covering where she ached for him and even the tiny piece of fabric was too much between them. Keaton, however, seemed to be in no hurry.

"Lena said lunch would be ready in a bit," she said, hoping he'd move faster.

"Doesn't matter," he answered, barely lifting his head. "I could stay here the entire afternoon, just doing this."

"I need you," she begged. "Please."

"You know, I never thought you'd be the impatient type."

"Only when it comes to you being inside me."

And still he didn't speed up or move. He kept on teasing her through the silk. When she tried to close her legs, he put a hand on each knee and kept her spread. Begging did no good, but she tried it anyway. Just when she thought he actually would stay put for the entire afternoon, he pulled back and ever so slowly, ran a finger around the edge of her thong.

"Fuck, you're so wet," he said.

"I know." She shivered at his touch.

He pushed his finger under the silk and teased her.

She jerked at the sensation of him finally touching her skin to skin.

"Oh yes," he said. "I can't wait to feel you. Is that what you want?"

"Yes, please," she said in a broken whisper he almost couldn't make out.

He came up on his knees, still not moving from his spot between her legs. She wasn't sure how he did it, but within seconds, his pants were gone and he was stroking himself.

"Oh my God," she said, because as he stroked, he seemed to grow thicker and longer.

He dug in his discarded pant pocket and fished out a condom. She tried to sit up. "Can I?"

But he pushed her back to the bed. "Not this time. I'm afraid if I have your hands on me, I'll lose it and that's not what I have in mind for today."

"What do you have in mind?" she asked, her fingertips dancing across his back.

"I'd rather show you." Without waiting for her to reply, he lined his sheathed cock with her and very carefully began to push inside her.

"Keaton." Her eyes drifted closed as she tried to contain the feelings he evoked in her body with his penetration. "So full. Damn."

"Just about halfway," he said, and she arched her back and lifted her hips to help him sink deeper. "Yes," he said.

He shuddered when he filled her completely and she realized how much he'd been holding back. She lightly touched his shoulder.

"You feel so good." She moaned when he swiveled his hips.

One eyebrow lifted. "Not too much?"

"No."

"Mmmm," he hummed and started a slow rocking rhythm that had her seeing stars.

"Ohh, yes." She tightened her legs around his waist.

He pulled out slightly and then drove inside her with a moan. She gasped in pleasure and clawed at his backside to try and get him deeper.

"Yes," she said in a half moan. "Again."

It was all he needed and he started a faster rhythm that had her panting in pleasure. She felt it was almost surreal that this was happening. How often had she imagined being in this very spot? And yet, even with as many times as she'd pictured it, the reality was so much more intense.

She could admit to herself that through the years, she'd held Keaton up as a yardstick against which she measured all men. Of course, it hadn't been the real Keaton, but one she'd made up in her mind. The other men hadn't even come close and now that she knew what the grown-up Keaton was like, he totally blew them out of the water.

She opened her eyes so she could watch him. She was in awe that it was her body that made him grow hard. Her hips that he dug his fingers into as he rode her. And her lips that he kissed just because he could and because he wanted to.

"You feel incredible," he said, going faster.

She wanted to tell him that he was the incredible one, but at that moment, he changed his pace, going slower, but being more deliberate, and in doing so, hit a spot within her that made her eyes roll to the back of her head and rendered her speechless with pleasure.

God, she'd never felt anything like this. He had been her ultimate dream and now he was her present reality.

The feel of him was incredible. The way his weight pressed against her, pushing her into the mattress, bringing them both pleasure. Truly, when she thought about it, he gave so much more than he took and if asked, she'd give him anything.

Thoughts like that used to frighten her about other people, but no longer. Not with him. Together they were more than they were by themselves. Something inside her knew that was how it was supposed to be. It was what her parents had. What she'd always wanted, but never thought she'd ever have. And now, it was so close, she could almost feel it in her hands. She realized in some ways that was even more scary: to have it within reach and to somehow lose it. Which would hurt so much more than if she'd never allowed herself the possibility of finding it.

"Tilly." He ran his hands up her side, leaving goose bumps in their wake.

Her orgasm was quickly approaching, which was a surprise because she never came that fast. Never. And, if she was reading his body language correctly, Keaton was close as well. His hands fisted on either side of her head. His breath came out in pants.

She planted both feet on the mattress and used it as leverage to meet him, thrust for thrust.

"Yes," he said. "Give it to me."

She came on his next thrust, feeling herself shatter around him as he held himself deep within her and released into the condom. Even after, he continued to surprise her, pulling her to him and holding her close. She couldn't help but think, *I could get used to this*.

He surprised her even more by holding her for several

minutes before getting up to dispose of the condom. "Stay here," he said, as if she had the energy to move.

He disappeared into the bathroom, returning with a washcloth. When she tried to close her legs, he simply said, "Stop."

No one had ever cleaned her after sex and while it felt odd at first, she decided after a bit that she could definitely get used to being taken care of.

"How long do we have before lunch?" he asked.

She rolled her head and glanced at the clock on his night stand. "Just under an hour."

"Good." He threw the washcloth onto the floor and crawled into bed with her. "Because I'm feeling lazy."

"You've never seemed like the lazy type to me."

He pulled her close. "Maybe lazy isn't the right word. I want to hold you for a few minutes."

"You won't hear any objections from me," she said, snuggling deeper in his embrace."

He kissed her shoulder. "God, you're beautiful."

She lifted her head and their lips brushed softly. The burning passion had passed, though Tilly could still sense it boiling just under the surface. She had a feeling it would always be like that. She could never imagine getting tired of him.

"What are you thinking?" he asked, after a few moments of silence had passed.

She rolled over so she was on her side and pushed up on her elbow, looking down on him. "I was thinking about how content I am. It's not a feeling I'm used to."

He closed his eyes with a big smile. "I can't tell you how happy that makes me."

She leaned down and kissed him, just because she could. "I'm happy, too. Happy and content."

Yes, she could definitely get used to this. She leaned

her head back, trying to remember the last time she felt this way. It was hard. Maybe before her mom died? It didn't make a lot of sense for her to feel it now. After all, two people she knew had been murdered, her apartment was a wreck, and though she was staying in the house where the guy she was dating lived in, a crazy debutante was also living there.

But none of that took away from her happiness.

She drew a finger across his chest and made lazy figure eights. His eyes were still closed.

"I do like the feel of your fingers on me." He chuckled. "Though I'm not sure I like it better than the feel of your legs around my waist."

"Evil," she said. "You're completely evil."

He cracked open one eye. "Sweetheart, you haven't even seen my evil yet and I can't wait to show you." He shut the eye. "Maybe after lunch."

"Now I see where the lazy comes in."

Moving so fast she yelped, he grabbed her and rolled her to her back. "Lazy? I'll show you lazy."

He then proceeded to kiss her until she was once more a raging ball of need and desire.

She put her arms around him. "I think lazy is my new favorite," she said between kisses.

"Excellent," he said with a laugh. He leaned down to kiss her again when a bloodcurdling scream broke the silence.

CHAPTER 9

"What the hell?" Keaton asked, sitting up.

Tilly was also sitting up, clutching the sheet to her chest. "It sounded like it was coming from right outside."

"Mr. Keaton!" Lena yelled from downstairs.

Keaton jumped out of bed and put his jeans on. His body worked on autopilot as he pulled his discarded shirt over his head. Tilly had gotten out of bed, as well, and within seconds, she was dressed.

"I'm coming with you," she said, and both her voice and expression told him it wasn't up for discussion. He wasn't going to argue with her, he simply nodded.

"Did it sound like Elise to you?" he asked.

"I'm not sure. I was too shocked to pay attention that closely. She left to go shopping right when you left."

"Let's go." He led the way down the stairs. From the top, he could see the front door was open, but the angle didn't allow him to see anything other than Lena standing just inside.

"I'll call 911," she said to someone outside. Elise, maybe?

He jogged down the remaining stairs, praying nothing had happened to Elise. He didn't like the girl very much and he certainly wasn't going to marry her, but that didn't mean he wanted her hurt.

"What's wrong, Lena?" he asked, crossing the foyer.

Everything seemed to happen in slow motion. Lena stepped out of the way. Elise stood on the other side of the door. She looked fine. Why had she screamed? He looked down and gasped.

A woman was sprawled on the bricks of the front porch. Her pale red hair covered her face, obscuring Keaton's ability to immediately see it, but whoever it was, she wasn't moving. What was even more disturbing was the blood staining the bricks, pooling out from a blanket that had been half tossed over her.

He fell to his knees and grabbed her wrist, looking for a pulse. Under his fingers, a faint pulse pounded slowly and he sighed in relief. From the cuts and bruising on her face, it appeared someone had beaten her within an inch of her life. He wasn't sure what internal injuries she had, but he was willing to bet she had some. Because of that, he didn't want to risk moving her.

She didn't have any sort of bag with her and Keaton didn't find any identification on her. He supposed it didn't matter who she was, but he would have liked to call her by name. Not to mention, the police would ask.

"Oh my God," Tilly said, dropping to her knees beside him. "It's Bea!"

"Another one of your women, Keaton?" Elise asked, with a pointed look to Tilly.

"Shut the hell up," Tilly told her. "This is Bea Jacobs. You know Brent Taylor?"

Elise nodded. Of course she did. Anyone with ties to South Carolina knew who Brent was.

"This is Bea, his half-sister. She's an attorney. I'm friends with Brent's fiancée."

"Rescue is on the way, Mr. Keaton," Lena said.

"Thank you." Keaton took off his shirt and tried to stop the worst of the bleeding.

"Bea," Tilly spoke softly. "It's me, Tilly, and this is Keaton Benedict. Can you open your eyes for me?"

He hadn't expected a response, so he was taken aback when she moaned. The eye that wasn't swollen shut opened a tiny bit. "Benedict?" she asked, and that one word seemed to use up all the energy she had.

"Yes, you're at Benedict House." Tilly glanced at him and he nodded for her to go on. "We've called for help. They'll be here soon."

Bea licked her lips and seemed to be struggling to say something.

"Shhh." Tilly stroked her forehead in an attempt to soothe and to keep her silent, but she shook her head. Finally, Tilly lowered her head, so her ear was near Bea's mouth. "Tell me."

Bea took a deep, shuddering breath before answering, "Knox."

She spoke so softly, Keaton was certain he heard wrong.

"What?" Tilly asked, obviously feeling the same.

"Knox."

Bea spoke it stronger this time and there was no doubt as to what she said. Keaton decided she must be confused. It was the only sensible answer.

"Knox is my brother," he explained. "I'm Keaton."

Once more, she shook her head. "Call Knox . . ."

Keaton froze. Beside him, Tilly sucked in a breath.

"What?" Tilly asked. "Bea?"

But speaking those few words had completely wiped

Bea out. Her eyes were closed, and though she was breathing and her pulse was steady, neither Tilly nor Keaton could rouse her.

In the distance, the wailing of sirens gradually became louder and louder.

Moving mechanically, Keaton reached in his pocket for his phone and dialed.

"Hey, bro," Knox said, picking up on the second ring. "What's up?"

Unable to take his eyes off the broken body of the woman on his porch, Keaton calmly answered, "We have a situation. You need to come home right away."

To say the hospital waiting room was tense was a vast understatement. It would be like calling the sun hot or the ocean wet. Tilly sat beside Keaton and they both watched Knox. He was pacing the floor and every so often, he'd move from his path in front of the window to make a detour by the clerk's desk to ask if there was any news, even though he'd been told repeatedly that they would alert him at the first sign of change.

The one thing Knox hadn't done was talk to his younger brother. Earlier, he'd arrived at the house after they'd put Bea in the ambulance. When Keaton told him she had been beaten within an inch of her life, Knox had spun around on his heel and climbed into his car. When Keaton and Tilly arrived at the hospital, Knox was already there, pacing.

Tilly placed her hand on top of Keaton's knee, trying to comfort him without saying anything. She knew there were no words she could say to help at this point. He gave her a small smile and took her hand in his.

"I know this sounds silly," he told her, "but I could

almost swear that blanket on her was with those abandoned homeless things I saw at the club."

"Really? I wonder if—"

Before she could get the words out, the waiting-room door opened and Kipling walked in. He glanced at Keaton and Tilly, but focused his attention on Knox.

"I received a call saying Bea Jacobs had been beaten and left on our porch and was taken to the hospital," Kipling said. "Why would anyone do that?"

"Not now, Kip," Knox said, speaking for the first time since Keaton had called him on the phone.

"Honest to God," Kipling continued. "Between you and Keaton, I don't know what the hell is going on with this family."

Knox stomped over to his brother, grabbed him by the collar, and shoved him against the wall. "Not. Fucking. Now."

Tilly had no doubt Kipling could pound Knox into the ground. Kipling's eyes flashed and for a minute, she feared he might. She breathed a sigh of relief when, instead, he calmly said, "Get your hands off of me."

Wisely, Knox listened. Kipling straightened his collar and stepped away from his brother. "I'm going to give you a pass this time since you're obviously upset and not thinking, but put your hands on me again and I'm kicking your ass."

"Did I come at a bad time?"

All eyes moved to the door where Alyssa and her partner stood.

"Would you leave if I said yes?" Kipling asked.

"Good try, but no," Alyssa said. "We came to find out what happened to Bea Jacobs. Do you know anything about her assault?"

"No. I didn't know anything had happened until Keaton called me," Kipling said.

She looked over at Keaton and raised an eyebrow. "Mr. Benedict. Ms. Brock."

Tilly felt Keaton tense up beside her. "When we saw her, she was already hurt and on our front porch," he said.

"You didn't see anything?"

"No, but our housekeeper and a family friend who's staying with us found her first."

"Thank you," Alyssa's partner said. "We'll go talk to them and then come back here to see if Bea's awake."

"She was wrapped in a blanket I think I remember seeing outside the club a few nights ago," Keaton said. "It looked as though it belonged to the homeless. It's still at the house."

"We'll look into it," Alyssa said.

Not long after they left, a door at the side of the room opened and a woman wearing green scrubs stepped into the waiting room.

"Knox Benedict?" she asked, looking at the brothers.

"That's me," Knox said.

"Come with me," the lady said.

There were numerous unasked questions on Knox's expression, but instead of voicing them, he nodded and followed her out of the waiting room.

As soon as he left, Kipling turned to Keaton. "Do you know what's going on?"

"I have no idea."

Kipling ran his hand through his hair. "They didn't say how Bea was. I hope she's okay."

Keaton entwined his fingers with Tilly's.

Tilly leaned her head against his shoulder. It was unfathomable to even think about something bad happening to Keaton and they had only been together for a matter of days. Not counting the years when they were kids, of course.

They stayed like that for a while. Tilly and Keaton sitting. Kipling pacing. It had only been about fifteen minutes when Knox came back to the room. He looked even worse than he had before he went back.

Immediately, Keaton stood up and Knox stopped pacing. Tilly held her breath, bracing herself for the worst.

"How is she? Is everything okay?" Kipling was the first to speak.

Knox winced. "Okay is a relative term. As for how she is, she's alive."

Keaton reached out to touch his shoulder, but Knox twisted away.

An uncomfortable silence fell across the room. Tilly wanted to disappear into the air. Whatever was going on between the brothers was private and she felt odd and out of place. She thought about leaving, but didn't want to draw attention to herself.

Knox sighed. "I'm staying here until she gets out. You guys might as well go home. No need for you to stay."

No one left right away. About half an hour later, the two police officers showed up again. Knox mumbled that they wouldn't learn anything from Bea.

But when they returned to the waiting room sometime later after seeing Bea, Alyssa pulled her and Keaton aside.

"Bea wasn't able to tell us much," Alyssa said. "But she did remember her assailant say something about Tilly being next."

Tilly froze in place and immediately Keaton put his arm around her.

"You need to find this guy and find him *now*," Keaton ground out.

"We're working as hard as we can."

"Work harder."

Instead of replying, Alyssa said, "We also looked into the blanket. It's an exclusive to an upscale shop on King Street. My boss doesn't believe a homeless person would have it in their possession."

Keaton cursed. "Of course the hell not. Didn't it cross his mind that someone might have donated it?"

"But," Alyssa continued, "I'm still looking into it."

"Thank you," Tilly said.

"It's my job." Alyssa shook their hands. "Stay safe and call me if anything else happens or crosses your mind."

When the police left, Keaton looked at Tilly and raised his eyebrows. She nodded, ready to leave. She had class the next day and with everything that had happened the last few days, she needed to ensure she was ready.

She stood up and waited while Keaton talked with his brother. They left a few minutes later and she held her breath as they approached the car. Keaton checked everything out, but nothing appeared tampered with. Apparently, the attack on Bea was all their unknown assailant had planned for the day.

Keaton had one goal the next morning when Tilly left for class—to stay away from Elise. He did well for the first hour. He called Knox, who said Bea was doing better physically, but still wasn't saying much. He did a bit of research on the charity he wanted to set up and patted himself on the back when he realized Tilly would be back in less than an hour.

He should take her out for lunch. They really hadn't been on enough dates and if they went out, they wouldn't have to worry about Elise hanging around. He left Kipling's home office where he'd been working and jogged up the stairs to his room, freezing completely when he found Elise sitting on his bed.

"Get out," he said, through clenched teeth. "I don't want you in here."

Elise had a sly little grin he'd like to wipe off. "Oh, Keaton. Honestly, you still think this is about what *you* want. You poor misguided fool."

"Out. Now." He was fed up with her.

"I don't think it's wise for you to kick me out without hearing my deal first."

"I've never made a deal with the devil and I don't intend to start now."

She still wore that damn grin. Like no matter what he said, she somehow knew this conversation was going to go the way she wanted it to. He hated to disappoint her.

"The devil?" She held her hand to her chest in mock outrage. "I don't think that's any way to talk about your future fiancée."

"You aren't my fiancée and you never will be."

Her grin got bigger. Damn it all. She seemed to be enjoying their conversation. That scared him more than anything else because he had the sinking suspicion he was missing something.

"A wise man knows not to use words such as 'never' and 'always.'" She patted the bed. "This is nice, but I think I'd like a firmer mattress. I find it much more conducive to sex."

He felt his blood begin to boil. She had some nerve. "Your opinion on my choice of mattress is irrelevant.

You will never sleep on it and you can be damn sure we won't ever have sex, either on the mattress or elsewhere."

"So stubborn. I'd better get straight to the point. You're going to marry me because I have some rather damning information about your dad." He started to protest, but she held up her hand. "Not only that, but if you refuse, I can work it to where it appears as if all the Benedict brothers knew about it. Benedict Industries will be ruined."

Was she serious? "I don't believe you."

She appeared entirely too joyful for his taste as she began. "The Benedict men are known for being players, don't even try to deny it. I know this is part of your nature and it's why I haven't put a stop to you and Tilly. But rest assured, it's coming."

He rolled his eyes. "Can we get to the point? I'm taking Tilly out to lunch."

He didn't imagine the ire in her expression that flashed briefly before she continued. "You could actually say it's in your genes. I'm not sure if you're aware, but your father screwed around on your mom."

He did his best to hide his grimace. He'd always suspected his father cheated on his mom, but to have it so well known that Elise knew about it was embarrassing.

"Of course, your father took the necessary precautions. After all, he didn't want to be bothered with bastard children." There was no denying it now, Elsie was positively elated to be sharing this story with him. "But, as you're aware, the only totally effective way to ensure no one gets pregnant is to not have sex. I think we both know that celibacy is not an option for most Benedict men."

He had a fairly good idea where she was headed, but

surely she knew it'd take more than an illegitimate child in his family's past for him to marry her.

"As was bound to happen, one of your father's mistresses got pregnant. Now, always before when this happened, your father paid handsomely for the woman to 'take care' of the child." Elise shook her head. "But this one decided, against your father's wishes, to keep it. Then, fearing for her life, as well as that of her daughter's, she vanished. You have to give it to her. She remained hidden for five years."

Keaton's heart pounded and sweat ran down his back. He had a sister? Granted, she would be a half-sister, but still. . . . He'd always wanted a sister.

"I'm not exactly sure what happened when the child turned five. If I had to guess, I'd say that the ex-mistress contacted your dad, perhaps believing he'd become enamored with the idea of a daughter after having three boys. Unfortunately, that wasn't the case. There was a hit-and-run days after she contacted your father. Both the ex-mistress and her daughter were killed."

The fact that she could sit there so calmly, only served to prove how cunning she was. "I don't believe you," Keaton said.

Elise shrugged like she didn't care one way or the other. "Funny thing about the truth. It doesn't matter what you think of it. It just is. Nothing you do can change that."

"You expect me to believe my father not only had a child with a woman who wasn't my mother, but that he somehow arranged for her and his own daughter to be killed in a hit-and-run?" It was beyond ridiculous. "No way. And you think I'm going to marry you because of this made-up shit? Get out of my room."

She laughed. Fucking laughed. "I have proof. Of

course, all I have with me are photos. I'm not stupid enough to bring you the originals. But not only do I have the originals, I have e-mails and bank statements. I have the ability to make it look as if the three of you were in on it with your father, or at least that you've been active in covering it all these years. Contrary to what you think, I learned a lot at college. And some of it was actually legal."

He told himself he would not panic. He would look over her "proof" and make a plan then. He'd show it to Kipling. Normally, he'd show it to Knox as well, but with Bea in the hospital, he was out of commission.

"Show me your proof," he told Elise.

"So impatient. You'll get it when I'm ready to show you. Right now, I want you to think about it and plan how we're going to announce our engagement. And, just so you know, there will be no discussing things with either Knox or Kipling. If I find out they know, the deal is off and I'll fucking crush Benedict Industries."

She smirked at him and ran a perfectly manicured nail down his chest. "I have an idea, come with me to my room. You can see the pictures of the evidence I took with my phone."

He felt like he was going to be sick. Fortunately, Elise didn't say anything further. She gracefully rose to her feet and walked out the door. As the sound of her heels grew faint, he realized just how much he underestimated her.

CHAPTER 10

Tilly smiled and waved to Keaton as she walked out of the building after her last class of the day. He stood by an oak tree with his hands in his pockets. He looked laid-back and relaxed . . . until she got closer to him. He was frowning and there were worry lines etched in his face.

She paused. "Oh, no. Is it Bea? Is she worse?"

"No." Keaton looked around like he was expecting someone to be watching or listening. It freaked her out. "Is there somewhere we can go that's private?"

"Your house?" she asked, not understanding why they needed to go somewhere when they had the huge mansion he lived in.

He shook his head.

"Empty classroom?" she suggested.

He thought about it and nodded. "Lead the way."

She walked back into the building she'd recently vacated, wondering the entire time what had Keaton so on edge. Not knowing where else to go, she led him to the classroom her last class had been in. It was a small room and everyone had left. She didn't even wait to sit down.

"What's up?" she asked.

This time he didn't hesitate. "Elise is blackmailing me."

"What? *Elise?*" The sad part was, she wasn't really that surprised. "About what?"

"It's crazy as hell, but she says she has proof that Dad fathered an illegitimate daughter and then had her and her mother killed."

"That's ridiculous. What kind of proof does she have?"

"She hasn't shown me yet, but she said she had photos, e-mails, and bank statements. She wants me to think about it." He spoke the words with disgust.

"What did Knox and Kipling say?"

He shook his head. "That's the thing. She says I can't tell them or else she'll set us all up."

"It sounds crazy as hell."

"I know, that's what I thought. But the thing is, it's so crazy, I can't see her making it up."

"Why is she blackmailing you? Doesn't her family have money? I mean, they're as rich as you guys, right?"

"It's not money she wants," he said quietly.

It took her a few seconds to register what he said and what it meant. "Oh, God," she said as understanding dawned.

"Yeah." He looked down and took a deep breath. "Exactly."

"What are you going to do?"

"That's what I wanted to talk to you about. I wanted to get your opinion. Obviously, I'm not doing anything until I see this so-called proof she has."

"That might be all it takes. For you to call her bluff."

"If only it would be that easy."

Tilly had a sinking suspicion that he was right. "So if it turns out it looks legit?"

Keaton clenched his teeth and growled out. "I'm not marrying her."

"You can't possibly think I'm suggesting that." She put a hand on his shoulder and felt the tension leave his body at her touch. "But we have to look at this as a serious threat. She might possibly have the power to destroy Benedict Industries and your entire family in the process."

Keaton took a deep breath and looked up at the ceiling. "If it looks legit, I guess I'll have to pretend to be engaged to her while I figure a way out. And I'm not sure what that will involve, but I'm sure I'll hate it."

Deep down, she knew it was the best plan. In all likelihood, it was the only one that made sense. But she hated the very thought of Keaton and Elise being engaged, no matter how pretend it was.

And she knew it wouldn't be pretend to Elise.

"I know it's the best plan. But if you're engaged, even if it's pretend in your mind, you and I can't. . . ." She couldn't get the words out and her eyes teared up. "I hate her so much. I mean, seriously? I just got you back."

"Hey." Keaton pulled her into his arms. "I'm not going anywhere and even if I have to pretend to be engaged, there's no way in hell I'm marrying that bitch."

"I know. My brain gets it, but just the thought of you and her . . ." She shivered just thinking about it.

"It's going to be fine. I promise." He ran his hands up and down her arms. "Let's get out of here. I don't want to go back to the house tonight."

She didn't want to go back to his house ever again, but she wasn't telling him that now. "A hotel?"

"Yes, but in town this time."

She knew what he was doing, flaunting their relationship. While she wasn't sure it was the smartest thing to do at the moment, she wanted to flaunt it badly.

"Let's go," she said, and held out her hand.

She'd expected him to take it and lead her outside, but he pulled her to him and kissed her. At the touch of his lips, she felt the tension leave her body.

"No matter what happens or whatever Elise says, know that my heart is yours and yours alone," he said when he pulled back.

When he spoke like that, she felt invincible.

After checking into the hotel, they decided to go for a walk. Tilly tried to drink in every minute with him because if there turned out to be any truth to Elise's claim's, she knew the time was rapidly approaching when she couldn't be seen out in public holding Keaton's hand. At least not for who knew how long.

Since they had ended up skipping lunch, they decided to grab a few to-go sandwiches and have an early picnic dinner. It was a typical Charleston summer day, which meant it was nearly unbearable to be outside for any length of time. They found a shady spot near the waterfront and sat on a bench, people-watching and making small talk.

As they finished eating, she cleared her throat and he looked up. "I was wondering if there'd be a place for me at the new division of Benedict Industries as an afterschool tutor? I love your idea about giving back."

His eyes grew wide with excitement. "That's a great idea. I love it and you'll be perfect."

"I want to be a part of this new venture with you." She felt her cheeks heat.

"Come here and kiss me."

She went into his arms willingly, amazed at how she'd become accustomed to his kisses in such a short amount of time. She didn't want to think about not having access to his lips if the plan played out with Elise. Even less did she want to think about Elise kissing him.

Keaton sighed and pulled back, smoothing his hands over her hair. "She's here, isn't she? Already between us."

Damn, was she so transparent? Even when they were kissing?

"I don't mean for her to be, but I close my eyes and I see her kissing you. I see her hands on you. It's like she's already got her claws in you." She shook her head. "No matter what happens, you have to resist her."

"I know. Believe me, I know." He ran his thumb over her lips.

She knew he got it. After all, he'd be the one who actually had to pretend like he liked Elise. At least she herself could continue with her undisguised disdain.

"Let's walk down to the port and then we'll go back to the hotel." His eyes danced with merriment. "I need your hands on me. Because they are the only hands I want on my body." He lifted her hands to his lips and kissed each one.

"I could so go for that."

Smiling once again, she told herself she wasn't going to think of Elise anymore for the rest of the night. That hussy had already tainted too much of her time with Keaton and she wasn't going to let her continue to do it.

"Should we get ice cream?" Keaton asked, pulling her away from her thoughts.

"You can. I'm still full."

They stopped so he could get a cup of ice cream and then laughed when she ate half of it.

"You can get your own, you know," he teased.

"That's all I want, any more and my hips wouldn't be able to make it out of your door."

"Good." He lowered his voice. "That means I get to keep you in bed. Which is fine by me, because I happen to love your hips. They're perfect for me to grab onto."

"Keaton." She swatted his arm, giggling because she knew he was telling the truth. Her giggles died as she looked out the window of the ice cream parlor and she felt rage start to boil inside. "Damn it."

What?" Keaton turned his head.

But the spot where Elise had stood seconds before was now empty.

Tilly nodded toward the window. "Elise was just standing there."

He leaned over and kissed her. *Take that, Elise.* "It's going to be okay."

"You keep saying that and I want to believe you, but at times I feel like she's the one with all the power and she's going to use it to tear us apart."

"I'm not going to allow that to happen." He stood up and held out his hand. "How about we run by the office on Columbus Street and then head back to the hotel where I can positively guarantee neither one of us will even think about a certain blond until sometime tomorrow?"

She put her hand in his. "Deal."

They walked down the street still holding hands. She loved how he was always touching her in some way when they were together. If any other man did it, she'd probably find it annoying, but when Keaton did it, it brought her comfort. Made her feel protected.

"Do you need to do something at the office?" she asked. Benedict Industries had a small office near the Columbus Street Terminal.

He nodded. "There's some paperwork I need to pick up. Normally, Knox would take care of it, but I told Kipling I'd get it since, you know, Bea and all."

Yes, she did. She'd tried to call Bea's half-brother the night before. She was friends with his fiancée, but she came to discover they were out of the country. Escaping wedding planning madness, if she knew Janie.

They were almost at the terminal and Keaton appeared to be focused on something else.

"I'm going to stay out here while you go in," she told him as they neared the office. "I'm going to go look out over the water."

"Do you think it's safe? I'd feel better if you came with me."

"There's a guard right over there." She pointed to the armed man standing nearby. "And there's a police officer across the street."

He didn't want to leave her, she could tell, and it was silly, but for some reason she felt like she had to stay outside. She tried again. "I need to prove to myself that I can be alone and not be terrified."

"I understand." He stroked her cheek with his thumb. "I'll be quick."

She rose on her toes and kissed him. "Thank you."

He was only gone for a few minutes. Before she knew it, he was back at her side.

She smiled and turned to put her arms around him. "I say we head back to the hotel and you make love to me so many times, I forget everything about this day except you."

Keaton gave her a small smile and cupped her cheek, his thumb stroking her cheekbone. She felt herself lean into his touch. "I think that's the best idea I've heard all day."

She turned her head and kissed the palm of his hand. "It should be. It was your idea, after all."

They'd barely made it into the room and locked the door before Keaton pushed Tilly against the wall. She gasped as he grabbed one of her wrist in each of his hands and held them above her. He shifted his weight so she could feel the length of him and how hard he was.

He was hanging on by a thread and he needed her to understand before they moved forward.

"I can't be slow or gentle right now," he said. "Tell me now if that's not okay or not what you want and I'll go take a cold shower or run five miles."

He half expected her to tell him to stop, but she surprised him by biting his earlobe. "Take me however you need. I'm yours."

He pulled back to see the truth of her words reflected in her eyes.

He wasn't sure what he'd ever done to deserve a woman like Tilly. She was accepting of him, even on his most unlovable day. She was quickly becoming vital to him. It shook him to his core to realize just how necessary she'd become. It was more than just the need to have her physically or even the need to simply have her in his life. He needed her to be safe and at that moment, he knew he'd give up his own life to keep her that way.

Keeping her hands immobilized in his grip, he took

her lips in a brutal kiss, tasting her, imprinting everything about her to his memory. She whimpered deep in her throat and lifted her right leg and hooked it around his waist, drawing him closer, even as he feared he should pull back.

Unable to stop himself, he let go of her wrists and yanked her shirt over her head. She looked at him with lust-filled eyes.

"You like it when I'm rough." It wasn't a question and she didn't answer.

His hands dropped to the waistband of her jeans and he hurriedly unbuttoned them. He growled as she repeated the action on him. He had hers pushed below her hips and there was only a scrap of silk standing between him and what he wanted.

He shoved the silk aside just enough to allow him to push two fingers inside her. "Damn, Tilly. You're soaked." He pumped in and out several times, but removed his hand completely when her body shook with an impeding release. "Not yet. I want to feel you shatter around me."

"Now."

He hadn't thought he could get any harder, but that one word proved him wrong. He bent down, taking her jeans with him, but stood up without removing his. She raised an eyebrow at him.

"I'm not even going to bother taking my jeans or your underwear off," he said. "I'm going to take you just like this: dirty, raw, and hard."

Her only reply was a shaky "Yes," that ended with a sharp intake of breath.

That was the only word he needed. "Turn around and face the wall."

She whimpered but moved into position, bending at

the waist slightly in order to give him better access. He stroked himself as he watched, wondering if she had any idea just how damn sexy she was.

True to his word, he only unzipped his jeans enough to remove his cock and she let out a moan when he pressed it against the silk on her backside.

"Feel how hard I am?" he asked, slipping on a condom. "You do this to me. Only you."

But it seemed that Tilly was beyond talking. She only nodded. He pushed the tiny scrap of material between her legs out of the way and with one hard thrust, buried himself inside her.

Her head fell back and she clenched around him as her climax overtook her.

"Damn, Tilly," he said in a half growl.

He started a rough rhythm, but listening to her gasps of pleasure, he could tell she didn't mind. Everything about her felt so good. He'd never been with anyone who could both capture his mind and make his body rise. He leaned over her back and in low whispers, he told her how beautiful she was, how sexy, and that she was made for him. But as he felt her second release approach in time with his own, he knew the truth. They were made for each other.

The next morning, Tilly woke relaxed and more rested than she'd felt in ages. Judging by the sunlight streaming in through the small crack in the window, it was still relatively early. She looked over Keaton's shoulder and saw it was just after seven.

Odd that she'd wake up so soon, she thought with a smile. After the night they had, she'd expected to be asleep until at least ten. Keaton was still snoring softly. She pushed up on her elbow and gave him a soft kiss on his forehead. A flash of light on the nightstand caught her eye.

Someone was calling him. Her heart pounded as she took notice of the name of the person calling. Derrick, the Benedicts' lawyer.

"Keaton." She shook his shoulder.

He didn't budge.

"Keaton. Wake up." She shook him harder. "Derrick's trying to get in touch with you."

"What?" He was fully awake now, looking around.

"Your phone just rang. It was him."

He grabbed the phone. "I have a voice mail," he said and held it up to his ear. After listening, he immediately made a call.

"Derrick. It's Keaton." He was quiet as the lawyer spoke, but his face turned an unhealthy pale color and she scooted closer. He hung up without saying anything.

"Keaton?" she asked, her concern growing with every second that passed.

He didn't look at her. "The police are looking for Kipling."

"Has he been threatened?"

"No, the other blond twin has been murdered. They think he did it."

CHAPTER 11

Keaton's phone rang almost immediately after he hung up. "It's Kipling." He answered it on speaker while going around the room packing their belongings. "Kip," he said. "Where are you?"

"I'm on my way home and why do I have all these calls from Derrick? I just tried to call him and got his voice mail." He laughed. "You aren't at the police station, are you? I thought for a minute maybe you'd been arrested."

Keaton didn't laugh, but stopped what he was doing and looked over to Tilly. She felt numb. Kipling didn't know.

"Keaton?" Kipling said, and worry now colored his tone. "You haven't been arrested, have you?"

"No. But listen to me. The police are looking for you. Tilly and I are meeting Derrick at home. Call him. We'll see you there."

"What? Keaton? Don't hang up."

Keaton picked up the phone. "The other blond twin was found murdered last night and the police want to talk to you. That's all I know. Call Derrick. We'll meet you at home." He disconnected.

To Tilly, it looked as if Keaton was in shock. She walked over to him and put her arms around him. "It's going to be fine. We know he didn't do it and I'm willing to bet Alyssa knows it, too."

They didn't talk much on the way to Benedict House, though Keaton seemed to relax at the sight of both Kipling's and Derrick's cars in the drive, with no police cruiser in sight. Once inside, they made it to the living room where Derrick sat on a couch and Kipling paced. The oldest Benedict looked up and gave a weak smile at their arrival.

Derrick waved for Tilly and Keaton to sit down. "I called that Officer Adams. They'll be here soon." To Kipling he asked, "You were *where* last night?"

Kipling stopped pacing. "I told you. Lena's youngest daughter had a ruptured appendix. Her husband is deployed and the regular sitter was busy. I volunteered to watch their two-year-old."

Keaton half snorted, half coughed. "You what?"

"He likes ships and we played boats for three hours until he fell asleep. Lena wasn't back, so I slept over."

"Oh my God," Keaton said.

Kipling rolled his eyes. "Do me a favor and don't tell anyone."

"I'm afraid we can't make that promise," someone said from the doorway, and they all turned to find Officer Drake standing at the entranceway to the living room with his arms crossed. By his side stood Alyssa, an unreadable expression on her face.

"Want to tell us what you were doing before you

went babysitting?" the policeman asked, walking into to living room.

Kipling looked to Derrick, but the lawyer only nodded.

"I went by the office and then walked down the docks." Kipling hesitated only a second, before continuing. "I ran into Mandy. We spoke briefly. She propositioned me and I declined. Right after that I got the call from Lena and I left."

Alyssa had recovered from her stupor at hearing Kipling say he babysat two-year-olds. "Was Mandy alive when you left her?"

Kipling spun around. "Yes, Officer Adams. Do you really think I killed her and then went to play boats with a two-year-old? Seriously?"

"Just doing my job, Mr. Benedict."

"You're doing it wrong," Kipling countered. "There's a killer running around out there and instead of finding him, you're harassing me."

"Mandy had traces of semen in her mouth," Alyssa said, and Tilly noticed her partner did not look pleased she'd shared that information.

Kipling didn't miss a beat. "Then you'd know it wasn't me because I didn't touch her."

Alyssa was silent and for a long second, they stood almost toe to toe, each watching the other. But then with a nod to her partner, she broke it with a bombshell. He handed her a flash-frozen black rose. She held it up to Kipling.

"Have you ever—" she started, but Kipling interrupted.

"Did you get that out of my car?" He looked over to Derrick. "Can they do that without a search warrant?"

Tilly wasn't looking at Derrick, her eyes were on

Alyssa and she looked stunned. At her partner's cough, she shook herself.

"It didn't come from your car," she said. "It came from Mandy's body. Kipling Benedict, you have the right to remain silent . . ."

Sitting in the Charleston police station with Derrick and Kipling hours later, Keaton wondered if he'd lost his mind completely.

"I strongly suggest," Derrick was saying, "that you hire another attorney. I'm not equipped to handle a capital murder case."

"It's not going to be a capital murder case," Kipling said. "I didn't do it."

"As much as I believe you, that's what everybody says." Derrick opened a file he'd placed on the table. "You need someone with expertise beyond what I have. Now, if you want me to act as co-counsel, I can do that. But you need to bring in someone else to be lead."

"Hell, you do think I did it."

"I would like to know how that rose made it from your car to her body," Keaton said.

Kipling's jaw tightened. "It's not what sounds like. I found that rose in my office days ago. I had it preserved and it's been in my car ever since. Obviously, someone took it from my car and put it on Mandy's body."

Derrick slammed his folder closed and stood up. "I'm not sitting here listening to this. Kipling, I'll be by later with some recommended names for you. In the meantime, keep your mouth shut."

The brothers watched him walk out. "He thinks I did it." Kipling sunk into his chair after Derrick left. "He honestly thinks I did it."

"How's it going securing the bail?" Keaton decided a change in subjects was needed. Heck, for all he knew, Alyssa was listening in on their conversation.

"Good as far as I know. Derrick's admin was working with our accounts people to get everything transferred."

"Sounds good. Maybe you'll be out of here soon." Keaton paused for a second. "We need to find out who got into your car. Do you think it was the same person who put it in your office?"

Kipling didn't have a chance to answer, because at that moment the door to the room opened and Alyssa walked in. "Time's up, gentlemen."

Kipling looked at the officer like she was prey to tease. "You know, Officer Adams, if you wanted to spend time with me, you only had to ask. You didn't have to arrest me."

"Mr. Benedict," she said and her voice was calm and even, though her flushed skin belied her otherwise composed demeanor. "Murder is a very serious charge. It may behoove you to take it seriously."

Kipling tapped the table. "Don't make assumptions, Officer. I'm taking it very seriously, I just happen to know I didn't do it and that's all I need."

"It would appear you also need an attorney," she said. "Yours told us he's advised you to select new counsel."

"Yes."

"Would you like to answer a few questions now?"

Kipling raised an eyebrow. "Do I look stupid?"

Alyssa crossed her arms. "You're sitting in jail, charged with murder. That leads me to believe you may not be as intelligent as you think yourself to be."

"Rest assured, there is no need to question my intelligence. I know I'm innocent, but I'm not so inept that I'm about to answer anything without an attorney present. Regardless of what you think, my staff is transferring the funds needed for bail and I'll be out of your hair shortly."

"You seem to think you've actually been in my hair. Trust me, you haven't been. You're part of my job, that's all."

"You know what the best part of your denial is?"

Alyssa smirked. "How it's the truth?"

"How satisfying it's going to be when you finally surrender to me."

"Keep dreaming, Mr. Benedict."

"Is it wrong how much it turns me on when you call me *Mr. Benedict?*"

Keaton kicked him under the table. *Are you insane?* he mouthed to his brother. Kipling shrugged.

"I'm not even going to justify that question with an answer."

Kipling didn't appear to be too upset with her statement. "Follow up and make sure everything's lined up for my bail. I really don't want to spend the night here."

Keaton nodded. He'd left Tilly at Benedict House before coming to the station. He wanted to go check on her. He thought Elise's internship started today and she wouldn't be there, but Tilly had been slightly uneasy about staying. "I'm going by the house, I'll make some phone calls from there."

Though Tilly wasn't thrilled to be alone at Benedict House, her discomfort was currently underscored by her concern for Keaton. He insisted he was fine, but it was her opinion that people weren't fine when their older brother was arrested and charged with murder in front of them.

"Truly," he'd told her, "I'm fine because the only other alternative is to have a breakdown."

So she'd agreed to stay at the house while he went to go meet with Kipling and Derrick. He'd also told her that Elise was to have started her internship today. If she had been at the house, Tilly would have insisted on going with him and staying in the car. She did not want to deal with Elise today.

After Keaton left, she went to the kitchen. She knew Lena was at the hospital and not in the kitchen, but that room had always seemed so warm and inviting. Just standing in it or walking through it could brighten her day.

Unfortunately, she had not thought about the one person who could ruin that feeling. Elise.

"I thought you started your internship today," Tilly said, instead of greeting her.

She knew she had to tread lightly. While Elise had told Keaton not to say anything to his brothers about the blackmail, she hadn't said he couldn't tell Tilly. They both thought it was probably an oversight on her part. Odds were, she didn't want Keaton telling anyone.

All that meant Tilly now had to put on the performance of a lifetime.

"I called and told them I wouldn't be in because of a family emergency." Currently, Elise's idea of helping during a time of crisis appeared to be filing her nails. "I figured my future brother-in-law being arrested for murder was an emergency, don't you?"

"I'm sure it qualifies." Tilly nodded to Elise's half-finished self-manicure. "And I'm sure Kipling appreciates you taking time to ensure your nails look good."

Anger flashed in Elise's eyes. "You're a real bitch, you know that?"

Tilly nodded. "In this case, yes."

Elise calmly went back to doing her nails. "I saw you two getting ice cream yesterday."

She hadn't imagined it after all. Some part of her really wished she had. "I thought I saw you when I looked out the window. You should have joined us."

"I should have, but I decided not to. When Keaton announces our engagement, I don't want anyone to think we're friends."

"Trust me, no one will ever think that."

Elise ignored her and kept talking. "And I hope you enjoyed your day with him because there won't be many more of those."

"Why, thank you. I did. I thoroughly enjoyed our day together, though now that I think about it, I'd have to say I enjoyed our night together so much more."

Tilly had only thought she saw Elise angry before, but the woman in front of her now appeared as if she'd slay her with her eyes alone. *Elise could be very dangerous.* Tilly wasn't sure where that thought came from, but she knew she needed to heed it.

And just that quickly, the murderous look passed and Elise went back to filing her nails. Albeit a bit intensely. "It doesn't bother me that Keaton's been with other women because I know two things. One, once we're engaged he'll be faithful to me."

The best thing Tilly could do was to get away from Elise. Staying anywhere near the conniving bitch was just asking for trouble.

"You tell yourself that, why don't you," Tilly told her. "Tell yourself that enough times and maybe you'll start to believe it. But I know the truth. And the truth is no matter how good it ever gets between you and Keaton, there'll always be a part of you that wonders. Maybe not during the day, but at night, when everything's quiet and it's only you and your thoughts. And you'll wonder as you lie in his arms if his mind is really with you or if he's thinking of me." She took a step closer to the table. "And when he's making love to you, you'll wonder if it's you he sees or if he's imagining me in your place. When you're touching him, you'll never do it without wondering if I touched him better."

Elise stood up so fast, she bumped the table and knocked over an open bottle of nail polish. She didn't turn back to pick it up or clean the mess, but stomped off out of the kitchen. Tilly didn't allow herself to feel victorious. She had the sinking feeling that no matter how good it'd felt to say that to Elise, she was going to end up regretting she'd done so.

Later that afternoon, Keaton was working on his proposal for Kipling. Derrick had notified him earlier that bail had been posted and Kipling would be getting out of jail within the next two hours. Tilly was studying in the library. He didn't know where Elise was, nor did he care. Tilly had filled him in on the conversation she had with Elise when he got back from the station. He thought she handled it as well as she could have, but he agreed with her that it hadn't been a good idea to piss Elise off.

"There you are," the woman in question said from his doorway.

He stopped typing with a big sigh. He had known this was coming. Best to get it over with now.

"I brought copies of the information I told you about," Elise said. "Want to look over them, see if you have any questions, and then announce our engagement?"

"You're awful sure of yourself." His stomach turned at both the thought of looking over the papers she had and thinking for a minute about asking her to marry him.

She tossed her hair back over her shoulder, and he wondered if she practiced that move in the mirror. "I have every right to be sure. It's win-win for both of us, Keaton. Eventually, you'll see that."

He doubted if he had all the time in the universe plus an extra million years added on, that he would ever think marrying Elise was win-win.

He went and took the papers from her, but didn't look at them. Elise didn't move, but stood there, as if waiting for him to do something. "Don't you have anything to do?" Seriously, was she just going to stand there in his doorway?

"No, not really," she replied.

"Well, I do." He closed the door right in her face. Like Tilly, he had a feeling that hadn't been the best way to deal with Elise, but it sure did feel good, he thought with a smile.

His gaze fell on the stack of papers he'd placed on his desk. Hell, he didn't want to look at them. He knew his father had been ruthless in business, but there was a huge difference between being ruthless and having someone murdered in cold blood.

To do the same to your own child signified an evil he couldn't comprehend.

No matter what the outcome, he knew after today, he'd never see his father in the same light. Jesus, what was it saying about him that he actually gave thought to the idea that his father was capable of such a thing? Hell, after today, he'd never see himself in the same light.

He remembered his dad so well. The senior Benedict had never been a soft man or one to show his emotions easily, but he had been fiercely protective when it came to his wife and sons.

The question was, did that protectiveness mean keeping a half sibling from his sons? And if so, how far was he willing to go to ensure they never knew?

Heart heavy with dread, he reached for the pile and began to read.

Tilly's head shot up at the sound of the library door closing. She breathed a sigh of relief at the sight of Keaton.

"Thank goodness it's you," she said. "I half expected to look up and see Elise."

He didn't smile or say anything, just walked over and sat down beside her. Her heart sank and her arms went automatically around him. He gave a soft sigh and, maybe it was her imagination, but she thought he relaxed a bit.

"You saw her evidence, didn't you?" That had to be the reason for his broken look. It hit her at that moment that this was more than his being blackmailed, it was learning something that rocked the very foundation of who he was.

She buried her head in his neck. "God, Keaton, I'm so sorry."

He embraced her as a sob ripped through his body. "I had a sister. A little sister."

Tilly knew he was not only crying for the sister he never had a chance to meet, but also for the man he thought his father was.

He kept his head buried in her hair. "How could he do something like that? Kill his own daughter? She was five! Five! She never even had a chance to live."

He had walked into the library empty-handed, but obviously thought whatever evidence Elise had provided was enough to prove her allegations were true.

"There's no way she could have falsified anything?" she asked, because truly, in her mind, it was the only logical explanation.

He pulled back. "There's nothing I'd like more than for that to be the case. Unfortunately, I don't see how that's possible. She has phone records showing calls were made from his office phone and bank records that clearly show the payout. I won't say it's not possible to create all that, but it wouldn't be easy. There's more too that she hasn't shown me. I'll need your help when I get it."

"Of course," she assured him.

He didn't say anything more, but she knew he was holding back. "Tell me."

"I went into the family's online banking records. I've never done that before, I've always left it to Kipling, but they matched." He pulled back and she saw the pain in his eyes. "They matched down to the last penny."

"Don't you think Elise would do anything it took to get her hands on you?" Tilly didn't see a little forgery standing in the way of Elise. Not when it came to Keaton.

"I don't see how she could do this. She'd have to have access to our accounts and there's no way she does." He took her hand. "Thank you for being here with me. I couldn't do this without you."

And she didn't want him to do it alone. "What are you going to do?"

"I'd really like to sit down with Knox and Kipling to get their take. I mean, they don't even know we had a sister. Who am I to keep her from them?" He took a deep breath. "But I have a feeling I'm going to piss her off enough as it is, so I really don't need to add fuel to that fire."

"How do you plan on pissing her off?"

He smiled for the first time since walking into the library. "I'm telling her I'm not going to marry her."

Tilly gave a low whistle. "Wow. That will totally piss her off. In fact, *piss off* is probably too mild of a way to put it." She'd never actually thought he'd marry her, but even the thought of a fake engagement had been enough to make her rage internally.

"The way I see it is, if I give into her demands, she wins, her dad wins, and my dad wins. After what he did, what do I care about his reputation?"

"But didn't she also say she could set up you and your brothers to make it look as if the three of you were in on it?"

"I think she'd have a hard time pulling that off. Even if it were to come out that she made up everything she had on Dad, that's a far cry from setting up three additional people. Especially when there's nothing there."

Tilly was well aware he was taking a calculated risk. The only problem was the stakes were so high. If he miscalculated and underestimated Elise, he and his brothers could wind up being charged as accessories to murder.

"I think this is about as good of a plan that we can come up with," she said. "I hate how risky it is, but I'll do anything I can to support you."

"Thank you. You don't know much that means."

Tilly had always thought of herself as a kind person. She was easy to get along with, and maybe it was prideful, but she thought most people liked her. Her mother had taught her to try to find the good in everyone.

All and all, when it came down to it, up until that moment, there had never been a person she hated. Oh sure, she disliked her fair share. And then there were those people you would never get along with, no matter how hard you tried. But to out and out *hate* someone? Never.

Except for today. Today she could honestly say she hated Elise.

His eyes lost some of the pain they'd held since he'd walked into the room. He took her hand. "Stay here with me. I can't do this alone."

Joy flooded her soul and she squeezed his hand. "Yes. There's nowhere else I'd rather be."

"I'm not telling Elise anything immediately," Keaton said. "I'm going to buy some time. See how long I can put her off. But one thing is certain, they'll build a ski resort in hell before I even pretend to be engaged to that woman."

CHAPTER 12

With Kipling back at Benedict House, things started to feel a bit more normal. Or maybe, Keaton decided, it was a new type of normal. He rarely made it through a few hours without thinking of the sister he never knew.

Bea was released in the hospital a few days after Kipling made bail. So far, she still refused to talk to Knox. Interestingly enough, he seemed to be staying at home more. But he was quiet and definitely not his normal self.

Elise had left to spend a long weekend with her grandmother. Keaton wasn't sure exactly what she was doing with her internship because she never actually seemed to be working. But he wasn't about to act like he was interested in anything pertaining to her.

After dropping the bombshell on him about his father, and giving him all the information to back it up, she had been relatively quiet. He and Tilly tried to take that as a good sign, yet the truth was troublesome. It likely just meant Elise was up to something.

He was still undecided about telling his brothers about their lost sister. For the time being he kept quiet.

After all, the only thing it served to do was destroy their image about their father. He figured his siblings had had enough heartache lately, they could do without having the additional burden of knowing their father's actions and the half sister they never knew.

And a part of him couldn't help but justify keeping it all secret. After all, if Knox and Kipling didn't know their sister existed, how could Elise possibly pin her murder on them?

"Hey, handsome," Tilly said, coming into his bedroom. "It's Friday night, let's get out of here."

God, he loved this woman. Already, he didn't know what he'd done without her. Nor did he ever want to go back to what he was before her. She grounded him. She understood him. She loved him. She hadn't said the words yet, but he knew.

It was evident in the way she looked at him. He could feel it in her touch. He tasted it in her kiss. And she wrote it on his skin with her fingers, every time she touched him.

Instead of replying to her suggestion, he asked, "Do you get the feeling it's been far too quiet lately?"

She crossed the room to where he sat and plopped down in his lap. "You mean like it's the quiet before the storm and there's a hurricane brewing?"

If there was anything better in the world than a lap full of Tilly, he didn't know what it was. "Yes, exactly like that."

"I've had that feeling since the day I moved in. I've just approached it like I have every other storm I've been through."

"And what is that?"

"I put up storm shutters, gather those that I care for, lock us all in a safe place, and wait it out."

Her eyes sparkled. She was so vibrant and lively. He pushed a lock of hair over her shoulder. "Would you gather me with you?"

"No," she said, shocking him until she added, "because you're my safe place."

That surprised him even more and he pulled her closer. "I hope I'm always able to keep you safe. I feel as if I've failed you in the past and it's only a matter of time before I really screw up."

"That's why you're afraid it's been too quiet lately? You think something's going to happen to me?"

He nodded.

"Don't worry about it. I promise I'm a big girl and there's no one and nothing that's going to come between me and you. I'm not going to let it."

"I know you're strong. I just worry."

"Let's not worry until we have something specific to worry about."

"I have a brother accused of murder. And I'm being blackmailed by a psychopath to marry her. I think we have plenty of specifics to worry about."

"Damn. When you put it that way, it makes me want to lock ourselves in your room and never leave." She took hold of his shoulder and pulled him toward her.

"Mmm." He shifted so she could feel his erection. "Much as I like the way that sounds, I did promise the guy who oversees the downtown shelter that I'd be by today. Come with me?"

"Of course." She hopped out of his lap and he resisted the urge to grab her and pull her back. "Let me go change."

They took his car to the shelter. Tilly recognized the location immediately. "I'm guessing it's not a coincidence that this shelter is so near the port terminal Kipling was at."

"Nope." Keaton parked the car and came around to her side to help her out. "I thought we could look around. I know the police already did their investigation, but you and I both know how I feel about the local police, aside from Alyssa."

"Are we snooping before or after we visit the shelter?"

"After, I think."

They were met inside the shelter by a frazzled-looking man with unkempt hair and disheveled clothing. He shook their hands and led down dark hallways cluttered with boxes. Most were taped shut, but a few had been opened.

"What is all this?" Keaton asked as the man moved several boxes off a threadbare couch in the office.

The man scratched his head and shrugged. "Donations? I don't have time to look through it all."

The phone on the desk rang and he picked it up. "Hello?"

Keaton caught Tilly's gaze and lifted his eyebrows. *Can you believe this mess?*

"I' m so sorry," the man said, interrupting their silent conversation. "We've had somewhat of an issue today and I need to take care of a few things. I'll be right back."

Keaton assured him it was fine. Tilly leaned over to him when he left and closed the door behind him.

"This place needs some help," she said. "I've never seen so much disorganization in one place before."

"Agreed," he said. "They need someone with some top-notch managerial skills to come in and take over."

He wrote that down on the pad he brought with him.

To suggest that any organization that was benefited by Benedict Industries also had some sort of board member oversight.

"You know," Tilly said, standing up. "I think I'll go see what they have in the way as far as women and children's services. I believe I saw a reception area to the side when we first came in."

It was on his tongue to tell her to be careful, but he refrained. Besides, what trouble could she get into at a homeless shelter?

"You know this place used to be a funeral home?"

Tilly turned at the question and found a teenager standing by a door marked STAFF ONLY. The girl was dressed all in black, with black lipstick, and blue-streaked black hair. But what struck Tilly the most were her empty looking eyes.

"Really?" Tilly glanced down the hall. The reception desk wasn't too far, but someone was being helped at the moment. "That's kinda creepy."

"They say there isn't any equipment still here, but there's a room downstairs they used to do the embalming in."

"Jade!" A sharp voice stopped the teen from saying anything else. If she were to guess, she would think the woman approaching was a resident, but Tilly hated to make that assumption based on how the previous employee dressed. Although she doubted an employee would wear such a huge hat. Tilly couldn't even see her face.

"Don't you have homework you could be doing?"

Jade huffed, but pushed back on the wall. "Yeah, I guess."

The lady waited until the teen was out of sight. "Sorry about that . . . teenagers, you know?"

"Yes, I most certainly do," Tilly said, and then waited for the woman to disclose the real reason she'd sent the teenager away.

"I saw you come in with that man." She looked around and then motioned for Tilly to follow her to a nearby room.

"Um." Tilly glanced over her shoulder to the office where Keaton was. She didn't think the woman beckoning her into another room was dangerous, but the truth was, you never really knew. "I better stay here. I'd hate for him to finish his meeting and not know where I went."

The woman walked closer and out of instinct, Tilly looked down to make sure her hands were empty.

"Gee," the woman said, holding her hands palms up. "Paranoid much?"

Tilly gave her a small smile and told her the truth. "I'm afraid so. It's been an interesting few weeks. I don't mean any offense."

"I understand. I have something I need to tell you, but can we step out of the line of sight from the front desk?"

"Back this way?" Tilly asked, heading back the way she came.

"Sure."

They walked down the hall, until the front desk was blocked by a storage cabinet. It wasn't completely out of the way, but they were alone for the moment. Plus there were enough people nearby that Tilly felt confident that the woman, whom she was almost certain was a resident, wouldn't try anything.

"What can I help you with?" Tilly asked.

"It's not what you can do for me. It's what I can do for you."

Tilly raised an eyebrow.

"That man you're with. He's one of those Benedict boys, isn't he?"

"Yes." Tilly couldn't think of a reason not to be truthful. Their visit wasn't a secret and the Benedicts were known locally. Probably most of the shelter's residents knew who Keaton was.

"I thought so. Handsome lot, all three of them."

Go on, Tilly wanted to say, but didn't.

"Damn shame the way they're trying to pin that girl's murder on the oldest boy. Especially since he didn't do it." The woman spoke with a knowing grin, fully aware that she now had Tilly's complete attention.

"Do you know something about what happened?" Tilly was doing her best to remain calm, but wasn't sure she was doing a good job of it.

"I know that girl was alive when Mr. Benedict left her."

Tilly felt like grabbing the woman and either shaking her or hugging her. "How do you know and why haven't you told the police?"

"I know because I saw him leave and she was unharmed. I didn't tell the police because things happen around here, if you know what I mean."

"No," Tilly said. "What do you mean things happen if you talk to the police?"

The woman looked at her as if she couldn't believe she'd been asked to explain, but even still, she leaned close and whispered, "When people here talk to the police, they disappear."

Everything inside Tilly wanted to jump up and down and then call the police, but she knew enough to understand she had to proceed with caution. As much as she wanted the world to hear what she'd just been told, she was also acutely aware that every word of it could be a fabrication.

"Why is it no one saw you?" Tilly asked.

"How often do you take note of the homeless?"

She had a point, but unfortunately, Tilly still didn't think it was enough to get the charges against Kipling dropped.

"I tell you what," Tilly said by way of a compromise. "Why don't you write down everything you saw and did that night, and when Mr. Benedict and I come back, you can give it to us?"

The woman bit her bottom lip, thinking. "No, I can't."

Which just seemed to make Tilly think the story was a fabrication. "Why?"

"How much press coverage do you think there is when a homeless person is murdered?"

She looked pointedly at Tilly, as if she was trying to get her to understand some hidden meaning in her words. Tilly remembered how careful she'd been about not being seen. She narrowed her eyes. "Are you saying that you're afraid someone's going to come after you? Because we can keep you safe. We can involve the police . . ."

Tilly stopped when the woman started laughing and held up her hands.

The woman glanced over her shoulder again. "I'm not saying anything other than there's no press coverage for dead homeless people. Besides, even if I was saying something, I wouldn't trust you people. They said on TV, a woman close to 'Saint' Benedict was attacked."

There would be no arguing with her. Tilly recognized a will of steel when she saw one.

"One more question," Tilly said and, at the woman's nod, continued. "What were you doing by the docks that night?"

The woman moved, as if to walk past her, but Tilly grabbed her arm. "Tell me, or I get Mr. Benedict and we have this conversation at the police station."

She bit her lip. "It was nothing, really. I saw the Benedict guy there with the blonde and I thought maybe I could sell some pictures. I mean, they ended up not doing anything, but she got on her knees for a while and it looked like she was going to blow him or something."

"You have *pictures?*" she asked in disbelief.

"Shhh." The woman looked over her shoulder as if she expected someone to come running. "I have this old cell phone. I don't have cell service or anything, but the camera works and no one seems to notice or care."

"But you have pictures? Of that night?" Tilly bit her lip so she wouldn't shout for joy. "I need that cell phone."

Tilly's mind spun, trying to think of how they could get the phone. Did they beg her? Go to the police? Heck, if it'd prove Kipling's innocence, she'd break into the shelter at night and steal the damn thing.

Tilly tugged her toward the office. "At least come with me to get Keaton and tell him—"

A loud piercing siren interrupted her.

"Fire!" someone down the hall yelled.

A fucking fire alarm? If that wasn't just great. People started pouring out into the hall. She couldn't smell smoke, but she knew that didn't necessarily mean there wasn't a fire.

Where was Keaton?

"Tilly!"

She looked behind her and saw Keaton jogging toward her. "Come on, we need to go."

Someone bumped into her hard, but she ignored it, wanting to keep her eyes on Keaton. There were so many people, she didn't want to lose him. Finally, he made it to her. She pulled him to the side. "Keaton, you have to meet someone." But when she turned, the woman she'd been talking to was gone.

Across the hall, watching her and not appearing to be in any hurry to make it outside, stood Jade, the teen with the empty eyes.

The Gentleman stood at the far side of the room. Unlike times before, today he wanted to see the faces of the men present. However, he still didn't want them to be able to recognize him. He glanced at the monitor providing video streaming from the hidden camera he'd placed in the room before everyone arrived.

They all stood, looking at his back. Several had no idea why they had been called to the meeting today. Including the man standing closest to the door. The man who was the main reason he'd gathered everyone together.

"Gentlemen," he finally decided to speak. "Do you remember my words from the last time we all gathered here?"

It was a rhetorical question, of course. No one was to speak in his presence unless he gave him leave to.

"The first part of the plan was handled competently." The Gentleman looked at the man who had killed the first blond dancer and the bartender. Hearing him say that, the guy took a deep breath of relief. "Not only was a liability taken care of, and a plan put into place, but a Benedict was implicated."

The man near the door had no idea what had happened following the death of the second dancer. He actually straightened his back, as if expecting to likewise be praised.

"Even better, the eldest Benedict has actually been charged with the death of the second dancer, which was beyond what we had planned."

Oh yes, the man was almost bursting with pride. Time for the truth to come out.

"However," The Gentleman continued, and a faint hint of worry showed on the man's face. "The scene was not as secure as one would have hoped. Indeed, it has since been discovered that there was a liability nearby snapping pictures the entire time."

The man's face turned nearly completely white in fear and shock. He shook his head. "No. That's not possible."

The Gentleman nodded and two security guards made their way to the door, ensuring no one tried to leave.

"I'm afraid not only is it possible, it is fact. I have moles everywhere." The Gentleman hadn't been sure installing Jade at the homeless shelter had been a good idea. He'd thought she was too noticeable, too recognizable. But as it turned out, most people gave who they thought to be an odd-looking teen wide berth.

The residents at the shelter weren't supposed to have cameras. Too much of a risk if someone took pictures of something they had no business taking a picture of. He had interests to protect at the shelter. It was where he found women that wouldn't be missed. He'd heard rumors that a few of the residents had ignored that rule, the no pictures rule, and he'd sent Jade in to investigate. She could be a brilliant actress when she tried.

Not only that, she was quick on her feet. Hopefully since she was able to pull the fire alarm while Keaton Benedict's whore was still chatting with the liability, they would be able to get the cell phone. Jade was searching for it at that very moment. It hadn't been handed off as far as she had been able to tell.

The liability had been dealt with. He had thought about disposing her, but she wasn't all that bad-looking. After a bit of training and getting cleaned up a bit, she'd make several of his clients very happy. And she would be able to spend however long they decided she was useful, thinking about how it never paid to snoop around.

Now it was time to deal with his incompetent hit man. Unfortunately, none of his clients wanted grown men. Which meant his usefulness was over.

"Even as late as last year, I wouldn't have taken action until we knew for certain the status of the phone." The Gentleman nodded to the security men and they moved forward, each taking hold of one of the man's arms. "However, like I said not long ago, I no longer give second chances."

"No!" The man struggled to break free, but he was no match for the two guards.

"Oh, yes. Time to go for a little swim." The Gentleman gave another nod and a third security guard appeared. Within seconds, the struggling man was gagged. The other men in the room watched the unfolding scene uneasily. Good. They needed to see that he was serious about not allowing any more second chances.

No one breathed a word as the man was led away. No one even fidgeted. He smiled. Excellent.

"You are all excused."

CHAPTER 13

Keaton was doing the best he could to keep his eyes on the road as he and Tilly drove back to Benedict House, but it was hard what with the fantastical story she was telling him about the homeless woman.

"We have to go back," Tilly said. "We have to get that cell phone."

Keaton tapped his fingers on the steering wheel as he waited for the light to change. "I wonder if we should call the police and tell them. They could get a search warrant."

"I don't know. I'm pretty sure she wasn't lying to me, but you never know. Plus, I don't know her name and she had on this ridiculous hat that covered her face." She bit her bottom lip. "The thing is, she seemed really scared about the possibility of going to the police. She seemed so certain someone was going to come after her if she did. I'd hate it if something happened to her because she gave me information."

As much as Keaton didn't want to, he had to agree with her. "Okay, we'll go back tomorrow. Maybe that will give the unnamed woman time to think and she'll be ready to hand over the phone."

"I wish I had at least gotten her name. I keep hearing her say no one notices the homeless and I didn't even get her name."

Keaton glanced out the side of his eyes to see a tear slip down Tilly's cheek. He put a hand on her knee. "Hey. You okay?"

Tilly nodded silently. "Yeah. I guess she just affected me more than I thought. I can't imagine why she ran off the way she did."

"Maybe that Jade girl scared her." Keaton had caught a glimpse of the teen. He couldn't explain it, but she gave off an evil vibe that had nothing to do with the way she dressed and everything to do with the soulless look in her eyes.

"I'm sure she's harmless."

"Maybe we could try to talk to her tomorrow."

"Yes," Tilly said, her excitement obvious. "And we can try to reason with the hat woman. If she still won't listen to us, then we can go to the police."

"I agree. One way or another, we'll get that phone," he assured her.

"I just know it has what we need to prove Kipling's innocent."

They arrived back at the house in silence not long after. He knew Tilly had homework to do and he needed to type up his notes from the meeting he just had and to work on the proposal for Kipling.

"Meet you in the kitchen in an hour?" he asked her as they walked inside. "I saw Lena's picked up some ice cream. We should make banana splits."

It had been a favorite summertime treat to share

when they were kids and he drank in the sight of her first smile since they'd left the shelter.

"Yes," she said. "Definitely."

He wanted to protest when she said she was going upstairs to do homework, but he knew how close she was to graduating and he was so proud. He didn't want anything to come between her and her degree.

Kipling was working in the downtown office today, so Keaton decided to take over his home office. Besides, he figured since it was a floor removed from where Tilly was, he wouldn't be as tempted to interrupt her.

He'd just turned on his laptop when Tilly flew into his office. He looked up to find her clutching something in her hands. Her eyes were wide with excitement.

"She must have dropped it in my bag when she bumped into me," she said.

"The phone?" He stood up. "Really?" He didn't want to get his hopes up, but felt them rise anyway.

His breath caught when she held up a cell phone. He knew right away it wasn't hers. This one was several years old and he'd never seen it before.

"Yes." She nodded in excitement. "I can't believe it."

"Have you looked yet?"

"No," she said. "It's off and I wanted to talk to you first."

He stood up and held out his hand. "Come here. Let's plug it into the laptop and see what we have."

She clutched the phone to her chest. "Be there. Be there. Be there."

He raised an eyebrow.

"It helps," she said. "Like hitting Refresh repeatedly."

Her hands shook as she handed him the phone. He

took hold of her hand. "You know that no matter what's on this, everything's going to be okay?"

"Yes." She sighed. "I just know he's innocent. There has to be a way to prove it."

He pulled her close and rested his chin on the top of her head. "We both know he didn't do it. Even if this doesn't hold what we hope it does, we have to believe the truth will come out some way."

"What if it doesn't?"

He dropped his voice. "I can't think that way. I have to believe our justice system works. Not just in putting away the guilty, but also in acquitting the innocent."

"I have just about zero faith in our justice system."

"Let's not wait any longer, then." He pulled away and neither one of them talked while he connected the phone to his laptop and turned it on.

He scrolled through the files until he came to the pictures.

"Be there. Be there. Be there," Tilly started chanting again as he opened the file.

An image of Kipling walking away from the dock was the last picture taken.

"That fits with her story that she only wanted pictures of Kipling having sex," Keaton said. "Too bad she didn't care about what Mandy was doing. If she had been, maybe we'd have a shot of the real killer."

He moved to the picture previous to that one and there it was. Tilly squealed and starting jumping up and down.

"I knew it! I knew it! I knew it!" she sang.

Keaton couldn't help beaming at her excitement, even as he couldn't keep his eyes off the picture of Kipling walking away from a kneeling Mandy.

"You know, technically, they could say he came

back and killed her." Keaton hated to bring it up, but he felt it behooved him to be honest. "All this really proves is he was walking away at that point. There's nothing to prove he didn't turn around right after the last picture was taken and kill her then."

Tilly stopped jumping. "True, but it's *something,* right?"

"Enough for a jury to find reasonable doubt, yes, I would think so. But enough to get charges dropped? Probably not."

"It's more than we had five minutes ago."

"Agreed. It's definitely worth giving to the cops and who knows, maybe they'll have better luck with our mystery woman than you did."

While he'd been talking, Tilly had moved to the stare at the computer screen. "Do we know how Mandy was killed?" she asked.

"No, they haven't released that."

"If it was by knife like the other two murders, we're in luck."

He spun around to look at the picture again. "What?"

Tilly had increased the size of the photo, which made it slightly distorted. She punched a few keys and pulled up the original resolution and put the two images side by side.

"See this?" she asked, pointing to the shadowy image of a man walking toward Mandy, coming from the opposite side of where Kipling stood.

"Yeah."

"If you blow it up, there's something in his hand. It kind of looks like a knife."

Keaton looked at the photo and squinted his eyes. It might be a knife. Or did it only look like one because he wanted it so badly? "It might be a knife."

"Come on." Tilly punched him. "What else could it be?"

"I don't know. Let's call Officer Adams up and give the photo to her."

"You're right. I know you are, but damn."

Keaton put an arm around her. "Don't be upset. I want us to be completely certain before we start celebrating."

"Call her."

Keaton took his cell phone out of his pocket and dialed the number on the card Kipling had out on his desk. "Officer Adams," he said when she answered. "This is Keaton Benedict. I have a question for you."

"What can I help you with, Mr. Benedict?" she asked.

"Was Mandy's throat slit?"

There was silence on the other end of the phone. He heard a door close in the background.

"Why do you ask?"

"Because if she was, I believe we just found a picture of our killer."

"I think you'd better explain yourself, Mr. Benedict."

The Gentleman slammed his phone down with a curse. Damn it all to hell and back, he hated incompetent people. And, unfortunately, the world was filled with them. Of course, this current mess brought up incompetence to a whole new level. He had an overwhelming urge to take his anger out on someone. He drummed his fingers on top of his desk and then reached for the phone.

"Amanda," he barked out at his admin. "Send Jade in."

"I think she just left, sir."

He closed his eyes and counted to three in his head.

He still felt like stepping outside to her desk and strangling her with the phone cord, so he counted to ten.

Better.

"Then I suggest you find a way to get her back here. I want her in my office in five minutes."

"I'll see what I can do, sir."

Fear and intimidation. He chuckled. That's all it took and the world belonged to him.

"Amanda," he started. "You will do more than see about it, you will have her in my office in five minutes. Do it as if your life depended on it."

"Yes, sir," she said, and then hung up.

The Gentleman set a timer and waited. Not surprising, there was a knock on the door, less than four minutes later.

"Come in."

Jade poked her head in. "You called for me?"

"Yes, have a seat."

"I was on my way out to get coffee. This couldn't wait?" Jade kicked the door closed and then spun around to glare at him.

She was one of the few people he allowed to see him. Partially because she was like a daughter to him, and partially because her secrets were almost as damning as his.

She wore jeans today and a cream colored tee, having ditched the all black clothes and wig in advance of the police stopping by the shelter to question everyone. Not only that, but she wasn't wearing the colored contacts that made her eyes appear to be brown. As always, her natural coloring made his breath hitch.

He shook his head. Focus. He hadn't come this far to be taken down by Jade's eyes.

"Charges against Kipling Benedict were dropped," he said in answer to her question.

"What?" She dropped into a nearby chair. "How?"

He thought that would get her attention. "They aren't saying. Only that new evidence points to someone else."

"I still don't see how that's possible. As far as anyone knows, he was the last person to see that dancer alive."

"But we know that's not the case, don't we?"

She nodded, and he could almost see the wheels spinning in her head.

"You never found the cell phone, did you?" he asked.

"No. Are you sure the woman didn't have it with her when you handed her over to her new owner?"

He shook his head. "She was naked and everything left behind of hers was searched."

Jade was uncharacteristically silent. Probably because she knew what he was going to say.

"From all appearances," he said, "we have to assume she somehow gave the phone to Tilly Brock. Who you were supposed to be watching and failed at. Therefore, it is because of you that we don't have it."

He had to hand it to the young woman; she didn't look the slightest bit fearful. "If it wasn't for me, you wouldn't even know that worthless employee of yours screwed up, much less that pictures actually existed."

"I'll admit it was quick thinking on your part to pull the alarm, in order to stop them from talking, but the fact remains, you left a loose end."

She leaned back in her chair. "Happens to the best of us."

He could laugh, but only because it was Jade who was teasing him. She was the only one who dared such a thing. It was a welcome change from the norm, but he still wouldn't allow anyone else to be so flippant with him. Even Jade knew to curtail the sass when others were nearby.

"That may well be the case, but neither one of us can afford to have it happen again," he said.

"So what do we do now?"

The question wasn't unexpected. After all, he'd been asking himself the same thing since the moment he heard Kipling was no longer a suspect. He stood up and walked to the minibar he had in his office, and poured them both a drink.

She watched him with those damn eyes of hers as he carried the glass to her. It was so unnerving, he almost looked away. He didn't, though. She could never know what they did to him.

"The endgame hasn't changed," he said. "The plan remains the same, we just need to move the time line up. It's not a Benedict death, but I find I don't even care. It will be so fulfilling to watch them suffer over her passing. Tilly Brock has to die and you're going to do it."

She smiled the smile she inherited from her mother and raised her glass. "Here's to the end of the Benedict empire."

He lifted his glass and joined in her toast. She was only partially right. But it wasn't enough for him to end the Benedict empire. He wanted to crush it beneath his feet, light it on fire, and watch it burn. Then he'd take the ashes and make any surviving Benedict eat them.

CHAPTER 14

Two days after he called Alyssa, Keaton sat in the living room with Kipling, Tilly, and Derrick, waiting for the police officer to show up.

"Where's Officer Drake?" Kipling asked once she'd arrived and Lena had shown her in. "Don't you need him to be good cop? Or are you just going to entertain us with your bad-cop impression? I have to warn you, I like it very, very bad."

Alyssa crossed her arms. "Your pathetic attempts to disarm me by using sexual innuendos aren't working."

Kipling seemed rather undeterred that she called him out. In fact, he appeared to like it. "You know, I did a little checking. I was wondering why your name sounded so familiar. It would seem I'm not the only one who likes bad."

"I don't know what you're talking about." But even Keaton could see that Alyssa did; her face was more guarded than it'd been seconds before, as if she knew what Kipling was talking about and desperately wanted to change the subject.

Unfortunately, Kipling saw the same thing and now

that he knew she had a weak spot, he'd use for all it was worth.

He rocked back on his heels. "Tell me, Officer Adams. How is it possible for an officer of the law not to know, or at least suspect, that her lover is a murdering sex trafficker?"

The question was so preposterous Keaton waited for Alyssa to volley an insult back, but instead, she threw her head back, looked him straight in the eye, and calmly said, "Love is blind, Mr. Benedict. Haven't you heard?"

"Perhaps. But I hadn't realized it was stupid as well."

Alyssa's lips tightened. "I don't see how my past relationship has anything to do with my current investigation."

"That's where you'd be wrong, Officer. It has everything to do with the current investigation. How do you expect me to believe you can tell which end's up when you didn't even know the man you were sleeping with had blood on his hands?"

Shocked at the turn the conversation had taken, Keaton tried to remember a news story even remotely related to what they were discussing in the foyer. Damn. He had no idea. That's what he got for never watching the news.

The corner of Alyssa's mouth quirked up. "Did you realize who I was when you first saw me or did you Google me after I arrested you?"

There were relatively few people who gave to Kipling as good as they got. Keaton hadn't expected the police officer to be one of them. His older brother must have felt the same. He laughed and replied, "Touché, Officer Adams. Touché."

Alyssa looked mildly amused. "I know your type,

Mr. Benedict. You think you're better than everyone else because you're wealthy. You think if something doesn't go your way, you can just buy your way out. Well, guess what? News flash. I'm not for sale."

"For the record, I'm not just wealthy. I'm insanely wealthy. And guess what? News flash. Everyone is for sale. Even you. All I have to do is find your price." His voice dropped a notch. "Would you like for me to try? Rumor has it I'm very thorough when it comes to something I want to buy."

Alyssa's cheeks flushed. She had to hate that. "I'm not interested, Mr. Benedict."

An uncomfortable silence followed. Derrick broke it by clearing his throat. "Officer Adams, was there something else?"

Alyssa snapped back to attention. "All charges against Kipling have been completely dropped. By digitally enhancing the photo, they verified the knife in the picture has a serrated blade, which is consistent with not only the stab wound on Mandy, but Mindy and the bartender as well."

"It wouldn't be enough to convict the man in the picture, but it's enough to let Kipling go."

It was the news they expected, but they let up a cheer anyway. Keaton took Tilly's hand and mouthed, *You did it.*

She squeezed back. *We all did.*

Derrick looked pointedly at Alyssa. "You're relatively free with the information."

If he expected an apology, there wasn't one forthcoming. "I don't see eye to eye with the Charleston PD on a lot of things pertaining to this case," Alyssa said. "And it's my job to see justice done. Unfortunately, the two don't seem to line up all the time. They wanted me to hold off on dropping the charges a few more days, but I didn't see why I should. He is innocent, after all."

"Told you I didn't do it." Kipling's smug side was back. That he'd lost it at all meant he hadn't been as certain of the outcome as he'd acted.

"You were very lucky," Derrick said. "And don't you forget about it."

"I'm a Benedict. We don't believe in luck."

"Call it whatever you want then. Most of the time, proof of innocence doesn't just fall into your lap. Or in this case, into your purse," he finished, with a nod toward Tilly.

Keaton knew Tilly enough to know something was still bothering her.

"What is it?" Keaton asked, dropping his voice.

"Have they been able to find the woman who took the pictures?"

"That's the other thing I wanted to talk to you about." Alyssa took a deep breath. "The shelter can't find anyone matching the description you gave."

"Okay," she said. "I can drop by the shelter tomorrow after class. Maybe I'll see someone or something that will help."

"I'll go with you," Keaton said.

"You don't have to."

"I want to. They still haven't been to track down the person responsible for trashing your apartment and threatening you."

"I'm sure they have more important things to do," Tilly said. "Like figuring out who really killed the twins and Raven."

"I'm no investigator," Kipling said. "But I'm guessing it was the guy in the picture."

"Right," Tilly shot back. "Or figuring out who he is."

"Regardless," Kipling said. "It no longer involves the Benedicts or you, so we can step aside and let the Charleston PD do its job."

"Is this a family meeting I wasn't invited to?"

They all spun around at the sound of Knox's voice. He stood in the hallway that led to the front door and he looked mad as hell. Beyond that, there were dark bags under his eyes that pointed to numerous sleepless nights.

"Knox," Kipling said. "Come sit down and join us."

"Nice to see you're back to treating everything like a joke now that you're no longer the prime suspect, asshole." Knox stormed into the room and stopped directly in front of Kipling. "Are you forgetting that we still don't know who attacked Bea and that Tilly seems to be their next target?"

Kipling stood up so that he was eye to eye with his brother. "I may be an asshole, but the one thing I take seriously is family and the second some bastard left Bea to die on our porch, she became my business. Just like Tilly is, so don't talk to me about what I do and do not care about."

A new voice came from the hall.

"What do you mean, just like Tilly?"

All eyes turned to the doorway where a pissed-off Elise stood.

"Fuck," Knox said.

Keaton glared at her. "Elise, this doesn't concern you."

Elise pointed to Tilly. "Well, she gets to stay."

"Now," Keaton said in a low and cold voice.

Elise shot Tilly a death glare and then turned and left the room. Kipling took a deep breath. "Keaton, that girl has become a problem. Deal with her tonight or I will."

Keaton had actually planned to talk to Elise tonight. He'd known the conversation was going to really upset her, but now . . . hell, he had no idea what she'd do. "I'll talk with her."

"Sounds like you're in for an interesting conversation tonight," Tilly whispered.

"We knew it was coming."

Seemingly satisfied, Kipling shifted his attention to the plainclothes officer in his living room. "Officer Adams. What. The. Hell? Going rogue are you?" He asked in that tone of voice he had that sounded even more dangerous the softer he spoke.

"I actually have more information for you. We have the name of your mysterious cell phone woman," Alyssa said. Tilly sat up straighter.

"Her name is Evelyn Dubious. She's twenty-nine and has been at that particular shelter for about two months. Other residents describe her as quiet, helpful, and has a tendency to keep to herself. I know you only had the one conversation with her, Ms. Brock, but does this possibly sound like the woman you talked with?"

"Sure," Tilly said. "But the same could be said about a lot of people. Why don't I meet you at the station or the shelter so I can see her?"

Keaton didn't miss Alyssa's wince and he moved his hand to Tilly's knee. He had the feeling she would need his support following whatever Alyssa said next.

"Unfortunately, Ms. Dubious hasn't been seen following the false fire alarm."

A faint shudder shook Tilly, but she didn't say anything immediately. When she did speak, Keaton got the impression she wasn't all that surprised at the officer's statement. Tilly nodded. "I've been thinking about it and I think she knew the fire alarm was fake. She'd just insinuated that she'd be in trouble if she told me too much."

"We have confirmed the alarm pulled was the one closest to where you were standing."

"You may want to talk to a teenager named Jade. She was hanging around, watching us," Tilly said. "I mean, I don't want to go around making accusations, but she seemed a bit shady to me."

"You're not the first person to mention her and we'd like to talk to her as well. Interestingly enough, she hasn't been seen since the false alarm, either."

Keaton shifted in his seat. "How long had Jade been at the shelter?"

"A week."

No one spoke the obvious, but Keaton was willing to bet everyone was thinking the same thought. Jade had appeared after the murder and disappeared after evidence was discovered.

"The security cameras." Tilly leaned forward. "They're all up and down the docks. What are the odds they captured the killer's face?"

"Fairly good odds, actually," Alyssa said. "In fact, there's one positioned in such a way as to record the exact spot Mandy was standing. Unfortunately, they were all shot out less than a week ago."

"Someone's good," Kipling said. "And knows what they're doing. You better hope you're half as good."

"Trust me, Mr. Benedict, I'm very good at what I do. Very, very good." Said by any other woman, it might have come across as a come-on, but here it seemed to just be Alyssa speaking the truth.

"That remains to be seen," Kipling added, appearing not at all ready for their verbal foreplay to come to an end. "But I have to say one thing."

Alyssa had shifted and leaned forward.

Kipling smiled. "As much as the thought of you holding a gun turns me on, remind me never to get on your bad side."

"Too late." She stood up, breaking the spell between them. "You reside there permanently."

"Do you have any further questions for any of my clients?" Derrick asked.

"No, I was just getting ready to leave."

Derrick struggled to his feet, using his arms to help lift his weight from the chair. "I'll walk out with you."

Keaton wondered if he had really intended to leave then or if he adjusted his plan once Alyssa announced she was leaving. They didn't appear to be talking as they left, but Kipling had a better view of the front door from where he sat.

Too bad all he was doing was staring at Alyssa's ass.

Tilly's hand drifted across his thigh and Keaton sucked in a breath. They had planned to cross-reference lists Knox had pulled of both the missing women and residents of the homeless shelter to see if there were any matches. Though now that Keaton thought about it, going over the lists on his bed probably wasn't the best way to be productive.

"Do you want to hand me that paper to your right?" he asked her.

Her hand moved up his thigh and she shifted closer to him so their lips were inches apart. "Not particularly."

"Mmm." He placed the paper he'd been reading

aside and kissed her. "Who came up with the idea to look over all this in bed?" he asked against her lips.

"You." She pushed on his chest until he was on his back and she leaned over him. "And I thought it was an incredibly brilliant idea."

He loved it when she took charge. "You did?"

"Oh, yes." Her hands were making quick work of his pants.

"I'm afraid I'm going to need some more evidence of my brilliance," he teased.

She sat up, moved the papers, and with her eyes on his, stripped off her shirt. She wasn't wearing a bra and didn't say anything, but rather, lifted an eyebrow.

"Damn, I'm a genius."

"I am, too," she said with a wickedly sexy smile. "Want to know why?"

"Tell me."

"I'm not wearing underwear, either. Want to see?"

God, he loved it when she was playful. When she teased him the way she was doing now. "I want to see so badly."

He'd thought she'd drag it out and make him wait. Or at least make him beg. But to his relief, she must have wanted him as much as he wanted her. And like him, she didn't seem to want to practice delayed gratification.

Not his Tilly. Not tonight.

"Watch," she said, as if it were possible for him to do otherwise.

She was so beautiful, he could only nod and when she lifted herself to her knees in order to shimmy her shorts down, it took all the self-restraint he had not to help. But even more than he wanted her naked, he wanted to watch her. His incredible and strong woman.

She took his breath away.

And when there were no more clothes between them, when she lowered herself on him with her gaze firmly on his, and as she began to slowly ride him, he kept his hands on her hips and let her lead them both to pleasure.

Only when her climax hit did she close her eyes and throw her head back. Her release triggered his and he didn't even attempt to hold it back, but rather let it wash over him. And for those few precious moments, there was nothing in their world except each other and the love they shared.

Sometime later, she rested with her head on his chest. "Are you really going to talk to Elise tonight?"

"Yes," he said. "I've probably put it off as long as I can."

"Will you do it here or go out somewhere?"

"I'm not about to go out in public with her and risk a big scene."

Tilly pushed up on her elbow so she looked down on him. "Should I stay in the house or would it be best for me to leave?"

"I don't want you to leave. I'd like for you to stay here. Preferably with a weapon nearby, but you'd better not because one arrest is enough for the week."

She ran her hand down his chest and sucked in a breath. "Maybe we'll both be surprised at how well she'll end up taking it."

They caught each other's eyes and they both smiled at the same time, saying, "Nah."

Keaton's smile faltered. "I can't decide if I'm making the best choice for the family or if I'm just being selfish." He leaned down for a kiss, only to be interrupted by a knock on the door.

"Keaton," Kipling's voice said. "This was not what I had in mind when I said to take care of the situation."

Keaton groaned. "I'm coming."

"There's a joke in there somewhere, but I'm not touching it," Kipling said.

"He didn't just go there, did he?" Tilly asked.

"Hey, Tilly," Kipling said through the door.

She blushed and it was beautiful. "Hey, Kip."

"I'm walking away now," Kipling said. "I have to stop by the office. Apparently, a pipe burst and there's water all over the floor."

"Trade ya," Keaton said.

"Negatory. Get your ass out of bed."

Keaton rolled out of bed after giving Tilly one last kiss. She flopped back and pulled the sheet up to her chin.

"I'm going to stay right here and keep your spot warm," she said.

Keaton pulled on a pair of jeans that had been thrown on the floor and buttoned up the shirt Tilly had taken off of him hours before. He wasn't sure if Elise was even in the house, but if she was, she knew exactly what he'd been doing since Alyssa left.

Probably wasn't the best idea that he was going to tell her to go to hell after leaving Tilly's embrace. On the other hand, it could be seen as the ultimate "fuck you." Either way you looked at it, though, one thing was almost certain. It wasn't going to be pretty.

He stepped into his bathroom and made himself as presentable as possible. He had to do this. To even think about giving into Elise's demands meant a lifetime of bowing to her wishes. He would never allow her to have that kind of power over him. He'd rather die than spend the rest of his life being her beck-and-call boy.

The door to the bathroom was open and through it, he could see Tilly. She'd grabbed a novel she'd left on his nightstand and was reading. While naked. He watched mesmerized as she lifted a hand to her head to push a lock of hair behind her ear. His eyes followed her finger as it dropped to the book to turn the page. He'd kissed that finger no more than an hour ago and yet, he still wanted more. He would always need more when it came to Tilly.

She was the main reason he was going to tell Elise where she could stuff it. He knew that in his heart, saying yes to Elise was the same as saying no to Tilly. It meant giving up Tilly, and he never planned to give her up again.

Suddenly, he didn't want to see Elise without Tilly knowing exactly how he felt about her. It was urgent she knew in order to feel secure of her place in his heart and in his life. Was it too soon for him to tell her he loved her?

Maybe.

Was there a possibility she wouldn't say it back?

Of course.

Did he care?

Not one bit.

She sat up and reached for him as he walked into the room. Going into her arms was as easy as breathing and once there, he was home.

He took her hands tightly in his. "I love you, Tilly Brock."

A few tears ran down her cheeks and he put his arms around her, crushing her to him. "Don't cry, baby. Please."

She sniffed. "They're happy tears. Because I love you, too."

He felt as if his heart was going to bust right out of his chest. She loved him.

She. Loved. Him.

"Kiss me, Tilly. Kiss me so I can go face Elise with the taste of your love on my lips. Because with your love, I can do anything."

Elise had shut herself in her room. He was ready to get this over with for numerous reasons, not the least of which was a naked Tilly waiting in his bed. His reward for setting Elise straight, he told himself.

He knocked on the door.

"Who is it?" Elise asked from within.

He rolled his eyes. "It's me." Seriously, who else would it be?

"Come in."

He cracked the door open. She'd lit candles. He pushed the door open a bit more. Elise stood off to the side of the bed, wearing a skimpy, silky robe.

Jesus. She had been expecting him.

But there was more than lust staring back at him with her eyes. Anger simmered not too far below the surface.

She put her hands on his hips. "You have some nerve coming here after leaving that slut's bed."

He bit back the irate defense of Tilly that danced on his tongue, telling himself he needed to keep his mouth closed. He hadn't expected this to go easy. "I need to talk to you."

She sniffed the air. "You should have showered first. You smell like her."

The thought made him happy and he tried not smile, but guessing from the anger that became even more prevalent on Elise's expression, he failed.

He took a deep breath. No need to drag this out or beat around the bush. "The thing is, Elise, I've made a decision."

A look of victory crossed her face, but only temporarily. Her eyes narrowed as she guessed exactly what he'd decided. "Go on."

"I'm not going to marry you," he said, as calmly as possible. "And I don't care what evidence you fling around or who you attempt to set up with what."

Whatever she was expecting, that wasn't it. "You're going to regret that decision."

"I really don't think so."

"You will because I'll see to it."

"Knox and Kipling don't even know we had a younger sister. How do you think you'll get a murder charge to stick?"

"You'd be wise not to underestimate me."

He had a sinking feeling she was right, but even more so, he knew he couldn't live with the alternative. Just looking at her made him sick to his stomach. Is that what she really wanted in a life partner?

"Elise," he said, thinking he might as well try to reason with her. "You're a beautiful, successful woman. You could probably have your choice of men. You don't need me."

"You don't get it, do you?"

"Apparently not. Why don't you try to explain it to me?"

"You're a Benedict, I'm a Germain. Our families are powerhouses separate, but together we could rule the world."

"Yeah, see," he said, "I have no need for world domination."

"Of course you don't. You've never been aware of

your full potential. That's what makes Kipling so mad. You have everything you need and you simply don't care."

How fucking dare she. "Don't bring Kip into this. I know for a fact he'd never want me to marry without love."

She laughed as if he'd just told the funniest joke she'd ever heard. "Love? Honestly, Keaton, you sound like a teenaged girl. Your concept of marriage is so old fashioned. Marriage is about alliances, power, and bloodlines."

"You would set aside love and marry for power?" He knew there were people like that and that not all marriages were rooted in love, but after feeling what he did for Tilly, he couldn't imagine settling for anything other than his soul mate.

"I'm quite fond of you, but I don't believe in love." Anger flashed in her eyes again. "But don't take that to mean you can keep on fucking Tilly once our engagement is announced. That shit stops now, understand?"

"Understand what? I just told you I wasn't marrying you."

"Because your thinking is all messed up. You're convinced in happily-ever-afters and rainbows and unicorns. Why do you think the divorce rate is so high? I'll tell you. Because everyone's bought into this 'love conquers all' BS. If people would just be a bit more logical, everyone would be much happier."

"I think that has to be one of the saddest things I've ever heard." He didn't want to think about how he might have actually agreed with her before Tilly came back into his life. But now that she had, he knew better. He knew love was real and, more than that, he knew he didn't want to live without it. "And if you truly believe that, you have to be the saddest person on the planet."

"Is this about sex?" she asked. "I think you're confusing love and sex. I may not love you, but I think we'd have a lot of fun in the bedroom." She slipped her robe off one shoulder. "Come here and let me show you how good it could be."

Before he knew what she was doing, the robe had slipped off the other shoulder and fallen onto the floor. In less time than it took him to blink, Elise stood naked before him.

He refused to look anywhere other than her eyes. "Put your clothes back on."

"Grow up. This isn't about anything other than biology. I spread my legs and you use your dick to make us both happy."

But it was so much more. He wanted to shout it. Biology was cold and clinical and if that's what Elise thought sex was, he felt sorry for her. However, he wasn't going to be the one to show her the difference.

"God, you are such a child," she finally said when he still refused to look below her neck. She bent and put on her robe. When she finally looked at him he was surprised to discover she no longer looked angry, she looked resolved, which, frankly, worried him more.

She methodically went to each candle and blew it out, turning on a lamp as she passed it. And when she spoke, there was no emotion in her voice. "I'd hoped you'd see things my way after I explained everything to you, but I see now that I misjudged you. You're actually far weaker than I imagined. My offer still remains, though, if you decide you'd like to change your mind. If not, you can't say you weren't warned." She shooed him away like a fly. "Go on. Get out of my room."

"Elise."

"I mean it. Now."

He didn't like leaving her the way he was. She seemed almost dangerous. He had the strange feeling that he shouldn't turn his back to her. But after what he'd just told her, he couldn't very well stay in her room.

She stopped in the middle of the room and stared at him. He had the feeling she wouldn't move again until he left. He turned and walked out of her room, knowing he'd done what he had to, but also feeling as if he needed to watch his back.

He still felt odd when he made it to his room and found Tilly still reading in bed. She looked at him with a million questions in her eyes, but he found he couldn't answer them at the moment. He held out his hand. "Come walk with me? I have to get out of this house."

Relief flooded him as she simply nodded and took his hand.

Jade sank back deeper into the shadows when the couple she saw at the shelter stepped outside into the lush garden that surrounded the massive house. She had one job to do. Kill Tilly.

She couldn't do it.

Once upon a time, she believed every word the Gentleman said and she was so starved for acceptance and love, she'd do anything he asked without question. After all, the Gentleman was her God and you didn't question your God.

But little by little, she became aware that he was all too human and she started questioning him, if only in her head.

She didn't like the answers she found.

She wished she could ignore her strange fascination

with the Benedicts. She wished she could be honest and talk to The Gentleman about it.

But he'd be angry and though she knew he'd never take his anger out on her, he'd take it out on someone and her conscience couldn't handle any more guilt at the moment. Unable to ignore it and unwilling to share, she chose instead to stay and watch.

All her life, or as far back as she could remember, she'd been taught that the Benedict family was evil, a blight on humanity, and needed to be taken down. But standing in the shadows of their garden, watching the youngest son and his girlfriend, they didn't look evil.

She of all people, however, knew that evil had many faces and most of them were pleasant, but she couldn't stop thinking that something wasn't adding up. How could the couple in front of her be evil when all they wanted to do was help people?

Even now, the way they acted toward each other showed nothing but love and kindness. They walked holding hands, their heads together as they spoke softly. She was too far away to hear what they were saying, but based on their body language, it wasn't evil.

The younger Benedict son had been upset about something when the couple walked out. He seemed better now; the occasional giggle could be heard from the woman. Once, she'd even heard Keaton chuckle. He looked down at the woman at his side and said something that must have been sweet and tender. The woman reached up and touched his face.

Jade lifted her hand up to her own face. No one had ever touched her with so much emotion. Nor had she ever touched anyone with such tenderness.

Nothing about them or this place appeared bad. On the contrary, it seemed warm and inviting. Part of her wanted nothing more than to be a part of it. Part of her wanted to walk up the long stone drive and be welcomed inside. The only thing was, if they were warm and inviting and good, then everything she'd ever been told was a lie and she wasn't ready to believe that just yet. She couldn't believe that.

She was still pondering that when the couple started kissing and shortly thereafter, made their way back inside. She was one breath away from leaving her hiding spot when a nearby movement made her freeze.

From her right side, a woman cursed and appeared from the shadows. Someone else had been watching the couple just like she'd been. She had the feeling the woman didn't find the scene warm and inviting. Even in the darkness, she could see the anger on the stranger's face and feel the heat of her hatred.

The Gentleman would not like it if he found out that Jade had been unable to detect someone beside her. He'd tell her he was disappointed and that he'd spent too much time and energy and money training her for her to perform so poorly. Then, because he refused to punish her, he'd torment someone in her place and make her watch. She couldn't be part of that again, so she made up her mind, standing in that garden, that The Gentleman would never hear of her failure. Not from her.

Jade couldn't explain it, but she had an overwhelming urge to protect the Benedict family from this unknown woman. She tried telling herself it was because if anyone was going to bring them down, it was going to be her and not some stranger who showed up from who knew where, but deep down, she knew that wasn't the real reason.

The real reason was she wanted a chance to see if warmth and family and love truly existed.

Either way, she was going to find out what this woman who also watched from the shadows wanted.

CHAPTER 15

The next Saturday, Tilly went with Keaton to the downtown offices of Benedict Industries. Much to Kipling's delight, Keaton had picked out an office space. He'd asked her to help him decorate, and though she knew nothing about interior design, she'd jumped at the chance to help.

"I thought you didn't have any experience decorating," Keaton said in a half-teasing, half-serious tone of voice, after she'd shot down his third choice of paint color.

"I don't," she replied, ensuring her tone matched his. "As it turns out, I'm just really, really opinionated."

"And bossy," he said, this time smiling. "Can't forget bossy."

"I thought you agreed with me that the second color you liked looked like dried snot?"

"Of course I did." He was walking toward her slowly with a predatory grin. "How could I ever see it as anything else after you so eloquently described it?"

"And this last one reminds me of vomit." She pointed

to the brownish orange color she hoped he'd been joking about liking.

"Does everything come back to a body fluid for you?" He'd reached her now, and grabbed her from behind, kissing the back of her neck.

"No," she said, reaching for the perfect color swatch. "I call this one 'happy.' It makes me smile when I look at it."

"Hmm. It is a pretty color, but I wonder if it'd be better suited for that office." He pointed to the office adjoining his that was also currently empty.

"Your admin's office?"

"No, I'm not going to have an admin."

"Oh?" she asked, with mischief in her eyes. She knew he was up to something, but obviously had no idea what.

"I've been thinking." He turned her to face him and ran his hands up and down her arms while he spoke. "You don't have to give me an answer today. And I don't want you to feel any obligation or pressure to say yes." He took a deep breath. "After you graduate next month, I'd like for you to come work with me."

"What?"

"I know you've been planning to teach and you brought up wanting to do afterschool tutoring. But I know you and I know you'd be the perfect partner for me and the charity division of Benedict Industries. You have such a kind and giving heart, but you know your mind and you refuse to be swayed or talked into something you don't think is right. At least say you'll think about it." He dropped his head to whisper, "If you say yes, I have the most perfect paint color in mind for your office."

Truly, she hadn't thought about not teaching. For the last few years, she'd not even given thought to doing anything else. But she couldn't deny that the idea held a lot of appeal. She'd be able to help so many people as an employee of Benedict Industries. That was what she wanted to do, help people.

"There have to be a lot more people who are way more qualified than I am."

"I don't know their hearts. I know yours and you'd be perfect." He kissed her forehead. "But don't feel like you have to give me an answer today. Take your time. Think about it." He pulled back. "Would you like to see your office? If you take the position, that is?"

"Trying to sway me?"

"Whatever it takes." The predatory grin was back and he reached out to take her hand. "I think you'll like it."

They had almost made to the empty office when her phone buzzed with an incoming text.

"Ignore it," Keaton whispered.

"I can't," she said, reaching into her pocket for her phone. "What if it's someone important?"

"I'm not important?"

"You are, but . . . oh my God." She checked the number to make sure she read it right. She held the phone up. "It's Bea."

What does she say?"

She read the text. "She needs to talk and wants to know if I'll meet her at Benedict House."

Keaton was frowning. "I talked to Knox last night and he still hadn't heard from her. She's not returning any of his calls or messages. Do you think this is a positive sign?"

"I don't know. I really don't know her all that well.

I can't imagine it's bad that she wants to talk, you know?"

"True. Are you going to drive?"

She'd met him at the office after school so they each had a car. He'd convinced her a few days ago to drive one of the extra cars the brothers had in their garage at home.

"Yes, and when Bea and I finish talking, I can come back here and help you."

He laughed. "Text her back and tell her you're on the way."

Five minutes later, he was kissing her good-bye and helping her into the car. "Text me if you can to let me know how it's going."

He was so excited. Tilly hoped the talk with Bea went well. As she drove off, she felt the weight of the expectations of all three Benedict brothers fall on her shoulders.

Jade's phone buzzed with a text. *Damn it, what was it now?*

Her irritation turned to dread as she read:

He wants you in his office in five minutes.

There was no question as to who had summoned her, only why. She made it to his office in three minutes and flashed his admin a smile. The fact that she didn't return it told her all she needed to know.

With her heart pounding in her throat, she lifted her hand to knock.

"Come in, Jade," he called from the other side of the door before her fist struck the wood.

She cracked the door open and slipped inside, hoping

against hope she'd misinterpreted why she was here. But one look at the scene set before her crushed that hope into a million pieces.

One of The Gentleman's hired thugs stood in the back of the room. His arms were tied above his head by chains from the ceiling. He glared at her. She forced herself to be still, not wanting either man to see her flinch.

The only good news, if you could call it that, was that The Gentleman sat in a chair, facing away from his hired hit man. She'd been in this room and in this situation enough to know that meant he wasn't going to kill the suspended man. That didn't mean he wouldn't wish for death before it was all over.

"This is Tom," The Gentleman said. "He's the one who sent Bea to the hospital. He did a great job. In fact, I'm going to send him out soon to finish the job. But first we have to deal with your actions. Tell Tom why he's here."

Damn. Shit. Fuck.

She curled her fingers into a fist so tight she felt her nails dig into her palm. It would do her no good to either play dumb or beg him not to hurt Tom. She'd done both in the past and the outcome had only gotten worse the more she protested.

"I went to Benedict House," she said.

"Yes," The Gentleman replied. "And you were supposed to do something and you didn't. Tilly Brock is still alive, isn't she?"

Because she was so conflicted every time she thought about it. Had she been fed a lie her entire life? She didn't know. And why was she questioning things now?

"Yes, sir," she said. "Send me back. I can do it. It won't happen again."

But she knew it wouldn't. Even now, standing in this room, she felt the urge to go back to the tall gates that surrounded the massive house, but not because she planned to kill Tilly. The house drew her. She frowned. Or was it the people within?

"Lies," The Gentleman spat out. "You tell me lies after all I've done for you. After I saved you and brought you into my house. After I treated you like my daughter. After all that, you have the nerve to stand before me and lie?" He took a deep breath and for the first time ever, Jade knew fear when she faced The Gentleman.

"Know this, Jade," he continued in a voice so cold, so soft, and so devoid of emotion, its very sound crept into her soul and possessed her body. "If I didn't still have need of you, if anyone else on this earth could do your part, you would be the one in chains in my office."

"Yes, sir," she said in a broken whisper.

"Watch," he commanded.

Tom's eyes looked wide and frightened. She kept her eyes on him, knowing she had to or else it'd be worse for him. She knew she appeared cold and distant to him, but she had no choice. Once, she'd made the mistake of mouthing *I'm sorry* to the person taking the beating for her.

The Gentleman had ensured she was truly sorry.

She'd been afraid once of what the men who took her punishment would do to her once they recovered. When she was thirteen, one of the men told her to watch her back. The Gentleman had slowly risen from his chair and turned to face the man. Just thinking about what happened next caused her stomach turn over.

"Begin," The Gentleman said, settling back into his chair to watch Jade's face. From the dark hidden corners of his office came two men. They didn't hold anything. They didn't need to. They could break a man with their bare hands.

Jade tried to zone out, to get to her happy place, but as thud after thud fell and Tom's grunts turned into howls of pain, she lost her way. And in that one instant, everything became clear. There was no heaven. There was no happy place. There was only hell.

And she was its queen.

CHAPTER 16

Keaton couldn't get Tilly to reply to his texts. It shouldn't bother him. Hopefully, it meant her talk with Bea was going well and maybe he'd turn around in ten minutes and see them walking into the office.

But when the front office door opened, it was only Knox. Keaton lifted a hand in greeting and looked at the clock. She'd been gone for almost an hour. Maybe the talk wasn't going well. That made more sense. It wasn't going well and she didn't want to tell him.

He walked into the office he'd claimed for her. It really would look perfect painted her happy color. He should pick a color that complemented it, but it'd probably be better to wait until she got back. That way she couldn't tease him that everything he picked out looked like a body fluid.

He heard Knox's voice floating down the short hallway. He'd wait and tell him about Tilly working with them when his brother got off the phone.

Restless, he walked to the front door and looked out the windows on either side. No Tilly. Nothing. He typed out another text.

Call me.

He deleted it before sending. He didn't want her to think he was controlling or trying to dictate her every move. He typed out another text.

Getting worried. LMK you're okay.

There. That was much better.

Except she didn't call. He knew he had to do something or else he'd start pulling his hair out. He went down the hall to Knox's office. His brother was still on the phone, but he lifted his hand and mouthed, *Give me one minute.*

Keaton couldn't wait a minute. He shook his head. *Off. Now,* he mouthed back.

Knox recoiled slightly, but ended his call. "What's wrong?" he asked. "And where's Tilly? I thought she was going to be with you today."

"That's what I wanted to talk to you about. Can you give me Bea's phone number?"

Knox's jaw tightened, but then relaxed. Keaton let out a deep breath. That went better than he'd thought it would. But Knox's reply brought him to his knees.

"I can, but it won't do any good. Her phone was stolen the day she was attacked. Her brother told me. Talking to him is the way I can get information about her."

For a long moment, Keaton couldn't move, couldn't talk. He kept seeing himself kissing Tilly good-bye and her excitement as she drove off. Would that be the last time he kissed her? The only thing he could do was think and all he thought was, *No no no no no no.*

"Keaton?"

He realized Knox had gotten out of his chair and was standing in front of him only when he shook him slightly.

"You're scaring me, man," Knox said. "What's wrong?"

"Tilly got a text from Bea, asking her to meet her at the house." Keaton was going to be sick. She'd been gone for an hour and he'd done nothing. Nothing. He dug in his pocket for his car keys. "Come on. We have to go. She's been gone for an hour."

"I'll call the police on the way. We don't know who's meeting her there."

She'd been gone for an hour and hadn't returned any text or call. Whoever she was meeting, it was probably too late. He shook himself. No, he wouldn't allow himself to think that. He had to believe she was okay, because nothing made sense without her.

Tilly stepped out of the car, noticing that there wasn't a car in the driveway. Bea must have walked. She wondered if she was waiting inside or outside, the house and grounds were so vast. Before she'd left she'd asked Bea where she'd be, but never received a response so Tilly sent another text, letting her know she'd arrived and asking again where to meet.

Tilly frowned when she received no response to that one, either. She sighed, deciding to go look. There was no one on the front porch, so she walked around to the side of the house. There were several nooks and crannies where a couple could sit and talk, but no one was in any of them. The bulk of the gardens were found in the backyard. She looked around quickly, but found no trace of Bea.

It made more sense for her to be waiting inside anyway. Tilly let herself in, and dropped her purse in the foyer. She peeked into the living room, but it was empty.

She frowned. "Bea?" Nothing. Maybe she hadn't

arrived yet, but it seemed strange that Bea would ask her to meet and then Tilly be the one to wait.

Bea definitely wasn't in the house. Tilly sighed. If she'd known she would have to wait, she would have stayed with Keaton longer. She reached for her phone to text and ask Bea what time she expected to be at the house, but her pockets were empty. Of course they were, she'd put her phone in her purse which was in the foyer.

She went into the hallway to get her purse, but decided to stop by the kitchen to see if Lena had seen or heard from Bea. It was strangely quiet. Usually, she could hear Lena doing something. The Benedict housekeeper loved to sing even though she couldn't stay on key to save her life.

Tilly was smiling just thinking about Lena, remembering both her own childhood and her newly rekindled friendship with the older woman.

"Hey, Lena." Tilly stepped in to the kitchen.

And screamed.

Lena was on the floor of the kitchen, clutching her belly, a pool of blood slowly spreading under her. At the sound of Tilly screaming, Lena's eyes opened in fear. Tilly dropped to her knees at her side.

"Hold on. I'm going to call for help." Tilly glanced around the kitchen, but there was no landline in the spacious room. "My phone's in the foyer. I'll just be a second."

"Run." It took Lena all her effort to force out the word. "She . . . has . . . gun . . ."

It suddenly hit Tilly that whoever shot Lena could still be in house and a shiver of fear ran down her spine. Damn it. Why had she left her phone in foyer?

"Run," Lena repeated. Her eyelids fluttered closed.

"Lena?" Tilly shook her shoulder just a bit, but the older woman's eyes remained closed. She felt for a pulse, breathing out a sigh of relief at the faint beat under her finger. "Hang in there. I'll be right back."

"I wouldn't count on it," said a cold and familiar voice from behind her.

She turned slowly and came face-to-face with a 9mm, held by a grinning Elise.

CHAPTER 17

Tilly slowly stood, her hands raised to show they were empty. "You shot Lena?"

"Totally unplanned, but yes."

"Why?"

"Because she found the suicide note I typed for you." Elise plucked a folded piece of paper from her pants pocket and cleared her throat. "'Keaton, I'm sorry. I don't know what to say other than that. I didn't want it to come to this, but my choices caught up with me and I'm afraid there's no other way for this to end. Before I go, I have to clear my soul. I'm the one who killed the twins and the bartender. They deserved it and I won't apologize for it.'"

Elise paused. Perhaps waiting for Tilly to compliment her on her flawless prose. It wasn't happening. Tilly tightened her lips.

Elise glared at her, while continuing to read. "'My one regret is leaving you behind, but I am comforted knowing I never deserved you in the first place. I hope you find happiness.'"

"He'll never believe I wrote that." Tilly couldn't believe she was even capable of speech. Was she really standing in the Benedicts' kitchen, being read a suicide note someone had written for her, all the while, one of the sweetest women she ever met was bleeding out on the floor *and* her childhood best friend was holding a gun to her head?

And where was everyone? Lately, there were always a ton of people around the house; why was it so quiet today?

Her brain hadn't yet come to terms with the reality of the situation, she supposed. Once it did, she'd probably completely freak out. If she was still alive.

"He'll have no other choice but to believe it," Elise was saying. "Now, what I need you to do is sign the note."

"Hell, no. If it didn't matter, you'd go ahead and shoot me." Tilly had no idea why she was still talking to Elise, but she must be doing something right; after all, she hadn't been shot yet. *Keep her talking.* How long would Keaton wait before he got worried? If she didn't text the way he asked, would he know something was up?

"How did you get Bea's phone?" Tilly asked.

She didn't think Elise would answer, but she seemed quite proud of herself when she answered, "I plucked it out of her hands when she was dumped on the porch. I figured she wouldn't know and I thought it might come in handy one day. I was right."

Tilly studied the woman before her, trying to see if any part of the girl she knew from childhood was still hidden somewhere. When had she lost her humanity and what had taken it from her?

Elise motioned with the gun. "Go over to the table. This is taking too long. Someone's going to show up soon."

Tilly had never wanted Elise to be more right. *Please let someone be on their way.*

But she needed to keep Elise talking. Stall. Tilly stepped toward the table to buy time.

"Why?" Tilly asked as she slowly made her way across the kitchen. "Do you want Keaton so bad you feel you have to do this?"

"Keaton would be mine no matter what. Killing you is just the cherry on top." Elise flashed her pageant-perfect smile. "He'll think you offed yourself, and I'll be there to put the pieces back together. He'll be so thankful, he'll propose."

There was no convincing her otherwise. Her twisted mind had somehow warped her brain into believing her lie.

"As to why," Elise continued. "Money. I need it. Lots of it."

"But you're wealthy."

"No," Elise nearly shouted, showing anger for the first time since she'd lifted the gun to Tilly. "My family is wealthy. Namely, my father. But the bastard has cut me off. Said I needed to grow up and take some responsibility. Apparently, he wasn't impressed with the hacking I did to get into the university's system to change a few grades. He said I needed to explore my true potential. I'm not sure this is what he means, but it's what I'm doing. Getting you out of the way, so I can marry Keaton and have all this."

The puzzle pieces slowly started to fall into place. "Were you the one who trashed my apartment? And slashed Keaton's tires?" Tilly had to keep her talking.

She glanced at the clock. She'd left Keaton about an hour ago. Surely, he was on his way. Surely, he knew by now something was off.

Elise looked confused for the first time. "No."

They'd both made it to the table and Tilly couldn't shake the feeling that her time was up. Worse, there didn't seem to be anyone on the way to save her. If she was going to make it out of the kitchen alive, it appeared as if she was going to have to save herself.

Elise shoved the pen at her. "Sign it. Now."

What should she do? If she signed, would Elise shoot her the second she finished? If she stalled any longer, would Elise shoot her anyway?

Tilly's gaze drifted back to Lena. If she focused enough, she thought she could make out the slow rise and fall of her chest. In a split second, she'd made her mind up.

"Call an ambulance for Lena," Tilly said. "I'll sign anything you want, but don't let her die."

"I can't do that."

"Why?"

"She saw me. She can't live. In fact . . ." Elise turned and pointed the gun at Lena.

Tilly knew she only had seconds to make a move. She took a step toward Elise when the world exploded around her.

Jade finished emptying her stomach in the tiny bathroom and splashed cold water on her face. Slowly, she looked up and into the mirror. What kind of a monster was she?

What kind of a monster had he turned her into?

Through the years, she'd dreamed about running. Of getting away from The Gentleman. Today was the first day she actually gave it serious thought. If she was going to do it, she had to make a move quickly while he was otherwise occupied.

Since he'd had to do away with the twins he'd used to satisfy his carnal needs, he'd been without sexual release for weeks. He had finally called a new club to request female companionship. The blonde had arrived to his office shortly after Tom had been released from his bonds and carried out.

Because it had been so long since he'd called for a woman, Jade hoped he'd stay locked inside for longer than normal. She ran through the list of what she had and could easily fit in a backpack, knowing she wouldn't be able to take everything she wanted. That was okay, though; as long as she got away, she'd be fine.

She took a deep breath even as excitement built inside her. Clothes, she needed clothes, but not too many. Maybe three outfits? She shoved them in the backpack along with underwear.

She looked over her weapons, knowing she had to be careful with her selection. The guns weren't registered in her name. While that might be a good thing since they couldn't be traced to her, it was too cumbersome to travel with a gun these days. Knives, however . . . She was better with a knife anyway. She picked her three favorites, strapped two on her, and packed the remaining two.

On her way out, she hesitated, stopping by the kitchen. If she was able to grab some protein bars, she wouldn't have to worry about food anytime soon. But a quick glance at the clock told her she was pushing it. Her assumption was confirmed seconds later at the sound of a groan coming from behind a closed door down the hall.

There was no one between her and the front door. She very nearly skipped to it and opened it for what felt like the first time, stepping into the light of her new beginning.

With every step she took away from the dark house that had been both her shelter and her jail, she felt lighter. It wouldn't last; eyes would be everywhere once he realized she was gone. She should move far, far away.

A bus passed her, filled with tourists. That was it, a bus. Cheap, yet effective. There was just one thing she had to do before leaving this city for good. Someone had to warn the Benedicts.

Keaton drove as fast as he could without being so reckless as to attract attention. Knox sat in the passenger seat, his hand anchored on the dash. He wouldn't say anything, though. He was perhaps the only person who understood exactly what Keaton was feeling.

Inwardly, Keaton cursed himself. How could he not know that Bea's phone had been removed from the scene? How could he have let Tilly go so easily after what had happened to her apartment and the girls who worked at the club? Hell, Bea had told them Tilly was next and he'd let her drive off unprotected. Damn it, if he wasn't the biggest idiot whoever walked the planet, he didn't know who was.

"Stop it," Knox said.

"What?"

"Beating yourself up over this." Knox moved his hand off the dash and settled back into the seat. "Don't even try to deny it. No matter what you think, this wasn't your fault."

Keaton scowled. "It *is* my fault, though. I just let her go off like it was nothing. I didn't even think."

"First of all, I know Tilly, and if you'd had told her she couldn't go, she probably would have told you to go to hell and then gone off anyway."

Keaton couldn't help the chuckle. "Yeah, you're probably right."

"I know I am." Growing serious, Knox asked, "Who do you think it is?"

"I keep asking myself that question and, honestly, I don't know." But in his gut, he had a sinking suspicion he knew exactly who it is. Her voice taunted him over and over. *Don't say you weren't warned.*

He'd always thought she meant to harm him, not Tilly.

"You're doing it again," Knox said.

Keaton didn't see any reason to deny it and they drove the rest of the way to the house in silence.

They pulled up to the house. Everything was quiet as they got out of the car, which made no sense. Typically, it would be quiet with all of them at work and Tilly in class. But today, even the air seemed eerily still. Waiting.

"Didn't you call the police?" Keaton asked.

"Yes, and I don't know why they aren't here yet."

He and Knox decided to walk around the house and look inside windows in order to try and see what was going on. Neither one of them wanted to say it, but Tilly might not even be at the house anymore. They split up and Keaton took the path that went through the garden, jogging, wanting to get to a back entrance so that he could burst into the house and hopefully have the element of surprise.

He turned a corner and froze.

"Who the hell are you?" He all but spat at the young

woman standing in the very spot he was headed for. "What have you done to her? Where is she?"

But as he drew closer, he realized he knew her. The young girl from the shelter, except she wasn't dressed casually in jeans today. "You! What are you doing here?"

He had to hand it to her. She didn't cower away from him. Instead, she seemed almost miffed that he was there at all.

"Shhh." She pointed at the window. "Your girl is holding her own fairly well, but that crazy-ass blonde will probably shoot her if they hear us."

Tilly?

He tapped the girl on the shoulder and she stepped out of the way, allowing him to peek into the kitchen. His relief at seeing Tilly alive lasted only a second because standing across the room, holding a gun, was Elise. He lifted his hand to knock on the glass, but the stranger grabbed his wrist.

"Are you an idiot?" she whispered angrily. "Or do you want her dead?"

"It's Elise," he said, wondering why he was arguing with her. "She probably doesn't even know how to use a gun." He had to tell himself that or else he'd be ripping the window apart with his bare hands.

"Tell that to the lady on the floor."

He looked to where she pointed and choked back a sob at seeing Lena's bloody body on the floor. His eyes flew back to Tilly. "We have to get Tilly out of there."

The girl looked uncertain for the first time. "You just can't go charging in there. That blonde has all the power right now. You need a plan."

He ran his hand through his hair. He didn't have

time for a plan. Elise had already shot Lena. He'd never forgive himself if anything happened to Tilly.

"The plan is, I get inside the house and get her attention off Tilly."

"How are you going to get inside?"

He'd had enough. "The back door. And I still don't know who you are, but if you're still here when I get back, I'm having you arrested."

"Listen to me. You can't go through a door, that's what she's expecting."

"You have any better ideas?"

"Yes, the secret passage that leads from the garden to the butler's pantry."

He glanced through the window. Elise was still talking. He had to get in there. "Look, girl. I get that you're trying to be helpful, but I grew up in this house with two older brothers. Trust me. If there was a secret passage, I'd have known about it."

She didn't say anything but simply grabbed his wrist again and pulled him away from the window and toward the back edge of the garden. She was surprisingly strong for someone of her size.

"What are you . . . I have to get to Tilly. . . . Damn it."

She stopped in front of an ivy-covered arbor and wiped her forehead. "Move it."

He wasn't sure why he did it, probably to prove her wrong, but he reached out and moved the arbor. His jaw dropped at the wooden door now freely exposed to the garden. "Holy shit."

She didn't even look smug, she just nodded. "Leads straight to the butler's pantry. I'm not sure how much noise you'll make going through, so go slow and try not to lose your patience. Do you even have a weapon?"

"No."

She sighed and propped her foot on a nearby rock. "Here." He watched, amazed as she drew a knife out of her boot.

"Who are you?" he couldn't help but ask, taking the knife.

She shook her head and glanced over her shoulder as if she expected to find someone there. "Later, Keaton Benedict." She tilted her head toward the knife. "Do you know how to use that without killing yourself in the process?"

He noticed for the first time how smooth with wear the knife handle was. The knife had been used enough that it probably fit the owner's hand like a glove. "Yes, but are you sure?"

"Take it," she said, looking over her shoulder again. "I have more."

Another time and another place, he would have questioned her more, but he had to get inside. He had to get Tilly away from Elise. He gripped the knife tightly. Whatever the cost.

"Thank you . . ." he said, wanting at least her name.

She hesitated only a moment before replying, "Kaja."

"Thank you, Kaja," he said, and opened the heavy door that would lead him to Tilly.

CHAPTER 18

Tilly would have laughed with glee if Elise didn't look so wild and unhinged. The gun had misfired. Elise had been completely prepared to shoot Lena again, but the gun misfired. The word echoed in her head. Misfired. Misfired.

It took her brain a second to absorb the reality of what that meant. Elise was unarmed. For the moment, at least, until she could get her gun working again, Tilly scrambled to her feet, but twisted her ankle in the process and fell back down.

Damn it.

Her heart pounded and she was having difficulty breathing. If she couldn't stand, she'd crawl. Sobbing, she all but clawed her way toward the butler's pantry. She only made it a few feet before she heard the metallic click of a gun. She froze and stood up. Elise stood between her and the butler's pantry.

"Good girl," Elise said. "Now, stand up and get back over here."

She slowly got to her feet, wincing as she stood on

her hurt ankle. Elise held the gun in her hand. Maybe
it wouldn't work. She'd stay right where she was.

Elise narrowed her eyes and pulled the trigger. The
wooden floor just to Tilly's left exploded.

"I just wanted to assure you that the gun is working.
If I wanted to hurt you, you'd be dead." She motioned
Tilly forward with the gun.

Tilly must have hesitated a bit too long because
Elise walked up to her and pressed the gun against her
forehead. "I'm not going to tell you again—get over
there and sign the paper *now*."

Elise's hand trembled, her finger looking danger-
ously close to pulling the trigger.

Tilly couldn't think of what else to do, she didn't
even have a way to leave Keaton a note. The finality of
her situation overcame her and she felt tears prickle her
eyes. This was not the way she planned to go out. Not
like this. Not at the hands of a crazy woman.

She held her hands up and took a step backward
toward the table.

"Hell, I'm tired of this," Elise said. "I'll forge your
name. Say good-bye."

From behind Elise came a soft click. It was faint, but
loud enough that Elise frowned and the gun dropped
the slightest bit. Tilly couldn't hold back her gasp as
Keaton flew up behind Elise and held her with one arm
around her chest.

"I have a knife," he whispered, all the while looking at Tilly. "Drop the gun and I won't kill you."

Get away. Get away, Tilly's mind chanted as she
took a step to the side.

"If you're smart, you won't move again." Elise must
not have thought he was serious, but from the way she

jumped and the way the last of her sentence was spoken in a high squeak, he obviously showed her otherwise.

Keaton spoke again. "I really don't want to kill you, but I swear to God, if you don't drop the gun now, I will." The icy chill of his voice and the determination in his eyes told Tilly he spoke true.

Sobbing, Elise tried to push away from Keaton, but his hold on her was too strong. Unfortunately, he couldn't grab the gun without either letting go of her or the knife.

The gun rose again and Keaton barely had time to yell, "Drop, Tilly!" before the shot was fired.

Jade wasn't sure why she gave Keaton her first name. No one ever called her by that name. They always used Jade, her middle name. "Princess of the gods," she remembered her mother saying. "That's what Kaja means because that's what you are." It was one of the only memories she had of her mother.

She didn't feel much like a princess today. She felt more like an outcast, and she'd be lying to say she wasn't scared of The Gentleman's men finding her. Damn it. She shouldn't have stopped by the Benedict House.

But still, she had talked to Keaton and that was something.

She dropped her head as someone walked by, knowing she was out of place in the well-to-do neighborhood. Hopefully, she didn't stand out so much that anyone would remember her later if The Gentleman sent his goons out to ask.

Once she was out of the neighborhood, she started to walk quicker. A glance at her watch told her she'd spent much more time than she'd planned at the Benedict House. She hadn't been thinking straight. Odds were, her leaving had been discovered. Even now, she might be watched.

Though originally she'd been excited to get on a bus and head for wherever the soonest departure happened to be heading, now she was just tired. Still, she stood back and scoped out the bus station. At first, she thought she was clear, but just when she was about to step out of her hiding place, one of the men who'd beaten Tom appeared from out of the men's room.

Jade took a step back and cursed under her breath. How did they catch up with her so quickly?

But of course she knew. The Gentleman had trained her and in doing so, had trained the way she thought. Of course he knew where she'd go to get out of town. By now, she felt certain he had men scattered all over the city and especially at bus stations.

Damn. Damn. Damn. Why had she gone to the Benedicts' house?

Because she was an idiot.

But the important thing was not to become a dead idiot. And to do that, she had to stay one step ahead of The Gentleman. It wouldn't be easy and it was probably damn near impossible on her own. Which meant she needed help.

Suddenly, she knew just who to turn to for help. It was a brilliant idea. Perfect. And, hopefully, it would be the last person anyone would think she'd approach for help.

She turned around, planning to put her new plan in motion, but instead ran straight into Tom's chest. She was so caught off guard that within seconds, he had his hand around her mouth and his other arm holding her tight to him.

She struggled, but it was no use. He was much too strong.

His deep chuckle sent shock waves of fear through her. "All he talks about is Jade this and Jade that. Makes you out to be some sort of superhero and yet, look at how easily I took you down. It's downright pathetic."

She couldn't allow herself to care about his insults. She had to focus on one thing and one thing only: getting away. Turning a deaf ear to him, she lifted her knee in a move she hoped he'd think was aimed at his groin.

He released his hold over her mouth and pushed her knee away as if swatting at a bothersome fly. "You really think I'm stupid enough to let you do that?"

"No." She reached for the knife in her boot. Moving quickly so as not to lose the element of surprise, she jerked it out and aimed it at his neck. "But you're stupid enough to let me do that."

He was smarter than she thought. He turned, which meant unfortunately she didn't kill him. However, the gash she left in his shoulder hurt him enough that he let go of her entirely.

As soon as she felt his arms loosen, she was off. Not once did she look back. Not until she was far enough away to be safe. Once she stopped, she bent over with her hands on her knees, gasping for breath. She didn't know a lot, but she knew one thing.

Charleston was no longer an option for her.

CHAPTER 19

"I like your hair," the blue-eyed blond little girl said to her. *"Mine's yellow and I don't like yellow. Except for bananas. Bananas are okay yellow."*

It was Tilly's first day of kindergarten at her new school. She had to leave her old one because Daddy had a new job. A big job, he'd said with a smile. And with it he'd be able to buy his girls anything they wanted. It always made her laugh when Daddy called her and Mommy "his girls" because Mommy was too big to be a girl.

She'd been afraid no one would want to be her friend at the new school, but she'd only taken one step into the room when the blonde approached her.

"I like ducks," Tilly said. *"And ducks are yellow."*

The other girl's ringlets bounced around her head as she nodded. Tilly liked her hair. She wished she could have curls, but Mommy said she couldn't do it with her hair.

"Do you like dolls?" the girl asked. Then without waiting for Tilly to answer, she continued, *"Want to go play house?"*

Tilly nodded and with a quick look over her shoulder to her mommy to wave good-bye, ran to catch up with the girl in front of her. When they made it to the dollhouse, the girl stopped, gave Tilly a hug, and said, "You're my new best friend."

Tilly wasn't sure she'd ever had a best friend before, but she threw her arms around her and said, "You're mine, too."

"My name's Elise. E-L-I-S-E. Mommy says it's smart of me to be able to spell my name."

"My name's Tilly. T-I-L-L-Y, not I-E. Some people do it with an I-E but that's not right."

Elise nodded. "We're going to be friends forever and ever, Tilly."

"Tilly! Tilly!" someone called, as the past faded from her mind, but from her place on the ground, she couldn't tell whose voice it was. There was so much blood. Blood everywhere. All over her. All over the floor.

Her ears rang, but she didn't hurt. Shouldn't she hurt somewhere if she was bleeding that badly?

Multiple hands gently pushed her onto her back and she looked up and found Keaton watching her.

"Are you okay?" he asked.

She glanced down at his shirt. He was covered in blood, too. She reached out a hand to touch him. Had he been shot? Was all the blood his?

He took her hand. "I think she's just in shock," he said to someone she couldn't see. "I don't think she was hit."

But if he wasn't hit and she wasn't hit, that meant . . .

"Elise?" she whispered.

Something a lot like pain, but closer to pity, crossed his face. "She's gone, Tilly. She shot herself."

Tilly struggled to sit up and see for herself, but the hands pushed her back down.

"In a minute," Keaton said. "Let's make sure you're all right first."

Knowing it was for the best, she let the paramedics poke and prod her until everyone was assured she was only suffering from shock.

"Lena?" she asked Keaton, in between sips of water.

The house that had been so eerily quiet before was now teeming with activity. There were medics and police everywhere. Not too far from her, someone was covered by a white sheet. She assumed it was Elise's body, but she didn't ask. There wasn't anything else covered in a sheet and she hoped that meant Lena was on her way to the hospital.

Keaton sat behind her, practically holding her in his lap. He leaned forward. His very presence calmed her. "Last I heard, she was in surgery. It's touch and go, but they're hopeful."

He wasn't able to say more because Alyssa came up to them. "Ms. Brock, I'm going to need to take your statement." She looked at her notes and frowned. "Mr. Benedict, you mentioned there was someone at the window when you made it here?"

Knox walked up behind the police officer. "I saw her, too."

"But neither one of you got any information?" Alyssa asked.

"She told me her name was Kaja, but it was very strange that she knew about the hidden passageway in the house and I'd never seen it." Keaton lifted his head to talk to Knox. "Did you know our house had a secret passageway?"

"No, never did, and that's a damn shame because I'd have loved to have played in there as a kid."

"I bet Kipling didn't know, either. There's no way he could have kept that information to himself." Keaton knew his oldest brother. Had the secret passageway been common knowledge, they would have tormented their parents and houseguests over the years.

"Unfortunately, I can't do anything with only a first name. No matter how unusual it is."

Keaton described her to Alyssa as best he could, but honestly, he told her, at the time he was more concerned about getting to Tilly and getting her away from Elise to have taken any sort of notice beyond the fact that she was female.

"And the fact that she carried a knife in an ankle holster?" Alyssa added with a raised eyebrow.

"That, too."

Alyssa finished up with a few more questions, told Tilly she'd be back later to interview her, and left. By that time, Kipling had made it to the house, muttering under his breath about the damn traffic and how the police almost wouldn't let him into his own house.

He gave Tilly a hug and looked with sadness at the white sheet covering Elise. "I should be the one to tell the Germains. They shouldn't have to hear about it from the cops."

Tilly imagined how upset the Germains would be. Elise had been their only child. And, it didn't matter that Elise had tried to kill her, no parent should outlive his or her child.

The coroner arrived to move the body. Keaton tried to shield her, but she saw it just the same. Without warning, she started to cry, even as he tightened his hold on her.

"I'm taking Tilly upstairs," Keaton said to someone, and the next thing she knew, she was being lifted into his arms. She clung to him as he carried her up to his bedroom and placed her on his bed. He joined her, holding her close as she cried.

She cried for Elise's parents, the child Elise had been, the loss of her friendship, and for the Elise who might have been. She cried because she was scared, because she almost died, and though she didn't understand why, because she felt guilty for being okay when Lena was fighting for her life, and Elise was dead.

She clung to Keaton as if he were her sustainer and savior, and when she'd finished crying, she smiled because he was both. She snuggled into his arms and with a voice hoarse from crying, she told him she loved him.

His voice shook when he answered, "I love you, too. And I've never been more scared in my life than today, when I thought I was going to lose you."

She turned to him. "I was scared I'd never see you again."

He kissed her forehead. "I think if I could hold you like this for the rest of my life, I'd be a happy man."

"I'm never letting you go, Keaton Benedict."

"I wouldn't go anywhere if you did, Tilly Brock."

CHAPTER 20

"Keaton!" Tilly was calling his name. She wasn't sure what Keaton was thinking about, disappearing right before the start of the big outside party to announce the new addition to Benedict Industries. Especially since the new division had been completely his doing.

Kipling told her that he thought he saw Keaton heading around the back of the house near the flower garden.

"And when you see him," he added just before Tilly went outside to look, "tell him to get his worthless ass to me ASAP."

He had a huge smile on his face delivering that last line. The smile didn't fit with his words and she stood there for a few seconds until Kipling said, "Tilly. Flower garden. Now."

"Right," she said, and headed outside. It was miserably hot, and the humidity hit her as soon as she stepped outside. It felt as if her body had been wrapped up in a steaming towel. Kipling had ordered tents for the party, but those had been set up on the other side of the garden. She hoped they had some sort of fans in them.

She rounded the corner of the house and was getting ready to call Keaton's name again when she saw him. He was turned away from her, but was standing in such a way that she could admire his profile. His hands were in the pockets of his navy suit while he stared at something that must be out of her line of sight.

She took a step and a twig snapped under her feet. Keaton spun around at the sound and smiled when he saw her.

"What are you doing?" she asked him as she made her way to him. "Guests will be arriving any minute, Lena is not resting like I told her, the caterer is mumbling something about missing shrimp, and Kipling said he wants your ass ASAP."

He looked completely oblivious to everything she'd just said. "Come here," he said, pulling her toward him so she was pressed against him.

"Did you hear anything I just said?"

"Oh, yes."

"Are you going to go back into the house?"

"Not yet."

"Not yet? But the party's starting and Lena . . ." her voice trailed off. He was smiling and nodding at everything she said.

"It can all wait."

She opened her mouth to speak, but couldn't think of anything to say to that, so she closed it.

"Almost losing you showed me that none of us are guaranteed anything other than the here and now. And the best part of my here and now is you. But I'm a selfish SOB and I want more. I want you to be the best part of my years to come. I love you, Tilly Brock."

He let go of her, reached in his pocket again, and

shifted to kneel on one knee. Tilly's hand flew to her mouth because surely he wasn't . . . but tears prickled her eyes, because *oh my God* he was.

"Will you marry me?" he asked, holding out a diamond solitaire.

The tears were no longer prickling, they were running down her cheeks and it felt silly because she'd never been happier than she felt at that moment. One word kept repeating in her head and she finally got her lips to move and say it.

"Yes."

The crowd gathered on the grounds of Benedict House hushed at the sound of silver tapping glass.

"Excuse me. May I have your attention?"

Keaton smiled and turned to his oldest brother.

"Thank you all for coming to help us celebrate this historic day for Benedict Industries. As most of you are aware, helping others has always been a passion for my baby brother, Keaton. For him, it's not enough to give to those in need, he wants to teach them to be leaders so they can in turn reach others. And that's what his new division of Benedict Industries, the Benedict Community Development Division, will do. Of course, he can't do it alone and he's smart enough to know a good thing when he sees it, which is why at his side will be Tilly Brock."

Keaton put his arm around Tilly and gave her a quick kiss on the cheek.

"Tilly graduated two weeks ago and we are thrilled to officially welcome her to Benedict Industries. And though she has always been family, I hope Keaton doesn't mind if I let slip that soon, she will become an official member of the Benedict family. Hold that hand up and show everyone your ring, Tilly."

"No, he didn't," Tilly moaned softly.

"So much for keeping it quiet for now." Keaton shook his head, but took Tilly's left hand and lifted it above their heads. A few of the men near him slapped his back and whispered congratulations. Everyone else clapped.

When everyone quieted down, Kipling continued. "This has been a difficult summer for the Benedicts and we truly appreciate you standing by us. I, for one, could not be happier that my little brother has found a lifetime companion in Tilly and I look forward to the day when she becomes my little sister." He raised his glass. "So would you all raise your glass and join me in toasting my brother, Keaton Benedict, and his fiancée, Tilly Brock, soon to be Benedict."

After that, it was a long while before the congratulations ceased. Tilly joked that she was smiling so much, her cheeks hurt. But she looked happy and that made Keaton content.

While Keaton knew she really didn't mind Kipling spilling the beans, he saw her flinch at the mention "little sister." With Elise dead and her evidence who knows where, he'd decided not to tell his brothers about the sister who'd died before they knew she existed. Tilly didn't like keeping secrets, but agreed there was no need for them to know. At least not now. Not while everything was so raw and exposed.

"Sorry about that," Kipling said, coming up beside him and giving him a one-armed hug.

"No, you're not," Tilly said, teasing him. "Don't even pretend to be remorseful."

Kipling laughed and Keaton realized it'd been far too long since he heard his oldest brother do so.

"Why, Mr. Benedict, I'm impressed. You might actually have a heart in that chest of yours."

The three of them turned at the sound of Alyssa's voice. Keaton was shocked that Kipling kept his smile intact.

"Officer Adams," he said in reply. "Have you been eyeing my chest? I'd be happy to take my shirt off so you can get a better look, but I'll warn you, I expect you to do the same in return."

Alyssa ignored him and turned to Keaton. "Congratulations on your engagement."

"Thank you." Keaton kicked his brother. "What can we help you with, Officer?"

"I apologize for stopping by unannounced, but we have an update on the murders of the club workers and I thought you would like to know."

"Did you find the man in the picture?" Tilly asked.

"We have." She winced. "Rather, we found his body. He appears to have jumped off a cliff on the Blue Ridge Parkway."

"He appears?" Kipling asked, crossing his arms across his chest. "You don't think he did?"

"I think it's a bit too tidy. He left a note confessing to their murders as well as the informant from the shelter."

Keaton glanced at Tilly, but she just nodded. She'd told him not too long ago that she assumed the wannabe photographer had been killed.

"He did tell us where to find her body, so we have a dive crew looking," Alyssa said. "I guess if we find her, that might be the evidence we need to put the cases to rest."

"And yet, you still don't think it was him who's the murderer?" Kipling asked again.

"I'm not sure, but I'll find out." Alyssa grinned at him. "You're not the only one who's thorough, Mr. Benedict."

"I'd say I look forward to seeing you in action, but the truth is, I'm rather glad you don't have any lingering reasons to stop by. No offense intended." He held out his hand.

Alyssa shook it. "None taken. Good-bye, Mr. Benedict."

Kipling nodded and watched her leave. Keaton was shocked when he turned back immediately without ogling her ass.

"Well," Kipling said. "There's that."

Keaton didn't think he imagined the melancholy expression Kipling had for a brief moment. He was getting ready to ask him about it when Lena called his name and waved for him to come to her.

She'd had a precarious and lengthy recovery, mostly due to her age. The brothers had offered her a hefty retirement package, but she'd scoffed and said she'd rather be dead than to not work for her boys anymore.

Keaton told Tilly he'd be right back and jogged over to see what Lena needed.

"I'm looking for Mr. Knox," she said. "But I don't see him out here."

"He went back inside after the toast. Is something wrong?" Keaton asked.

"Mmm," Lena said. "I think I need Mr. Knox."

"Why?"

Lena pointed to the approaching figure he hadn't seen before. "Ms. Bea."

"I'll handle this," he said, giving her a pat on the

back. "Will you go tell Tilly I'll be a few more minutes?" He waited for Bea to make it to him. "Knox isn't free at the moment. Is there something I can help you with?"

He didn't mean to sound confrontational, but he was afraid he did. He couldn't help it.

He could definitely see why his brother was captivated by the tall and willowy attorney. She was pale with a few barely there freckles across her nose, with red hair and piercing blue eyes. He wouldn't be surprised if it turned out Knox had made a pass at her.

She bit her bottom lip and glanced nervously around the lawn at the numerous guests. "I forgot this was today."

So Knox had invited her. Interesting.

"Bea?" Knox asked, appearing from the side of the house.

Bea looked relieved that Knox had shown up, but regardless, Keaton wasn't leaving them alone. No way. Not when this woman had the ability to rip his brother apart emotionally.

"Knox," she said, looking sideways at Keaton. He stood his ground and crossed his arm. It wasn't until he raised an eyebrow that she continued. "I'm sorry to just show up without RSVPing." She took a deep breath. "Oh, God. This is harder than I thought. I should go."

"Bea. Stop." Knox sounded more pained than he had in weeks. But when she turned back, there were tears in Bea's eyes and she was trembling. "What's wrong?"

Belatedly, Keaton realized Alyssa hadn't said anything about the note the alleged murderer left containing any mentions or taking any responsibility for the attack on Bea.

She took a deep breath. "I had roses delivered to me today. I thought they were from you, but they . . ." She blinked the tears out of her eyes. "The note said, *Just a little RSVP to let you know I'll be back to finish what I started.*"

EPILOGUE

There was one empty chair. He'd ensured it stayed that way.

"As you can see, Jade is not with us." It still made him mad enough to breathe fire that she'd taken off the way she did. How dare she? After all he'd done for her, this was how she repaid him?

"We aren't sure where she's hiding at this time, but we don't believe she's left the city. Everyone not assigned to Bea will be out looking for Jade. This is your top priority, but she must be brought back to me alive."

Tom cracked his knuckles, though he seemed to be favoring one arm over the other. "I'll find her, boss."

"I said *alive*."

"No problem," the large man said. "As long as you give her to me when you finish with her."

He knew Tom. If Tom put his mind to it, he'd have her located in less than two weeks. "Done."

AUTHOR'S NOTE

I know as writers we're not supposed to have favorites, but I do and Keaton and Tilly are two of mine. They were a couple that simply clicked. In writing their story, once they came together, they stayed that way. I've written couples I wasn't sure I'd be able to get together and it's very freeing when they instead hold hands, look at you, and say, "Just try to tear us apart."

The only thing missing with a couple like Keaton and Tilly is that because they share so much history, you don't get to see everything in the main story. For instance, when we see them reconnect in *Darkest Night*, they've already had their first kiss. If you're anything like me, that just won't do. So I persuaded our happy couple to share that memory.

FIRST KISS

"Keaton," Tilly said and he didn't have to look at her to know she was rolling her eyes. "You're not paying attention. Do you want to fail this test?"

They were sitting at the kitchen table at Benedict House the way they did almost every day after school. Lena had baked her famous maple oatmeal raisin cookies and set half a dozen of the warm, delicious treats in front of them.

"Sorry," he said, but he wasn't at all. "Read it to me again."

Tilly took a deep breath and read, "A plane takes off from Miami and flies 347 miles against the wind in 4 hours. Flying home and with the wind, it flew 330 miles in 3 hours. Find the rate of the plane in both directions."

Keaton leaned forward. "Tell me why I need to know to do that and you won't hear a peep out of me for the rest of the year."

He thought he had her until she gave him that simile of hers that melted him every time. "To prove to the world that you're more than just a pretty boy with a ridiculous trust fund and that you want to make your

own way instead of Daddy Benedict paying your way
for everything."

"Now you make me sound like I'm a spoiled brat."

She put her hand off top of his. "You'll note that I
said, 'prove to the world,' not 'prove to me'."

He wished the rest of the world saw him the way
Tilly did, but he knew that to most them, he'd never be
more than another entitled playboy. "I don't care
what the rest of the world thinks of me, Tilly," he said.
"As long as you know the truth."

"And what truth is that?" She stood up. "That you
have so much potential and you refuse to do anything
about it. Why is that, Keaton? Afraid you might make
something of yourself that has nothing to do with shipping?"

"Sit down, Tilly. Please don't go."

She looked at the clock on the wall and shook her
head. "It's almost four and I have to go to ballet."

"Ballet, huh?" he said, and he wasn't sure why he
said it other than something she said hurt him inside
because he knew she was telling the truth. "You're a
fine one to stand there all pious. When are you going
to tell the truth?"

She didn't look at him, instead, she gathered her papers and math book and put them into her backpack.
"I don't know what you're talking about."

"When are you going to tell Mama Ann the truth
about how you hate ballet?"

She looked up at him then and he wished she hadn't
because he knew he'd hit on something that caused
her pain. He promised himself then and there that
he'd never say anything that put that look on her face
again.

"It's not the same and you know it," she whispered.

"Tilly, I . . ." he started, but didn't know how to finish.

"Mama wants me to take ballet because she never had the opportunity to take it when she was growing up. She worked on her family's farm until her parents demanded she quit high school to work full time for them. But she refused, and ran away from home at fifteen." She shook her head. "I forget sometimes how different you and I are."

"Tilly," he called again, but she was already walking out of the kitchen. He started to go after her, but someone put their hand on his shoulder. He looked up and saw Lena.

"Best let her go for now," she said. "Girls like Tilly, they have hearts that run really deep. That's a good thing because they will love you forever and ever once they put their mind to it, but it's bad because they can also be hurt just as deeply."

Keaton watched the retreating figure of Tilly wishing he could have the last five minutes back. "I love her, Lena. I do. But sometimes it scares the sh . . . crap out of me."

"Watch that mouth, young man." Lena gave him a playful shove. "Go on up to your room and finish your homework. You can go tell her you're sorry after dinner."

Tilly flattened her mashed potatoes into a pancake and then piled her peas on top of them. She hated pot roast and peas and mashed potatoes. When she had her own place, she was never making pot roast for dinner.

"Tilly," her dad called from the head of the table. "If you don't want to eat, you can be excused, but you're not going to sit there and play with your food."

"Sorry, Daddy." She stood up to clear her plate. "I'm going to go upstairs. I have some math to finish."

She sighed. She didn't want to finish math, she wanted to talk to Keaton. Problem was, she didn't know what to say. Her father cleared his throat and she looked up to find him smiling.

He pointed for her to put her plate down. Confused, she did so and waited to see if he'd explain why he was smiling the way he was. "Is something wrong?" she asked when he didn't say anything.

"I forgot to tell you that you had a visitor before dinner. Came by while you were taking a shower after ballet."

"Who?" she asked, almost afraid to ask for fear it wouldn't be *him*.

"Keaton Benedict. He said he'd be waiting for you in the rose garden . . ."

Her dad might have been saying more, but she didn't hear it. She was out the back door by the time he finished saying "garden."

She forced herself to walk once she made it past the fence the surrounded his house. He sat on a bench in the rose garden, just like he said he would be. His head was down and the fading sunlight glowed behind him. It was that second Tilly knew he was the best looking boy she'd ever met. And that she was completely in love with him.

"Keaton?" she whispered.

He stood up and shoved his hands in his pockets. "Hey, Tilly," he said, but he was watching his toes as he kicked some dirt.

"Daddy said you came by?"

He looked up and the sadness in his eyes made her gasp.

"Come sit down with me," he said and waited for her to have a seat on the bench before he joined her. When he did sit down, everything felt all awkward and she desperately wanted things to be the way they once were between them.

But he had sought her out first and she swore she'd sit there all night before she talked first. He finally looked at her.

"I'm sorry about this afternoon," he said. "Everything you said was true and instead of telling you that you were right and letting you help me with math, I was a jerk. I'm sorry and I'd like to say I won't ever be a jerk again, but," he smiled, "we both know that'd be a lie. However, I do promise to never do anything to knowingly hurt you again."

He moved his hand as if he was going to take hers, but he stopped and all the awkwardness came back. She took a deep breath and figured the only way through the awkwardness was to march straight in it.

"You were right about ballet. I told Mama on the way home I hated it and didn't want to go. That I was only doing it for her."

Her mother told her all she ever wanted was for Tilly to be happy and if she didn't like ballet, there was no reason for her to keep going.

"Really?" he asked and she felt the world lift off her shoulders at his grin.

"Really."

They sat there for several seconds and all at once she was aware of him in a way she'd never noticed before. How close he was. How warm he felt. How strong.

A slight gust of wind blew a few wayward strands of hair in her face. Before she could reach up to move them, Keaton already did. But instead of dropping his hand, he stroked her cheek.

"Tilly," he whispered and she hoped he couldn't feel how fast her heart was beating. Then he leaned forward and everything flew right out of her head because he was kissing her. Before she even knew what she was doing, her arms were around his neck and she was kissing him back.

A nearby light suddenly flooded the garden and they both jumped away. One of the back doors opened and Lena's voice filled the night.

"Tilly, your mama just called and said to tell you to come on home."

Tilly groaned, but Keaton laughed as he pushed the same wayward hair back into place.

"I better go," she said. "Algebra tomorrow, three o'clock, your place?"

"Please. I have a test to ace."

WANT MORE *SONS OF BROAD*?

Read on for the first novella
in this swoon-worthy series

SHATTERED

FEAR

PROLOGUE

He strolled along the cobblestone path, his casual step a stark contrast to the energy pulsing through his body. He didn't look at anyone, but rather kept his attention focused on the path before him.

Numerous questions ran through his head. Why had The Gentleman called him so soon after the last delivery? Was there a problem with the package? Surely he didn't require another one so soon. But damn, what if he did? The last one was a struggle to deliver and he'd been hopeful it would have lasted longer than three weeks.

"Hey, watch it."

He stepped back just in time to narrowly miss being mowed down by a student on a bicycle. The near miss made his heart beat even faster and he shook himself, knowing he needed all of his mental capacities for where he was going. He pulled out a handkerchief and wiped his brow, cursing the humidity of July in Charleston.

Paying closer attention to his surroundings, he turned down a side street and walked up to the house with the horrible monkey door knocker. Fortunately, he didn't have to touch the monstrosity because, as always, the door opened before he had a chance to knock.

The man who opened the door was also familiar, but he'd never been given the butler's name. In fact, the man had never spoken a word in all the times he'd visited. He would simply stand there, his ebony skin in sharp contrast to his spotless white uniform, looking him up and down, as if the cat dropped a half-eaten bird on the porch. Then he'd nod and turn to walk down the hall, never once looking back to ensure he was being followed.

They came to a stop before a set of wooden doors. After a quick knock, and the "Enter" given in reply, he was shown inside the main meeting room. He knew his guide wouldn't follow him, but would wait outside to escort him back to civilization when the meeting was finished.

The Gentleman stood with his back to him. Once, he'd asked The Gentleman why he never turned around. His answer had been a deep chuckle and a softly spoken, "Do you really want to know the answer to that?"

"You asked me to come this afternoon, sir," he stated, which was stupid, but then again, so was talking to someone's back.

"The last delivery was unacceptable," The Gentleman said, confirming his fear.

"I was sure this last one was sturdy," he said, his voice only cracking at the end. It was neither an apology nor an outright challenge. He wasn't stupid. He coughed. "Surprising it didn't last three weeks."

Silence was his only answer, but then again he hadn't asked a question.

He shifted from foot to foot. Shit. He didn't want to

make The Gentleman angry, but damn. Still, he knew as long as he talked to the guy's back, he was fine. It was if the man ever turned around that he'd be in serious trouble. Or that was the rumor, anyway.

"The last delivery was unacceptable," The Gentlemen repeated.

His fingers itched to take his handkerchief and wipe his brow again, but he refrained. The Gentleman might have his back to him, but he knew he was being watched. He could not show fear.

He took a deep breath. "I'll see what I can do about getting a replacement. Maybe by the end of the month . . ."

"Try again."

He figured as much, but he thought he may as well try. "Sir."

"Next week."

Next week? That was going to be nearly impossible, but he could tell The Gentleman wasn't going to take kindly to hearing that. He swallowed his sigh and said, "Yes, sir. Next week."

"Very good. And, a word of warning: the Charleston PD has a plant at a certain popular club."

He not only knew that, he knew who it was. "Not a problem, sir," he said. "I've got it under control." But it was a lie because he didn't have it under control, and he had no idea what he was going to do about it.

"Very good. That's what I like to hear."

A small sense of relief started to weave its way through him. Maybe, he would be able to leave soon. The whole house gave him the creeps. He would much rather take his chances at the club, even with the police plant, than stay in this house for a minute longer than necessary.

He waited for the door behind him to open and for the other man to lead him outside. But there was nothing. He looked over his shoulder to make sure he hadn't missed it. Why wasn't the door opening? When he turned back around, it was almost as if he could sense The Gentleman smiling.

"Before you leave," he said. "There's the matter of the unacceptable package to deal with."

He grit his teeth, knowing it would do no good to argue. He hated this part of his job. Whom was he kidding? He hated all parts of his job. He was just buried too deep inside to get out now. Damn gambling addiction. And damn himself for thinking he'd ever be free. Truthfully, he only had himself to blame. No one forced him to get half a million in debt.

Though he felt the weight of what he was getting ready to do and what he had already done, he forced himself to put on a neutral face. "Where is it?"

The Gentleman laughed. "You think I have it here? The body is being delivered to your house as we speak. Deal with it."

CHAPTER ONE

Janie Roberts figured she had about three minutes' worth of patience left before she vaulted over the bar and smashed something over the head of the guy currently trying every cheesy line he knew in an attempt to get her number. She eyed the shelf behind her, mentally calculating the price of liquor in each opened bottle. She'd have to use something cheap since it was doubtful the Charleston PD would allow her to expense it.

Unfortunately, she was working undercover and if she started breaking bottles, the bar would probably kick her out on her ass. Serial kidnapper or not.

"Damn, honey," the half-drunk dweeb tried again. "You are H-O-T, hot. Why don't you come over here and warm me up?"

She considered complimenting his spelling, but discarded that idea almost immediately. No doubt her sarcasm would be lost on him in his current state. She opened her mouth to tell him no, *again,* when a man she'd served a beer to about an hour earlier stepped in between her and the hardheaded drunk.

"Seriously, man," he said, with a nod in her direction. "Have some pride. She said no. Many times."

Drunk Guy looked like someone had kicked his puppy, but Janie hardened her scowl and put on her best *don't mess with me* face.

"But . . ." he said with a hiccup.

Her white knight crossed his arms and shook his head as the lights in the club dimmed slightly. Janie nearly laughed. He towered over Drunk Guy. Heck, he looked as if he could snap him in half with that icy glare alone.

Drunk Guy hiccuped again, sized up his competition, and turned away. He half stumbled toward the back of the club where dancing was getting ready to start.

When she was certain he was gone and wasn't going to come back, Janie faced the guy who'd run him off.

"Thank you so much," Janie said, taking the time to get a good look at the guy. Earlier, when she'd served him, the crowd at the bar had been too thick for her to pay attention to anything other than his drink order.

He was classically handsome in the guy-next-door look. Of course, she had no idea where that phrase came from; none of her neighbors had ever been half as good-looking. His hair was a messy, dirty blond, and his eyes were a warm brown. She estimated him to be a few years older than her twenty-nine because he had a few laugh lines barely visible. On another man, they might have aged him, but it only added to his character and they painted him as someone who enjoyed life.

"It's no trouble," he said. "Truly."

"He must have heard the Aristophanes quote and thought by being drunk he was being clever."

His eyes widened in surprise. "You mean, 'Quickly, bring me a beaker of wine, so that I may wet my mind and say something clever'?"

Now it was her turn to be surprised. "You know Aristophanes?"

His laugh was soft and seductive. "I could ask you the same."

"Theater minor."

"Ah," he said in understanding. "I spent several summers in Greece with my grandparents."

His response flustered her a bit. Spent summers in Greece? Who did that? But he, apparently, thought nothing of it as he tipped his glass back and drained what was left.

"Let me get you a refill." She nodded toward the empty glass in his hand. "Stout, right?"

"Thank you, but that's really not necessary."

"It may not be necessary, but you probably saved my job. Before you showed up, I was trying to decide which bottle would be the least likely to get me fired if I busted it over that guy's head."

His smile was back. "I can't turn you down when you put it like that."

She took his glass to refill, watching him from the corner of her eyes as she poured him another beer. He leaned casually against the bar, but she had the underlying feeling it was a rouse. The air around him pulsed with a restrained energy.

The realization was enough to shock her back into the reality of her situation. She wasn't here to flirt or meet men. She was working the bar in an attempt to discover information on the disappearances of several young women while they were working at the club.

And something about him suddenly had alarm bells going off in her head. The way he stood, perhaps. Confident. Self-assured. Or maybe the way his eyes swept over the club, always watching. Definitely not typical.

No matter. She'd been a cop long enough to know not to ignore those warning bells.

She schooled her features before turning to hand him the beer.

"Thank you," he said, taking the offered glass. "Will I be too much like the guy I chased off if I ask your name?"

"Janie Roberts." She didn't offer to shake his hand since she'd picked up a dishrag as soon as he'd taken the glass from her.

"Brent Taylor," he said, and she couldn't stop the little gasp she gave when she recognized his name. She thought he looked a bit disappointed that she knew who he was.

"Thank you again, Mr. Taylor." She had spent enough time talking to him; there were other customers to attend to. And she didn't miss the manager on duty standing not too far away with his arms crossed and giving her *that* look. The *I don't care if the Charleston PD wants you here, when you're behind my bar, you're to be working* look.

Brent nodded, probably catching sight of the manager's expression. "I'm going to head out. Hope to see you again soon."

He was gone before she could reply. Shaking her head, she shifted her attention to the men waiting for her to take their orders.

Two hours later, Janie groaned as the last club patron left and the door was locked behind them.

"Talk about a long night," Tilly, one of the club's waitresses, said as she slid onto a barstool beside Janie.

Janie enjoyed talking with Tilly, who was young, vivacious, and funny. Normally she tried to stay emotionally detached when she worked undercover, but Tilly had the type of personality that naturally drew people to her. All except one person, Janie hoped. Tilly didn't fit the profile of the women the kidnapper was focusing on. So far, he seemed to target blondes with little to no family, and only one had an education beyond high school. Tilly was certainly pretty with her wide blue eyes set against her light brown skin and wavy dark hair, but she didn't fit the profile. Except, she didn't have any family.

"You can say that again," Janie said. "I think it was the busiest since I started."

"I did happen to notice a few men with an interest in hanging out by the bar," Tilly teased.

"The drunk guy who wouldn't take no for an answer?"

"Not only him, but the blond guy, too."

Her white knight in shining armor, who just happened to be a well-known philanthropist. "Brent Taylor?"

Recognition flashed in Tilly's eyes, even though she said, "Oh, I don't know his name. I just thought he was very interested in you."

Interesting. But Janie played along. "From what I've heard, he's the biggest playboy in the South. He's a trust-fund baby." As soon as she said the words, it struck her that this might be the man they were looking for. Well-educated. Wealthy. Good-looking. Come to think of it, he fit every item the profiler had told her to look for. Could he also be the type to enjoy playing the double life? Magnanimous on one hand, calculated killer on the other?

Was it possible he thought himself above the law and went about kidnapping women to prove it? She'd seen it happen before, particularly among the very wealthy. It was almost as if they saw other people as beneath them.

In the last year, six women had gone missing. Four had some sort of tie to this club. Janie had been the first person to connect the dots and when her boss asked her to go undercover three weeks ago, she'd jumped at the chance. She was also trying to find a link between the club and the other two girls.

Her mind drifted back to the feeling she'd had in the bar earlier.

Well, damn.

Was he the reason behind the disappearance of so many women? It made her sick to her stomach just thinking about it.

"Hey." Tilly waved her hand in front of her eyes. "Are you there? What happened?"

"Nothing. Just thinking of some things I need to take care of when I get home."

"This late at night?"

She knew for a fact Tilly was in school. "Don't give me that look. I know somebody who's going to home and study for about three hours before they turn in."

"Guilty."

"Are you two going to stay here all night?" the manager asked. "Or do you plan on leaving sometime in the near future?"

Tilly grabbed her purse and Janie's hand. "We're leaving."

CHAPTER TWO

"Run that by me one more time," Alyssa, her friend and coworker, requested after Janie gave her the high-level details of the night before.

Janie sighed and excused herself to Alyssa's kitchen where she poured herself another cup of coffee. "You want it all or just the highlights?" She tried to keep the irritation out of her voice. Unfortunately, after spending the night before wide awake, unable to shut her brain off, she wasn't sure it was possible.

"I'm sorry." Alyssa followed behind her. "But *Brent Taylor*?" She asked like it would make far more sense for the kidnapper to be the vice president of the United States. Hell, it probably would.

"I know he's done a lot for the city." At Alyssa's lifted eyebrow, Janie conceded, "And for the state of South Carolina. But you have to agree, if you were going to get your hands dirty by kidnapping women, it wouldn't hurt to have a stellar reputation for being one of the most charitable men in the South. Besides, usually it is someone with power and they end up exerting that power in unsavory ways."

Alyssa didn't say anything, so she continued. "It's always the people you least expect. You never hear the next-door neighbor saying, 'I could tell he was a whack job the moment I laid eyes on him. Everyone knew he was batshit crazy and it was only a matter of time before he snapped.'"

At least that got a hint of a smile out her friend.

"Admit it," Janie said. "You know I'm right."

"I'll admit it does happen like that most of the time. But," Alyssa added before Janie could gloat, "you know we get plenty of calls from neighbors who just plain despise each other. In fact, I think it's about time for old man Green to call and ask if he can have his neighbor's dog arrested for trespassing."

Since Janie had been called to Green's home more often than she cared to remember when she was new on the force, she had to admit there was truth behind Alyssa's statement as well.

"I think it's wise not to let Brent Taylor's reputation cloud your judgement," Alyssa said. "But make sure he's not the only one you're keeping your eye on."

Janie would have been offended if she thought Alyssa was telling her how to do her job, but she knew it was only her friend's personality. Deciding to turn the topic away from Brent Taylor as a suspect, she sighed. "It'll be hard to keep my eyes on any other man. Do you know how hot that guy is?"

"Brent Taylor?" Alyssa's forehead wrinkled and Janie nodded. "Only from what I can tell from pictures. I've never had the privilege of seeing him up close and personal."

"See what up close and personal?" Alyssa's boyfriend, Mack, strolled into the kitchen, swiped an apple from the fruit bowl at her elbow, and gave her a quick kiss. Janie couldn't help but feel just a little jealous.

"Nothing." Alyssa smiled and pushed a strand of dark hair out of his eyes. "Just girl talk. You heading out?"

"Yeah." Mack frowned. "But I'll make it quick. Meeting your cousin for dinner at seven, right?"

Alyssa nodded, and both women watched as Mack walked away.

"I've said it before," Janie said. "You got one of the last great men."

"I'm a fortunate woman."

Alyssa and Mack had been dating for over two years. Alyssa confided in Janie recently that Mack had been dropping hints about getting married and starting a family. But she didn't feel the same pull.

"I'm an idiot for not agreeing to marry him, aren't I?" Alyssa asked when the front door closed behind him.

"I'm sure you have your reasons." Janie knew Alyssa always had a reason for everything she did, but she hadn't shared the reason she was hesitant to marry him. "If you don't hear your biological clock ticking and if you're completely happy *living in sin,* then by all means, keep it up."

Alyssa looked sideways at her. "You're kidding me, aren't you? I hate that I've known you for so long and I still can't tell."

"I kid. I kid." At least, she was half kidding. She really didn't think she'd be able to turn a man like Mack down.

"Back to you and Brent Taylor," Alyssa said.

"There is no me and Brent Taylor." She said the words, but if that was the case, why did her stomach get all excited just speaking his name? And why was she actually looking forward to going back to work in the club tonight just in case he happened to be there?

Which he wouldn't be. Last night was the first time she'd seen him in the weeks she'd been working there. And there was no way possible she'd have overlooked him.

Alyssa looked at her with that *you can't fool me* look, but she didn't say anything.

"You still think it's for the best you went in as a bartender instead of a dancer?" Alyssa asked.

When they had first set everything up, the original thought was that Janie should be a dancer, but after a few nights spent observing, it was decided she'd work behind the bar. She was glad, too. Not that she would have minded dancing, but the dancers didn't have the opportunity to see and talk with customers the way a bartender did.

She was thankful as well that it was an upscale gentlemen's club. Though the crowd ran anywhere from college boys to middle-aged men, for the most part they were well behaved and not scummy like she'd feared.

"Definitely for the best," Janie said. "After all, Brent Taylor wouldn't have even seen me last night if I'd been a dancer. He spent all his time at the bar."

The corner of Alyssa's mouth quirked up in a slight grin. "I think that was because he was smitten with you. If you'd been dancing, he'd have still found you."

"Smitten." Janie rolled her eyes. "Really?"

"What time do you go in tonight?" Alyssa asked, instead of answering.

"Eight." *Twelve hours to go,* she thought, looking at her watch.

"Text me when he shows up."

"He's not going to show up."

Alyssa crossed her arms. "How about we make it interesting? He shows up, you owe me dinner at the new farm-to-table."

Just to call her bluff, Janie added, "And if he doesn't, we go shopping for wedding gowns."

But Alyssa didn't falter. She stuck out her hand. "Deal."

Holy hell, he was going to show up.

The first few hours of her shift passed by in much the same way as every other night she'd tended bar at the club. It started out slow, with a sparse crowd that gradually grew over time. As the clock neared midnight, she excused herself for a quick bathroom break. She stuck her phone in her pocket, planning to text Alyssa and ask her what day she wanted to go wedding-gown shopping.

She tried to plan her text in her head. She wanted it to be snarky with an *I told you so* attitude, though she wasn't in the mood at the moment. It pissed her off how much she'd actually wanted Brent Taylor to show up.

No. Scratch that. What really pissed her off was how much she'd been looking forward to seeing him again.

This was why she shouldn't get her hopes up, she told herself as she turned to head down the hall leading to the restrooms. Because she always felt like warmed-over, day-old hell when nothing lived up to her expectations.

"Janie?" the seductive voice that haunted her fantasies all day asked.

She shook her head. It must be her fantasy this time, too.

"Janie Roberts."

It was the addition of her last name that made her stop. Interesting. There was no need for her fantasy Brent to use her last name. Even so, she turned slowly, wanting to draw out the feeling that he had returned to see her.

She'd done such a great job at convincing herself he wouldn't show up, it took her brain a few seconds to comprehend that yes, he had returned and yes, he sought her out.

Well, damn.

CHAPTER THREE

"What are you doing here?" she asked and then cringed, because out of all the things she could have said, out of all the things she'd planned to say, that wasn't one of them. The only reason she could think of was she'd just convinced herself he wasn't coming.

It obviously wasn't what he'd expected, either. His smile left and the light that was in his captivating eyes dimmed.

"I'm sorry," she managed to stammer out. "That was horribly rude."

"I caught you off guard," he said. "It's fine."

But he didn't look like he was fine and he wasn't smiling. Two things struck her at once. One, she didn't want him to leave, and two, if he was the man she was looking for, she couldn't allow him to leave.

She placed a tentative hand on his arm. "Let me get you a drink."

Something in her words or demeanor must have struck a chord, because the tension left his body.

"I'm not myself tonight. I didn't sleep well," he

admitted, and she wondered if he tossed and turned the way she had. "I can't stay long, either. I have to get home. But I wanted to know if you'd like to go to dinner with me sometime?"

"You want to have dinner with me?" She hoped he didn't hear the croak in her voice.

"Yes. It's not every day I find someone who will quote Aristophanes at me, especially someone as bewitching as you." His tone sounded normal, but his eyes danced with mischief.

He thought she was bewitching? She suddenly felt like she had in high school when the boy she'd had a crush on admitted he liked her. But she couldn't allow herself to act like a schoolgirl whose crush just asked her to prom.

"Thank you," she said. "But I think it was actually *you* who quoted. I merely inferred."

"Semantics."

At least he said the latter with a smile. But looking over his shoulder, Janie noticed the manager on duty did not have a smile on his face.

"I have to get back to work," she said. "Boss is watching."

Brent nodded and took his phone out. "I have to be going, too. Why don't you give me your number and I'll call you. Tuesday night sound good for dinner?"

She nodded as they walked back to the bar and she gave him her number. Seconds later, her pocket vibrated.

"That's me," Brent said at her slight jump. "Now you have my number."

She waited until he left to check and then, with a

shake of her head but wearing a smile, she sent a text to Alyssa.

Dinner is on me.

On Tuesday morning, Brent called to tell her the dinner they'd planned for that night had to be postponed.

"I feel like such an ass," he said. "Believe me, I tried everything I could to get out of this, but I have to fly to Manhattan for the day."

His voice still carried the easy confidence she'd noted before. She didn't think he was trying to get out of the date, but she'd be lying to say she wasn't disappointed. She'd been looking forward to spending time with the man she was just starting to get to know. More importantly, she was looking forward to getting to learn more about him and see if he was potentially the kidnapper.

Not for the first time, she asked herself what the hell she was doing getting involved with a potential suspect. In the past, she'd always thought such people needed professional help. So what did that say about her?

"I'll be right there," he said to someone. "Give me three minutes. Yes, go ahead and get it ready."

"I won't keep you," Janie said. "I can tell you're busy."

"I swear I'll make it up to you. How does Thursday night sound?"

Thursday was her night free from the bar. "Thursday will be perfect."

There were voices in the room with him, but she couldn't make out what they were saying.

"Great. I'll call you when I get back." He hastily said good-bye and then disconnected.

Janie stared at her phone for several long seconds, shocked at how much his change of plan had affected her. And the worst thing of it all was she really didn't want to spend the evening by herself.

She called Alyssa to tell her about the change of plans and to see if she happened to be free.

"I don't know," Alyssa teased. "I'm not sure I like being your second-choice dinner companion. But as it just so happens, Mack has to work late and I'm free."

"Which makes me your second-choice dinner companion."

"That makes us even."

Janie rolled her eyes at the phone, smiling. "Let's do easy. You want to come over here, watch a chick flick, and order pizza?"

"Best idea you've had today."

It wasn't too often Janie and Alyssa were able to get together for more than a hurried meal. Janie tried to think back to the last time they were both off and able to get together for girl bonding, but she couldn't. They were seriously overdue.

Alyssa said the same thing when she arrived hours later, holding up a brown paper bag that Janie knew would contain her favorite ice cream. "I so need this tonight."

They ordered the pizza to be delivered and turned on their favorite Jane Austen movie. It didn't take long for the rest of the world to dissolve into hot men with accents and horse-drawn carriages.

They were getting ready to open the ice cream when Alyssa's phone rang. With a huff, she pulled it out of her purse and frowned when she read the display. "Damn it. I told them not to call me if it wasn't an emergency." She hit the answer button. "This better be good."

It obviously wasn't good news judging by how fast her face went pale. In a tight voice, she replied to whomever was on the other line, "I'll be there in ten."

She hung up with a sigh and stood up. "There's been a body found. No identification yet. Young female."

"You better go," Janie said, giving her friend a hug. "We'll do this another time."

When Alyssa left, Janie felt bad knowing the night her friend had ahead of her. Death was never easy. Especially in the case of a young person killed before they had a chance to live. But she also knew that Alyssa wouldn't have to deal with the aftermath alone. She had Mack and he'd seen her through rough cases before. He'd be there again this time.

Janie turned the movie off and planned to get to bed early, but all that changed when Alyssa called her with a shocking update.

"It's your case," she said. "The body is the last girl who went missing."

Janie didn't need Alyssa to go into details. Though several women had been reported missing before now, there had never been any further trace of them. The assumption had been they were being trafficked. But now that one had been found murdered, they would have to relook at their entire investigation. It also meant Brent might be more than a kidnapper. He also might be a killer.

Janie didn't sleep hardly at all that night. The thought kept running through her head that she could be dating a murderer.

His hands trembled as he opened the letter. His name, written in a flowing script on the outside of the envelope, told him who it was from. Surely, though, if they were going to kill him, they would have sent an assassin instead of a letter.

The paper inside was made of a pure white linen without a speck of dust to mar the finely handcrafted stationary. He dropped the letter on the table when he realized his hands were sweating. *Idiot. It's just a letter.*

He wiped his palms on his thighs and looked around to make sure no one was watching. They weren't. As always, everyone was too caught up in their own world to notice his. Taking a deep breath, he unfolded the paper and read.

My instructions were clear.

The only reason you're still breathing is because she was so decomposed when they found her, there will be no evidence.

Mess up one more time and I'll deliver the next letter by hand.

In his mind, he saw it happening. He'd open the door and The Gentleman would be standing there waiting, a strange combination of pity and pleasure on his face as held up the weapon. Would it be a knife or a gun? Probably a knife. A gun would have everything over much too quickly.

He shot up from his desk and ran to the men's room as his stomach flipped and his lunch reemerged.

CHAPTER FOUR

Thursday night, Janie and Brent met in the historic district since that was where he'd been working. She'd spent her time window shopping, strolling along the cobblestone streets, trying to enjoy the near constant buzz of tourists, and peeking into windows. The truth was, she was a wreck of nerves. She stopped in front of a high-end clothing shop and admired the cocktail dress in the window, trying to imagine ever going somewhere that would justify wearing such a gorgeous gown, while at the same time taking deep breaths to calm down.

"You should try it on," a familiar voice said.

She jumped at the sound of his voice, but forced herself to smile when she turned. "You've vastly overestimated my social life."

He chuckled softly, but didn't mention the dress again. "I thought tonight would never get here."

She couldn't help but notice the looks of admiration he received from a group of women walking past them. Looking at him through their eyes, it was hard to imagine him as evil.

"I agree," she said looking up at him. "How was New York?"

"Busy, like always." He pointed to a nearby seafood place. "This okay?"

"Sure." She recognized the place, but had never been in it.

They walked up to the hostess stand and Janie inhaled the mouthwatering taste of perfectly grilled fish and fresh baked bread.

Brent dropped his head as they waited for the couple in front of them to give their name. "If it wasn't so hot outside, we could sit out here."

Delightful shivers traveled down her spine from the way his warm breath tickled her neck. "That's too bad," she agreed. "I love to people watch."

"Me, too."

The hostess quickly led them into the restaurant where the air conditioner kept it blessedly cool. Brent pulled out her chair for her and she covered her surprise. She didn't know guys still did that except in movies.

They made small talk while looking over the menus. It wasn't until they ordered that Brent turned his brown eyes to focus exclusively on her.

"Tell me about yourself," he said. "Besides the fact that you're a bartender who reads Aristophanes."

She shrugged. "There's not much to tell. I'm working the bar at night, while looking into other opportunities during the day."

That wasn't much of a lie. In fact, if you stretched it, it was sort of the truth. She had a feeling Brent Taylor wasn't going to reveal much of himself, either. Which meant she had her work cut out for her.

"Any family?" he asked. At the shake of her head, he added with a smile, "Dog, cat, goldfish?"

"None of the above, but I'm looking into getting a dog." Since turnabout was only fair, she asked, "How about you?"

"Neither," he said. "I'm allergic to both dogs and cats, but I have strongly considered a goldfish."

She laughed at the image of someone like Brent Taylor considering getting a goldfish. "Just one?" she asked. "I would have thought you'd get a huge saltwater aquarium."

His eyes danced with a playfully naughty look. "Maybe there's more to me than you read about in the society column."

She started to protest that she didn't read the society column, but quickly closed her mouth as she felt her face heat. No doubt he knew the effect he had on women and guessed from the way she'd reacted to his name when they first met that she did read those columns.

"I'm sure there is, Brent Taylor," she said. "After all, aren't we all more than mere words on paper?"

He raised his wineglass. "Touché."

"Now it's your turn," she said. "Tell me about yourself."

"I have one half sister. She's younger than me. My father died when I was four and my mother married a pastor. Shocked the hell out of everyone. I mostly stayed with my dad's family."

She nodded. All of that were things she could gather from reading about him in the paper. She wanted more. She wanted the Brent Taylor who was known to very few. "Boring. Tell me something that will never be printed in the papers."

"I'm considering a move to Washington, DC."

Her glass of wine stopped halfway to her lips, and before she could reply, their entrées were delivered.

After the waiter left, Brent sat across the table, silently watching her.

But was he watching her as a man who wanted to get to know her or as a hunter studying his prey?

Had he guessed she was a cop? Or had he invited her to dinner because he suspected something? Dinner might not have been the best decision.

Her mind spun trying to unravel the tangled ball of yarn the investigation had become. If he was the man they were looking for, would he be thinking about moving? Maybe the discovery of the last girl's body had scared him and he'd decided to change locations.

Or maybe, he was just your average guy, looking to expand his horizons.

Like Brent Taylor could ever be called *average*.

"You're thinking about something awfully hard," he said.

"Sorry, it's hard to shut my mind off sometimes."

"I do the same thing," he assured her. "The trick is, I need to get your mind on something else so it doesn't wander away."

She tilted her head. "Why Washington?" she asked, not ready to give up control over the conversation yet.

"I've been approached to head a joint committee with the government and several special interest groups on transparency in food labeling. It's something I've always been passionate about."

"Sounds like an exciting offer." She recalled he'd funded several grants dealing with the subject.

"It is. I'm just not sure I'm so tired of South Carolina summers that I'm ready to trade them in for DC winters."

"Good point," she conceded. "How long do you have to decide?"

"A few months," he said.

She didn't have months to solve this case. There were too many lives at stake. If they waited it out and the disappearances stopped, it wouldn't be enough to say with absolute certainty that it wasn't him. On the other hand, if DC started seeing similar disappearances, even though it would be circumstantial, it would still be telling.

"Not much time to decide," she said.

"No, and I'm heading that way tomorrow to look at a few properties."

"Oh." He was already looking at property? That meant he was strongly considering the move.

They passed the rest of the meal in compatible conversation. Janie found herself thinking of him more as Brent than *the* Brent Taylor and was surprised to find him charming and down to earth. The more she talked with him, the more and more she wanted to believe he wasn't the guy she was looking for. But she couldn't rule him out, which meant she might be dining with a killer.

The thought was enough to keep her focused on her objective: to get more information on Brent Taylor.

After dinner, he asked if she'd like to walk around the Battery. Since the sun had gone down, the temperature had dropped to a more comfortable level, and she agreed. Besides, a casual walk might mean he'd lower his guard.

Several couples and families had the same idea they'd had and the historic district, while not being crowded, definitely wasn't empty. More than once, they had to sidestep a group of tourists who had stopped to take pictures.

For a while they walked in silence.

Janie's senses were on high alert as they walked out of the heart of the historical district and into less occupied areas. Brent chatted about the neighborhoods he planned to look at in DC and how he feared they wouldn't measure up to what he was used to characterwise, after living in Charleston. After a few minutes, the tourists were gone. A few more minutes and they were basically alone. Was this how he seduced the women? If she wasn't a cop, would she have noticed how secluded they were?

Either way, she was a cop and she couldn't get out of her mind that he'd been out of town the night another woman went missing. She was an idiot to walk this far alone with him.

"Are we going anywhere in particular?" she asked as they turned down another nearly deserted street.

He looked around and cringed. "I'm sorry, I was so involved in talking, I didn't even realize how far outside of town we were." He held out his hand. "Let's go back."

She tentatively took his hand. He seemed genuine enough, but could it be an act? His hand was warm and powerful. Yet, not the sort of power that terrorizes, but rather protects. Or was she only projecting what she wanted to feel?

"Would you'd like to get coffee or something?"

She wanted to. She wanted to badly. But it wouldn't be wise right now, not when she was so uncertain. He ran his thumb over her knuckles and it felt so good. Why did he have to be so perfect?

Focus, she told herself.

She looked at her watch. "Can we do it another time? I have an appointment in the morning and I should go to bed soon."

Technically, she didn't, but if she stretched it, Alyssa would call her in the morning to see how her date went. That could be a meeting in the loosest sense of the word.

"Sure—"

He was interrupted by his phone ringing.

"Do you need to get that?" Janie asked. "I don't mind."

"No. It's my sister's ringtone. I asked her to call me. I haven't told her about the DC offer yet." He sighed. "She won't like it and it's not a conversation I feel like having right now."

She was momentarily shocked speechless. He'd told her about DC before he told his sister? "Why . . . why won't she like it?" she finally managed to get out.

"No particular reason. Just being a typical younger sister. Not wanting me to be that far from her. I love her to pieces, but she has a tendency to worry and over-think things."

"Are you close?"

He nodded, his expression lighthearted and filled with affection as he spoke of his sister. "We are. She's one of my best friends and that's another reason I didn't want to pick up. She knew I had a date tonight and I'd hate for you to hear me babble on and on about what a great time I had."

They approached her car as she turned to look at him. "You did?"

"Yes." He lifted a hand to gently stroke her cheek. His touch felt so good, she closed her eyes to savor its feel. His thumb drifted lower to brush her upper lip. "In fact, I'd like to know if you want to do it again when I return from DC?"

"Yes." The reply fell from her lips without giving her brain a second to think.

"I wish I was already back," he whispered, and then he dropped his head and kissed her far more gently than she wanted.

She hesitated only a second before putting her arms around him and pulling him closer. "Me, too." And when he kissed her again, he wasn't as gentle.

Her brain shouted that this was wrong and she shouldn't be kissing him, but her heart wanted him. She'd always prided herself on keeping emotional distance between her and her job. So what was she doing in the arms of a potential suspect?

She remembered they were on a public street and forced herself to pull away before she did something she'd regret or that might be seen. "I need to go."

"Call you when I'm back?" The moonlight danced in his eyes and his smile filled her with anticipation of when he'd be home.

"You better."

The next night at the club, she was still reliving memories of the day before. Brent Taylor was nothing like she had imagined and he was nothing at all like the playboy philanthropist newspapers painted him out to be. He was so much more.

For once, being hit on by intoxicated patrons didn't bother her all that much. Of course, it probably helped that she couldn't get Brent out of her mind.

"I don't think I've ever seen you smile so much at one time," Tilly said. "Word around the club is that you went out with Brent Taylor last night."

"For once, word around the club is right." She couldn't hide the big grin that she gave the petite server.

"That's it? I don't get the details or anything?"

"There's not much to say. We went out to dinner."

Tilly crossed her arms and raised an eyebrow. "Dinner put that smile on your face?"

"Not just dinner. We went on a walk, too."

"I see." Tilly smiled. "Now the truth comes out."

"What? There's nothing else to tell. We didn't do anything. He's on his way to Washington." Those were the last personal questions she was going to answer tonight. "What about you? Do you have a boyfriend?"

She had asked it as a harmless question. Just something to break the ice and get the focus off her. Instead, Tilly's face grew flushed.

Janie thought she should apologize, but she wasn't sure what for. "I'm sorry. You don't have to answer that if you don't want to."

Tilly took a deep breath, and the corners of her mouth lifted slightly. "It's okay. You didn't say anything wrong. It's a common question."

Janie waited.

"I don't go out very often, but not for the reasons you might think. In my mind, there's only been one man for me. I used to think we could actually happen, but I'm older now." There was a sadness to Tilly's voice that was very much at odds with her normal jovial personality. "I never talk about it, but I probably should."

Janie looked around. It was a slow night at the club, and the normal manager wasn't on duty. The one in charge tonight spent most of his time watching porn in his office. No one was paying any attention to her and Tilly. They could spend a few more minutes talking.

"Tell me about him," Janie said.

"Goodness," Tilly said. "I don't even know where to start."

"Does he have a name?" Janie said with a laugh. "That's normally a good place to start."

But Tilly wasn't laughing. "The thing is, you've probably heard of him."

"Really? Okay, now I have to know."

Tilly bit her bottom lip and whispered, "Keaton. Keaton Benedict."

Janie only blinked. Surely she had not heard right. Tilly couldn't have been talking about *those* Benedicts. That would be crazy. Even crazier than Brent Taylor taking her out to dinner. The Benedicts were Southern royalty. The epitome of blue bloods. And Tilly knew one of them? Not only knew one of them but, apparently, had a major crush on him.

"You don't have to say anything," Tilly said. "I know it's crazy. But believe it or not, Keaton and I grew up together. There was some bad business between our families, and then we weren't friends anymore."

The Benedicts were notorious for their ruthlessness in business. She would not want to be on the bad end of a deal with them. She could only assume that's what Tilly meant. "What happened?"

Tilly shook her head. "It's been so long I don't remember."

But Janie didn't believe her, Tilly just didn't want to tell her right now. And that was fine, everybody deserved his or her secrets.

"You ever talk to him?" Janie asked.

"Not in years," she said softly.

Janie didn't want to pry. It was obvious the woman was hurting. She had her head down, her long dark hair hiding her face. She sniffled and looked up with a smile.

"When I first started working here, I had this fantasy he would come in one day and find me. Rescue me. Silly, right?"

"I don't think so," Janie whispered.

"But it's silly of me to put my life on hold, waiting for him to reappear."

"I think if the right man came along, you should be open to the possibility of a relationship and not let Keaton Benedict hold you back."

Tilly's gaze drifted to the clock. Her break was almost over. "Fortunately for me, between this job and school, I don't have time for any relationships."

Before she could walk away, Janie reached for Tilly's hand. "The right one's out there. Just be patient."

"Listen to you," Tilly said with a laugh, obviously deciding to bury the past for a bit longer. "One date with Mr. Taylor and you're a relationship expert." She wiggled a finger at her. "Be nice to that man; there aren't a lot of good ones left."

Janie laughed back and shooed her away. "I hear you. Go on and get ready."

Brent was never far from her mind as she worked that night. Of course, that was to be expected since she had spent a good portion of her day researching him. From everything she'd discovered, there were no dark corners or hidden closets in his past or present. Heck, not only had his biological father left him a shit ton of money, but his stepfather was a well-respected minister.

But in the back of her mind, was that lingering thought that he'd cancelled on a night someone disappeared.

Her digging had also found some interesting facts, though. He hadn't been lying about spending summers in Greece. After his father died and before his mother remarried, his paternal grandparents had him stay with them in Athens for three months.

He'd graduated as valedictorian of his private high

school and summa cum laude from the University of North Carolina at Chapel Hill. She couldn't help but think the universe really hadn't been fair to other men in bestowing so much on Brent.

As she left the bar that night, she couldn't help but wonder if he'd call tonight. She hoped he would. It was silly, but she missed him. How was that even possible? They hadn't known each other that long.

She'd parked on a side street and walked part of the way with Tilly. Tilly didn't have a car. She took a bus, and Janie always felt bad about leaving her at the bus stop in the wee hours of the night, but Tilly just laughed it off and said she'd been doing it for years and the drivers all looked out for her.

Janie reassured herself Tilly didn't meet the profile of the kidnapped girls, but that only brought a small measure of comfort. The world didn't always treat women well. Especially those sitting alone at a bus stop alone at two in the morning.

Tilly was still on her mind when she turned the corner to get to the street she'd parked on. She sniffed the air. Odd. It was a man's cologne or soap. She was certain she'd smelled it before, but she couldn't remember where. Very distinctive, though, like minty cedar. Looking around, she didn't see anyone. But it had rained earlier and the low-hanging fog drastically cut her visibility.

A faint scuffle sounded as if it was coming from the location of her car. She patted her gun, safely concealed by the large tunic style shirt she wore, and hurried down the street.

At first she thought it was just two guys talking. But as she drew closer, she heard the bigger one cursing at the other. The smaller man was Charlie, a homeless guy she recognized.

He often hung outside the bar. Between her and Tilly, they managed to sneak him food on a regular basis. He was a gentle soul, though he always turned down any offers of shelter or job.

When she first met Charlie, she'd hoped he either had or would soon come across something that related to her case. So far, though, he hadn't seen anything.

She approached carefully, keeping her hand on her weapon, but not drawing it. Who would be cursing at Charlie and why? He was harmless. The men still hadn't noticed her.

"Hey!" she called out.

The stranger turned and saw her. There was a flash of something silver as his hands made their way to his pockets. He took a step back, shoved the older man into the brick wall of a nearby building, then turned and started running down the street.

She could either go after him or check on Charlie, but she couldn't do both. The other man was out of sight and Charlie was crumpled on the street. She hesitated for a second before turning to the more critical matter.

She dropped to her knees beside Charlie. "Are you okay?"

"Yes," he said in what sounded like a wheeze. "Little punk ass didn't have to throw me into the wall. I don't think I broke anything, but it hurts like the devil."

"I bet. Do you need anything?" she asked.

Charlie patted her hand. "You're such a good girl. You and Tilly. Looking out for me."

"Tell me what happened," she said, digging in her purse for a tissue to wipe up the blood from his forehead.

"No need to worry about it, Miss Janie. It's not a big deal."

Typical response and one she anticipated he'd use.

"Do you know of those women who have gone missing?" she asked.

He nodded. "Damn shame that whole situation."

She leaned closer as if she was going to tell him a secret. "You haven't seen or heard anything, have you?"

His eyes grew wide in understanding. "You think that was him?"

"I think you probably see a lot more than you think you do. And yes, I think it's possible. Why else would he be hanging out on this secluded street?"

Charlie was visibly shaken. Though he always had a slight tremor in his hands, it became more pronounced as she spoke. He kept looking around the darkened street as if expecting the man to come back.

Was it possible she'd just let the man they were looking for slip through her fingers? But she'd made the call to attend to Charlie; second-guessing herself wouldn't do any good.

"Let me drive you to a shelter, okay?" She gently helped him to his feet, surprised when he didn't protest about getting in her car.

He looked uncomfortable and out of place in her sedan and was totally uninterested in the radio. She eventually turned it off.

"Did he say anything to you?" she asked.

"He just told me to move. Said it was his turf." He scratched his arm. "Don't see how a fancy man like that would want any part of that dirty street. Don't make a lick of sense."

"Fancy man? Did you notice anything that would help identify him?" She couldn't help but think this might be the break they were looking for. She debated taking Charlie straight to the station, but feared he might freak out thinking she was going to have him arrested.

Charlie just chuckled. "You know I can't see for shit. Everything's a hazy blur. I said he was fancy 'cause he sounded fancy." He chuckled again. "That's right."

Of course. They had one potential eyewitness and he was blind as a bat. No need to think about a side trip to the station now.

She pulled into the drive of the homeless shelter a few minutes later. "Let me know if you need anything."

"I'm good. And you know I'll do anything to help you, Miss Janie."

"I know you will, Charlie. I know you will."

She had just entered her apartment when her phone rang. She rummaged in her purse, finally pulling it out and smiled as she read the display.

"Hiya, handsome," she said.

Brent chuckled. "You worked tonight, right? I didn't wake you up?"

"Just walked in the door. How's DC?"

He sighed. "It's okay. The position is what I've been wanting to do and there are some really nice properties for sale, but I'm just not sold on it yet."

It was ridiculous that should make her happy, wasn't it? Seriously, they hadn't known each other that long. She couldn't expect him to stay in Charleston for her. Shouldn't she want him to be happy? Even if that meant he moved to Washington?

"You'll make the right decision," she told him. "And when it's right, you'll know it."

"I know I thought about you all day."

His smooth, seductive voice stroked the embers that always threatened to ignite when he was around.

"I thought about you, too," she admitted. If the man who attacked Charlie was whom they were looking for, she hoped that meant it couldn't be Brent.

"I'll be home early in morning. Want to meet for lunch?"

"Tomorrow?"

"Yes, if you're able to. I thought I'd take you on a picnic."

"A picnic?"

"Are you going to keep answering me with questions?" he asked, a smile in his voice.

"And what if I do?" she asked, matching her tone to his.

He laughed heartily then and she couldn't help but join in. She couldn't remember the last time she had such a good time talking about absolutely nothing in particular with a man.

They finally agreed that he would pick her up at noon and said their good-byes. Not long after, she crawled in bed, looking forward to what the next day would bring.

CHAPTER FIVE

After a delicious picnic the next day, Brent suggested they go back to his place to talk. He said he lived nearby in the historic district and she could follow him in her car.

"I've always wanted to tour one of these." Janie looked up at the historic building he called home. It was white, with a huge wraparound porch and massive windows. It blew her mind he lived there. "I have to be honest, though. If I did own one of them, there's no way I'd sell it and move to DC."

"Who said I was going to sell it?" he asked, his hand brushing against her lower back as they walked up the steps of his porch.

She rolled her eyes at him. "Right, I keep forgetting you're wealthier than some countries."

"Only a few of the small ones, though," he said, flashing her a grin.

She wasn't able to say anything smart back to him, because at that moment, the door opened and she felt like she'd been transported back in time. Thick, rich rugs covered the hardwood floors and the majority of the furniture were antiques. Her eyes jumped from piece to piece, trying to take everything in.

"I would never leave my house if I lived here." She turned to look at him. "Brent, this is gorgeous."

"Thanks, I wish I could take credit for it, but I hired someone to do it for me."

"It's an interior decorator's dream home."

He smiled and rocked back on his heels. "My sister said almost the same thing."

Heaven help her, what his smile did to her. It made her belly fluttery and turned her knees to jelly. It really wasn't fair if you thought about it. She just had to make sure her head was on straight because she feared she was losing her objectivity when it came to Brent.

Take for example, she really didn't need to be in his house. Not like this. Not when he was so disarming. It left her vulnerable and that could be a dangerous thing.

He gave her a quick tour and she oohed and aahed over most of the house. Historical homes were one of her weaknesses and she yearned to study every antique piece he had. He actually laughed at one point when she was examining a sideboard and teased that if only he had dovetails maybe he'd get some attention.

She gave him a playful punch on the arm. "You probably don't even know what half of your furniture is."

His eyes danced with mischief. "You know, you're right, but it brings me pleasure to see you so taken with them."

They strolled into a sitting room and he waved toward the couch. "Have a seat. Can I get you something to drink?"

"Do you have iced tea?"

"Coming right up."

While he was gone, she picked up a picture from the

arm table. It was Brent, standing with a woman that had
to be Bea. They looked so similar, although while Brent
had the olive skin of his Greek ancestors, Bea was
much paler.

In the picture, Brent had his arm around her and she
beamed at the camera, holding up a diploma. She tried
to read which university the degree came from, but the
writing was too blurry.

"That's Bea and me the day she graduated from
Duke with her law degree." He handed her a glass of
iced tea, pride for his sister obvious in his tone, and sat
down beside her. He didn't sit down at the other end of
the couch. Oh, no. He sat down in the middle so his
upper thigh was pressed against hers. She felt the heat
from his body and his spicy masculine scent filled her
senses. "I'll have you both over so you can meet."

It was obvious the two half siblings were close, even
if he hadn't told his sister about the DC position first.
She could tell by the way he spoke of her and the affection in his eyes when he did so. "I'd like that."

"I know she'd love to meet you. Probably so she can
tell you horribly embarrassing stories about me."

"It's what all the best sisters do." She laughed. "Or
so I've heard. I can see the family resemblance." She
took a sip of tea, trying to get her mind off Brent, his
scent, and his body. Her grandmother always told her
you could tell a lot about a person by how they made
iced tea. Brent's was superb. "Also," she said with a
wry smile, "it's obvious you're a family of underachiev-
ers." She held up her glass. "This is good."

"Thank you." He draped his arm across the back of
the couch. Her body naturally moved closer to his and
he cupped her shoulder as she drew near. She thought
they would talk, and she wanted to question him more

about the night he was gone, but suddenly every word she ever knew flew straight out of her head. Which made lifting her face the natural thing to do when he softly spoke her name.

He ran his thumb along her cheekbone and her skin felt electric where he touched it. Her eyes fluttered closed as his thumb continued along her face and brushed across her lips. Unable to stop herself, she parted her lips slightly and bit the tip of his thumb. She smiled at his sucked-in breath.

"Tease," he whispered.

"Not yet," she replied.

He hadn't moved his thumb away from her lips yet, so she drew it into her mouth, sucked it. And smiled at his softly whispered curse.

But if she thought she had won, she was sorely mistaken. He removed his thumb from her mouth, shifted on the couch so that he pressed her into it, and framed her head with both his hands.

"You want to play that way?" he whispered.

He was hard and warm against her, and it had been far too long since she had a man touch her that way. She couldn't help but lift her hips and grind them against his.

"Oh no," he teased. "It's not going to be that easy for you."

She groaned.

"Good things come to girls who wait." He then proceeded to methodically unbutton her shirt. He took his time and went so slowly, she swore to herself that the next time they went out, she would wear a pullover.

She was desperate to feel his hands on her, and she imagined he felt the same. She began working on his shirt in the same manner he was working on hers. Little by little, she exposed his skin, and when she had it half-way undone, she took both hands and placed her palms on his chest.

"You feel so good," she said.

"I know it's a cliché," he said, "but you haven't seen anything yet."

She untucked his shirt from his pants. "Promise?"

But instead of answering her, he dropped his head and nibbled the sensitive skin at the curve of her neck. His ministrations sent waves of electricity through her body, which only served to remind her how empty she was. And how desperate she wanted to be filled.

She ran her hand down his chest and lightly cupped his erection. "When do I get to see this?" she asked, playfully.

"You can see it whenever you want, but if you want me to last longer than ten seconds, it would probably be a good idea for you not to do anything other than look. At least until I get something resembling control back."

Had they been together longer, she might have teased him by continuing to palm his erection. But on the off chance he was being honest about the ten-second thing, she moved her hand.

He flashed her a deliciously evil grin and took both her hands and pulled them above her head. "Now, let's see if you can keep them here."

"Why would I want to do that?" She couldn't touch him if she did that.

"You'll have your turn. Right now I want to explore every inch of you."

He shifted them on couch a bit more, so he had better access to her body. He gave her a brief kiss on the lips, and then started kissing his way across her shoulders and down to her breasts. The man had a deliciously wicked tongue, and his lips weren't that bad, either.

As his mouth closed around her left nipple, there was a knocking on the windows. She stiffened immediately, but Brent didn't seem fazed at all. Probably it was nothing. She closed her eyes, determined not to be bothered by it.

Brent moved on to her right nipple and when the knocking came again, she couldn't ignore it.

She sat up. "What is that?"

"Probably some neighbor kids. Don't worry, they can't see in."

She still felt like she should probably pull her shirt together, but she didn't want to move. Not when Brent was looking at her with that look of his like he wanted to eat her alive.

He moved away from her and she moaned with the loss of his body against her, even as her mind was saying it was a good thing they were interrupted and she should take it as a sign and leave before she went any farther with a potential suspect. But, no, he wasn't going anywhere. He simply held out his hand to her and when she took hold of it, he pulled her up and brought her close to his chest.

"Let's go upstairs," he whispered in her ear, and ended the sentence by nibbling on her earlobe.

His fingers brushed up and down her arm, barely touching her, but electrifying her body and sweeping away any lingering resistance.

"Lead the way," she murmured.

"I can do better than that," he said, and lifted her in his arms.

She'd never been carried to bed before and if she'd

thought about it beforehand, she probably would have been self-conscious. She tried to protest, but he silenced her with another kiss.

He put her down once he crossed the threshold of the bedroom. She took a few seconds to simply admire the way he moved. He walked over to the bedside table, opened a drawer, and took out a condom.

As he walked back to her, she slipped both shirt and bra off her shoulders, and let them fall to the floor. She was thankful that she had the foresight to put her service revolver in her purse, and not carry it on her body.

He wrapped his arms around her and she could have sighed with how perfect they felt wrapped around her. "Now, where were we?"

Obviously, it was a rhetorical question. He cut off any chance of her talking by covering her lips with his. His lips were strong and demanding, showing her exactly how it would be with him. She had no doubt he was just as strong and demanding in bed as he was out. She'd spent so much of her life doing what was right and what was expected, she wanted to lose herself in him. Even if it was just once.

He walked backward to the bed, stopping only when the back of his legs hit the footboard. "Ah yes, I think we were about here."

He put his hands around her waist and lifted her onto the bed, pushing her down so her legs were hanging off the edge. She watched appreciatively as he situated himself between them.

"Yes," she said. "This is much better than the couch."

He laughed. "I thought you might think so."

"There's only one thing that could make it better."

She ran her hands down his back, making sure her nails scratched the fabric of his shirt that he was still wearing. His moan of pleasure made her do it again.

"What's that?" he asked.

"Me waiting for you take this shirt off."

He had it off and on the floor within seconds.

She could only stare. Dear heaven above. Every inch of him was perfect. She scooted up the bed and pulled her legs up so she was sitting.

"Now the pants," she said.

He pointed toward her. "Panties first."

"I asked first," she said.

He crossed his arms over his chest, a teasing look in his eyes. He knew he had her right where he wanted her.

"Fine." She shimmied her panties down and took them off. "You win."

His eyes were dark with lust and need. "Oh, but you have that wrong, my Janie. I can assure you, *you're* the one who's going to win this round."

She didn't have a chance to question him because the next thing she knew, he'd grabbed her ankles and pulled her right back to the edge of the bed. She barely had time to take a breath and let out a whimper before he'd buried himself between her legs.

Her eyes nearly rolled to the back of her head because she had vastly underestimated his mouth and tongue skills earlier. Within seconds, he had her dancing on the edge of release. She stretched her arms, desperate for something to grab onto and almost as desperate to figure out how the hell he managed to get her there so quickly.

She was neither a virgin nor a prude, but orgasms had never been easy for her to obtain. In fact, most of the time, she faked. It'd always worked in the past. Her lover would be satisfied, he would think she was satisfied, and when he left or went to sleep, she would then get herself off.

Never in her entire life had one crept up on top of her so suddenly. Her hands found purchase in his hair and as he licked, nibbled, and sucked her, she fisted his blond locks.

He moved just enough to bring a finger up to rub her clit while he continued to nibble and lick her sensitive flesh, and that was all it took. Her release crashed over her so hard, her breath left her for several seconds.

"Oh my god," she said, when she could speak again. "That was. . . . oh my god."

He looked altogether pleased with himself, and rightfully so. Anyone who could do what he just did deserved to be a bit prideful. She was coherent enough to notice he still had his pants on.

"Why don't I take those off you?" She crooked a finger at him. "Come here."

He got up on the bed and came across on his knees to where she waited. She unbuttoned his top button and slowly dragged the zipper down, making sure she palmed him as she did so. Her efforts were rewarded with a low hiss.

"Careful," he said.

"Why? Is it going to bite me?" She'd finished unzipping and was tugging his jeans down.

He chuckled. "No, but I might."

"Is that a promise?"

But he couldn't answer because she had lowered his boxers, allowing his cock to spring free. She debated putting her mouth on him. He must have sensed what she was thinking, because he fisted his hand in her hair.

"No. I want to come with you this time." He handed her the wrapped condom. "You can put this on me."

She ripped the packet open. "Next time, I'm taking you in my mouth and I'm not letting you go until I swallow you down completely."

She made sure to tease him with her touch a little bit as she rolled the condom on him. He filled her hands and she couldn't stop touching him. "Oh yes, I can't wait to get my mouth on you."

He seemed to grow larger and longer at her words. She sat back once the condom was in place.

"I had no idea you were such a dirty talker." He fisted his erection. "That's so fucking hot. Get on your hands and knees."

She never thought of herself as a woman who enjoyed taking direction in bed, but his demands turned her on. She moved fast enough so he could see that she was following his request, but slow enough so that he would know she only did it because she wanted to.

She wiggled her butt when she got to position. "Like this?"

"Oh, yes." He ran a hand across her backside. "This way, I can stare at your ass while I fuck you." His fingers trailed down to between her legs. "Or maybe I'll just tease you. Judging by the evidence, you enjoy it."

She couldn't very well argue with him, not with his fingers as wet as they were from her arousal. "Yes, but I'd enjoy having you inside me so much more."

"An impatient dirty talker," he said. "Even better. Maybe I'll just stay here and tease you all night."

It certainly appeared as though he was going to do just that. He took his cock and swept it across her slit, teasing, never pushing inside and within minutes, she was rocking against him, desperately trying to get him inside.

"Brent . . ." She couldn't keep the whine out of her voice. "Please . . ."

"Please, what?"

"I need you inside me."

He slowly entered her. She leaned forward and pressed her elbows into the mattress, bracing herself as he continued pushing into her.

"Yesss, so good." He gave a sharp thrust, setting himself inside her fully and holding still. "I could stay inside you forever. Just like this. Enjoy the feel of you so hot around my cock."

He started a lazy thrust. Retreating out an inch or two, and sliding back inside her. Yet never hard enough and not quite deep enough.

Almost.

Almost.

Almost.

He held still inside her again and, with one hand, reached between their bodies to find her clit. She bucked against him at the sensation.

"Not quite yet, my greedy girl." He removed his hand. "I'm not finished fucking you yet."

She moaned in reply to his statement, certain she'd be nothing but a puddle of girl goo by the time he finished.

"Do it then," she urged. "Hard."

He muttered a curse under his breath, but complied, moving faster and stroking into her harder. Unbelievably, she felt her release build once more inside her. She'd been almost certain after her previous orgasm that if she had another one—a big if—it would pale in comparison to the first one. But under Brent's knowledgable body, that didn't seem to be the case. It was as if each stroke into her body increased the intensity of her approaching climax.

She fisted the sheets at her hands and pushed back, urging him deeper, while at the same time not knowing how she could withstand the pleasure if he did. Behind her, his breathing grew choppy and she knew he was close.

His hand once more came between them.

"You going to come for me again?" He rubbed her clit with his thumb.

She was on the brink and it wasn't going to take much to push her over. Not with the way he was playing her body. She tried to answer him, but the only thing that came out of her mouth when she tried to speak was something that sounded like a mix between a whimper and a meow.

He rocked his hips, hitting a new spot inside her, and she was gone. Pleasure ignited within her and she came so hard, she saw stars. He followed seconds later. Overwhelmed by sensation, she collapsed onto the bed, not realizing Brent joined her until he rolled them so she rested on top of him.

He stroked her hair and peppered kisses along her forehead while his breathing returned to normal. In his arms, she felt secure and the rest of the world seemed so far away. She wished they could stay in his bedroom forever.

The shadows were growing long. Pretty soon, she would have to leave. But for now, with Brent under her and their passion temporarily abated, she could take him up on his earlier offer.

She lifted herself up on her arms and ran a finger in a figure eight across his chest.

He cracked one eye open. "What are you—"

"Shh." She pressed a finger to his lips. "My turn starts now."

"I wish you didn't have to go." He held up her right hand and kissed it, hours later. "I'd like for you to stay the night."

She had already stayed too long. She had her weekly report to write for a meeting with her boss, Martin, at nine the next morning.

"I wish I could, too. Maybe next time?" She hooked her finger around his waistband and pulled him toward her. "Because there will be a next time."

Just thinking there might be a next time was more than batshit crazy. It was risky and dangerous. To speak it out loud even more so. But there it was and she couldn't help it.

"Oh, hell, yes," he said, and dropped his head to capture her lips for a kiss that almost convinced her to forget the report and meeting. She groaned, though, because she knew she couldn't. "I have to go," she whispered against his lips.

He sighed. "I know. At least allow me to drive you home."

"My car's right outside."

He gave her one last kiss. "Okay, I won't push you, but next time?"

"Yes."

It was full dark as he walked her to her car, holding hands. Even though night had fallen, the air was still thick with humidity. A group of crickets chirped, adding their particular music to the night.

"Thank you again for a wonderful day." They had made it to her car, but she wasn't quite ready to go home and face an empty bed.

"You're welcome." He started to say something else, but his eyes widened in shock. "No!" he screamed, grabbing and pulling her to the ground. He covered her with his body, seconds before a gun sounded and her car window exploded.

Reacting totally on instinct, she reached for the revolver she carried when she was off duty and groaned in disgust when she remembered she'd put it in her purse so Brent wouldn't see it. And at the moment her purse was stuck under her and Brent.

"Are you okay?" Brent asked.

"Yes." She tried to push him off of her. "Let me up so I can see."

It was doubtful the gunman had stayed nearby. As soon as the shot was fired, yard lights began to flicker on, drowning the area in artificial light.

"We don't know if he's gone," Brent said.

"Trust me. He's gone." She didn't see anything suspicious or out of place. The only thing out of place was how fast Brent moved. Her heart still raced with the thought of how close she came to being shot. "How did you know?"

"I saw someone behind me with a gun. It was all reflected in your car window."

She stood up slowly, still looking around, still trying to find out who shot at them. "We need to call it in."

"I'm sure someone already has." Brent fumbled in his pocket for his phone anyway.

While he talked to the 911 operator, Janie stood near the car, watching as people peeked out windows and cracked open doors. She scanned the area for any possible security cameras on Brent's property, but she knew the best thing to do would be to look into any footage neighbors had. Surely in an area as wealthy as this one, people other than Brent had outside security cameras.

"Police are on their way," Brent said. He came over to her and it wasn't until he put his arms around her that she realized she was trembling. "You sure you're okay?"

"Just a bit of shock." She sighed and felt her body relax in his embrace. He still smelled like sex. "Why would someone shoot at us?"

It was the question she didn't feel comfortable voicing until she was in the security of his arms. Yes, she was an undercover cop, but he was a wealthy, well-known local public figure. The gunman could have been aiming for either of them.

"I've never had anyone come after me with a gun," he said, his unspoken question hanging in the air, *Why would anyone want to shoot you?*

She shivered and huddled closer to him, not wanting to answer, but her mind was working overtime. Was her cover blown? How? Had she stumbled upon something she didn't realize the significance of? Did someone know who she was?

The wail of sirens sounded before he had a chance to voice his question. Janie shut her eyes, wondering who from the department would respond to the call.

Two car door slammed nearby and Brent pulled away from her to address the officers.

"Mr. Taylor?" a familiar voice asked.

"That's me." He moved in front of Janie, as if to shield her, but she stepped around him and faced her two coworkers.

"Can you tell me. . . ." The rookie's voice trailed

away and his eye widened as he recognized her. She shook her head and he coughed, directing his attention back to Brent. "Can you tell me what happened?"

Brent gave his statement and the other officer made a call. Probably to alert someone that she was involved. She couldn't help but watch Brent. How was it possible that a little over an hour ago they were in bed, without a care in the world? And why had she thought it was a bad idea for her to spend the night? They could be on another round of hot sex instead of standing here, in the aftermath of being shot at.

She felt sick knowing that the guy got away because she had dropped her guard.

"Sir? Ma'am?" the officer who'd been on the phone asked. "We're going to need you to come down to the station."

Of course they would. Damn it all to hell, could this night get any worse?

An hour and a half later, she could have kicked herself, because she should have known. Things could always get worse. Like now, she was sitting in her supervisor's office, waiting for him to talk with her. From the way people were looking at her as they walked past the open door, it wasn't going to be a pleasant conversation.

She didn't know where Brent was. They had been split up as soon as they arrived. What had he been told? Was he still here? There was no one to ask and she wasn't about to step outside the office to look.

"Roberts," her boss said, coming into his office. He had a folder tucked under his arm and he closed the door. "Tell me what's going on."

She sat up straighter. "With the investigation or the shooting?"

"Neither." He slammed the folder on his desk. "I want to know what the hell you're doing traipsing around town with a potential suspect."

She flinched. There was no answer she could give. Especially since she'd done so much more than traipse for the last few hours. She decided to remain silent.

He crossed his arms and pierced her with his gaze. "If that's too much for you to handle, let's start with why you were at his house so early in the morning?"

She thought that was rather obvious so she decided, once more, not to say anything.

With her sitting down, he towered over her. "Did you or did you not meet him at the club while working undercover?"

"Yes, but—"

"Don't interrupt me." His eyes flashed and she swallowed. Damn, this was a mess.

"You're a good cop, Roberts. One of the best. That's why you're on this case. But I'll be damned if I'm going to let you screw it up because you've become involved with a suspect."

The phone on his desk rang. "Martin." He barked his name out, while still watching her. "Tell her to come on in."

His door opened and all the air left Janie's body as Alyssa walked in. Her friend didn't look her way, which was odd, and suddenly Janie had a bad feeling about what was getting ready to happen.

"Thank you," her boss said, as Alyssa handed him a file and remained there while he opened it and read the papers within it.

It seemed like forever, but surely it was only about two minutes or so until he looked up. "Is this everything?" he asked Alyssa.

"Yes, sir," Alyssa said. "May I leave?"

"No," he said. "I need you to stay here for a few minutes more."

Alyssa still wasn't looking at her, but her boss certainly was. "Not too long ago," he said, "you identified Brent Taylor as a person of interest. Is that true?"

"That's what I put my reports, sir," Janie said.

"And yet two weeks later you were at his house very late at night. Two weeks." Without waiting for confirmation, he continued, "Brent Taylor meets several of the criteria identified by our profiler." Her supervisor flipped through some more pages in the file. "Way too many, for you to be cavorting with him outside of work."

"When I first met Mr. Taylor, I thought the same thing." Janie forced herself to remain calm, a feat that grew harder with each passing beat of her heart. She knew, *she knew*, Brent wasn't their man. Yet, she'd messed up by getting involved with him. "But—"

He held his hand up. "Skin scrapings were retrieved from underneath the fingernails on the woman we found." He tapped the report Alyssa had brought in. "The DNA doesn't match Taylor's."

Oh, thank God.

She let out a sigh of relief. While her gut had told her that he wasn't the one they were looking for, her mind still wouldn't let her forget that he could be. At least not until now, when they had tangible proof that he wasn't their suspect.

"This does not negate the fact that you were involved with a potential suspect." His eyes blazed with anger. "Officer Roberts, consider yourself on suspension. You are not to go anywhere near the club, or look into this investigation any further. Someone will be in touch with you later about the details."

The look on Alyssa's face gave her some relief. From all appearances, her friend was just as shocked as she was about the suspension. Janie wanted to say and argue, but the fact was, she was exhausted and she knew she would only make things worse. Best to get a few hours of sleep and try to talk reason into her boss then.

She had to talk with Alyssa, too. What was she doing at the station this time of night? Something wasn't adding up right and she couldn't shake the feeling that something else was wrong. Unfortunately, she wasn't in the right frame of mind to work it out at the moment. Maybe after some rest and lots of coffee, she could try to put the puzzle pieces together into something that made sense.

Alyssa looked everywhere except at Janie. That was fine, they could talk later. Come to think of it, she hadn't told Alyssa about the altercation at the club with Charlie. Since it appeared Alyssa had taken the case over, she would definitely need to be aware of what happened.

She stood up. "Is Brent still here?"

Martin looked a bit shocked that she didn't argue with him. He shook his head. "No, he left about an hour ago."

She shot Alyssa a *we need to talk* look and went out the door. This night had certainly gone downhill fast. Brent was gone. Her car hadn't been released yet. And she'd been suspended. Abso-freaking-lovely.

She stepped out of the building, planning on calling a cab, when she heard her name being called softly.

She looked up and smiled. Brent had waited.

He made his way toward her and as he neared, all of the emotions of the last six hours caught up with her and she started to cry.

"Hey," Brent said, hurrying her way and putting his arms around her. He stroked her back and was so damn kind and gentle, it made her cry harder. "It's okay. You're safe. I'm right here."

She would have to explain everything to him, sooner rather than later. She didn't know how well he'd take it. But that could wait. For now, this moment, she only wanted him.

He pulled back. "What took so long? I was out an hour ago."

She sniffled. Now would be the perfect time to tell him, but she didn't want to do it like this. Not in the parking lot where she worked and not after she had just been suspended. "They had to deal with something else before they could talk to me."

He nodded and seemed to accept that reasoning. He softly stroked her hair. "I'm sorry. That's so unfair."

She looked into his eyes and shoved aside the guilt she had over lying about why she'd been inside so much longer. "I've changed my mind. I don't want to be alone tonight. Can I crash at your place?"

He wiped her lingering tears away and kissed her forehead. It was altogether soothing, and not sexual at all. "Yes, of course. You can stay for as long as you wish."

She let him lead her to his car, where he opened the door for her and saw her settled before getting in the driver's seat. For the first time in hours, she let herself take a deep breath and relax. Her mind was filled to the limit with what she saw as multiple pieces of string, each one representing a person or a thought. She needed to sit down, detangle, and lay them out flat so she could see if anything matched or could somehow be linked together.

All that she would deal with later. For right now, in this moment, she was going to take Brent up on his offer to take care of her. There were worse ways to spend the few short hours before she had to deal with the fucked-up mess her life had become.

He disappeared into the shadows at the police station, holding his breath until the headlights of their car passed by. He didn't think they saw him, but it had been damn close. He wiped the sweat off his forehead. He hadn't expected her to come out when she did, and it had probably been a mistake to follow them here, but he had to know. Had to know if they recognized him.

He was still riding the high of a recent kill—that was the only excuse he could come up with for why he came to the station instead of heading home. As he waited in his hiding place, he recalled the events of the last twelve hours.

Charlie was blind, but he was always underfoot. If he ever took the time to think about what he'd heard on the streets, it was possible he could implicate him. When he'd come across the homeless man in the alley, he'd only meant to give him a warning, but then Janie showed up. She'd put him in her car and taken him to one of the nearby shelters. If he knew Janie, he knew she'd be back in the next day or so to talk more with him.

And that wouldn't do.

So Charlie had to die.

He had waited until the old man stepped into the alley beside the shelter. It was empty and even though Charlie was blind, his hearing was sharp. The old man called out a tentative "Someone there?" as soon as he fell into step behind him, but of course there was no reply. It was too much fun seeing the look of fear in the old man's eyes. He watched from a quickly located hiding spot as Charlie tried to decide if he really heard something or if it'd all been in his head. Standing there, unable to tell if he was alone or not.

These things required patience. He didn't move from his hiding spot until the old man turned away. By the time Charlie realized his mistake, he had a knife at his throat.

So yes, he'd thought Janie would have been in the station longer. Especially with the gift of Charlie's body he'd left her at the homeless shelter.

That old man would be telling *Miss Janie* nothing. He smiled just thinking about it.

The only downside to the night had been the missed shot at Janie. His mind raced with how he could explain it. The important thing was to act as if everything was going according to plan. Yes, of course he missed. That was his intention the entire time. They didn't actually think he was going to shoot a police officer, did they? He didn't have a death wish. Oh no, he'd planned to miss. Let her off with just a warning.

That was it. A warning. It was just crazy enough to be believable.

He would tell The Gentleman he waited until the guy she was with saw him and then he shot. Of course her lover would save her. Of course he would. Besides, how crazy would it have been to shoot two people?

Though, now that he thought about it, he could have shot them both. Made it look like a mugging gone wrong. Yeah, he could have done that. And maybe . . . maybe that's what he'd tell them. He'd planned to shoot them both, but who knew so many neighbors would have heard and turned on their lights?

No, he couldn't use that excuse. The Gentleman

would want to know why he hadn't used a silencer. He'd have to go with a warning shot after all.

His phone vibrated, catching him off guard. Lately, he'd been jumping at his own shadow.

His fingers fumbled with the phone and he almost dropped it.

"Hello?" he finally asked the person who only showed up as UNKNOWN on his phone.

"Busy night tonight," The Gentleman said.

"Yes, sir," he said. "I was going to call you."

There was an ominous chuckle from the other end of the line. "I suppose you're going to tell me it all turned out the way you planned?"

He froze, resisting the urge to look over his shoulder. How did the man get inside his head like that? "Yes, sir," he answered cautiously. "I wanted to scare her."

"I think your plan may have backfired on you."

He wrinkled his forehead because that statement didn't make sense. "I don't understand, sir."

"I didn't think you would, but that's okay. You will." Something in The Gentleman's tone scared him more than getting the letter about messing up again, more than standing in that room staring at his back, praying he didn't turn around. "Trust me. You will."

CHAPTER SIX

Alyssa called her four times on the drive to Brent's house. After the fourth, Janie took her phone and shoved it to very bottom of her purse. Brent looked at her sideways. "You sure you're okay? You actually looked better before you entered the police station."

She didn't know what to say. Did she tell him she'd just been placed on leave from her job? Or that she felt like her best friend was keeping something from her? But neither of those explanations would work, not without revealing what she really did for a living.

"I know," she managed to get out. "I'll feel better once I've had a shower." She bit her lip and turned her head to look out the window, telling herself she was not going to cry again.

"Hey." He pulled into his driveway and stopped the car. "Look at me."

His touch was gentle on her shoulder and she risked a glance at him. "I don't know where to start," she said with a sniffle.

"Stay here for a second."

He hurried out of the car and crossed in front to get

to her side and open the door. The way he gathered her in his arms brought back memories of how safe she had felt in his embrace just hours before. She felt herself relax.

He kept his arm around her as he unlocked the house and got her safely inside. "Now, do you want food, shower, bed, or wine?"

Much as she'd like wine and bed, she felt grimy. "I need a shower."

No sooner had the words left her mouth did she realize she didn't have anything else to wear. Damn it. Had she been thinking, she would have had Brent stop by her house to pick up some things. That was her problem lately, she wasn't thinking.

"But I don't have any clean clothes," she said, half in exasperation, half in resignation.

"Not to worry." Brent walked toward one of the spare bedrooms. "I'm pretty sure Bea left a few things here. Let me see if I can find something. Why don't you go ahead and get in the shower? I'll put what I find on the bed. Take your time."

She loved that he was taking charge and looking after her. How long had it been since someone—anyone—did that? Certainly, not one of her exes ever came close. She turned the water on and let it get as hot as she could stand and then proceeded to stay in, just letting the water wash over her until her fingertips grew wrinkly.

The house sounded unnaturally quiet when she turned the water off. So much so that it freaked her out for a minute. She told herself to stop being silly—it was the middle of the night, what did she expect? Surely, Brent hadn't gone to bed yet. She'd hoped they could talk a little before turning in. Though she should be exhausted, the emotions of the day hadn't quite hit her yet.

She tiptoed out of the bathroom and found a soft tee and cotton shorts waiting on the bed. From the picture she'd seen, Brent's sister was taller than she was, but the clothes still fit.

Feeling much more human, she peeked into the hallway and saw a light coming from the kitchen. Brent was still up. She scurried down the hall, ready for the glass of wine he'd brought up. Maybe after she had some, she'd tell him about her job. It was time to come clean once and for all. Especially if she wanted a future with Brent. Which she did.

But when she stepped into the kitchen, she knew the wine would have to wait. Brent sat at the kitchen table. In front of him was her gun.

He looked up as she entered. "I don't mind you having secrets, but I believe I have a right to know why you're bringing a firearm into my house." She wanted to know why he felt entitled enough to go through her purse, but before she could ask, he held up her phone. "First, though, I suggest you call your friend Alyssa. She gave me an earful when I answered your phone. Damn fool thing wouldn't stop ringing."

"I don't want to talk to her," she said, feeling like a child as soon as she spoke the words.

"It's either talk to her, she said, or she's coming over."

Janie nodded. "She can see me later today. Right now I need to tell you a few things."

"Would you at least text her?" He gave her a half smile. "Because if I hear that ringtone one more time . . ."

She appreciated his attempt at humor. Quickly she

typed a text to Alyssa. **Exhausted. Going to bed. Come by after 11.**

There. That should take care of one thing on her to-do list. She looked toward Brent and took a seat beside him. Now for the most important thing.

"I'm not really a bartender," she said.

"Could have fooled me." He leaned back in his chair, looking much too good at such an ungodly hour in the morning. "I'm very sure you were tending bar when we met."

She took a deep breath. "I was undercover, working on the disappearances of several women."

He sat up straighter. "You're a cop?"

She nodded. "That's why I have a firearm in my purse. I always carry, even when I'm off duty."

He didn't say anything for a few long seconds that felt more like hours. Finally, he broke the silence. "Are you supposed to tell me? I thought that was secret?"

"As of an hour and a half ago, I've been taken off the case."

"Oh, Janie. I'm so sorry." His face contorted with understanding. "Wait . . . the shooter tonight?"

She nodded. "Was probably after me."

"But why? And how did he know you were here?"

"I don't know. I have those same questions." Suddenly, she remembered something. "The knock on the window."

Understanding flashed in his eyes. "I have a security system, with cameras." He stood up. "Let me pull the footage and see if it caught anything."

She jumped up. She tried not to get her hopes up as he motioned for her to follow him down the hall and into a small office, but it was pointless. Part of her couldn't help but think that she could solve the case tonight. Her body buzzed with excitement.

Brent pulled a second chair up to his desk so she could see the computer screen, too. He typed in a few words and within seconds, the outside of his house came into view as recorded by four cameras.

"Wow, paranoid much?" she asked, mostly kidding.

"I know it looks obsessive, but I like to be safe."

"In this case, I'm glad you are."

"Okay, this is about fifteen minutes before we arrived this afternoon. Or yesterday afternoon, more accurately." He hit a few more keys and the view pulled back, showing more of the yard.

They watched a squirrel scamper along the yard and two kids run after a wayward kick ball.

"Next-door neighbor's grandkids are in town," he explained. "That's who I thought it was."

Brent's car pulled into the screen. Hers was parked along the street and just out of the camera's view. She watched as she walked up the drive and joined Brent. On the screen, he settled his arm along her lower back and they disappeared into the house.

"I think we heard the first knock maybe about thirty minutes later," he said.

She wasn't sure either one of them breathed as they sat glued to the screen, watching and waiting for anyone or anything out of the ordinary.

"Oh my god," she said as a hooded figure came into view. They watched in silence as he approached the front window. It had to be man she was after, it had to be. Chills traveled down her spine. He had been so close to her and she'd been making out with Brent on the couch.

"I think I'm going to be sick," she said as the figure walked around the house to another window.

She looked up at Brent. His face was stony, showing no expression, but she felt the anger radiating off him.

"Who is he?" he asked through clenched teeth.

"Quite possibly the man we think is responsible for the disappearance and possible murder of several local women. From the case I'm on," she said, then added with a whisper, ". . . was on."

He cursed under his breath. "I wish you would have told me."

"I couldn't."

"This whole time, I never knew who you were. Is Janie even your real name?"

It appeared all her secrets were catching up with her. It'd finally sunk into him that she'd deceived him about who she was, what she did for a living, and now she'd led a criminal to his house. She wanted to tell him she was sorry, but she couldn't. If she had to do it all over again, she knew she would go about it the same way. Her responsibility, first and foremost, was to the hunted women.

Brent had turned his attention back to the computer screen. The only emotion visible on his face was the vein on the right side of his temple that pulsed.

"He kept his head down and his hood on." He turned the computer off. "This is worthless. Maybe tomorrow you can ask my neighbors if they'll hand over any footage they have."

"I've been suspended and I'm off the case. I have no authority."

"In that case, I'll ask them." He smiled, but it didn't

reach his eyes and she wondered if it was forced. "I think it's time we called it a night and got some rest."

Was he still upset? He was so hard to read, she couldn't tell, and it made her uneasy. "Sounds good. Where do I . . . I mean, do you want . . ." Damn, it shouldn't be this hard to ask where he wanted her to sleep. Not with everything that had happened between them in the last twenty-four hours.

"I'd like you in my bed. I know you said you didn't want to be alone."

They were silent as they got ready for bed. Janie felt like she should say something, but every time she opened her mouth, nothing came out. They crawled into bed and there in the darkened silence it felt like there was an ocean between them. Tears filled her eyes because only a few short hours ago, they'd been making love on this very bed.

She sniffled and felt the bed move as he rolled toward her.

"Hey." He put a hand on her shoulder. "What's wrong?"

"I've been such a wreck, keeping who I am a secret from you. I keep feeling like I should apologize for not telling you I was a cop, but I was undercover and the truth is, I couldn't tell you. I couldn't compromise the case. Then I feel I should apologize for sleeping with you this afternoon, but it was incredible. I refuse to degrade it by acting like it was a mistake because it wasn't and if I had it to do over again, I wouldn't change anything."

He pulled her into his arms and she burrowed into the warmth of his embrace, sighing when he kissed her forehead.

"I'll admit I was a bit taken aback," he said. "But I

know you did what you had to do. You couldn't very well tell me the first time we met that you were under-cover."

"I had made up my mind to tell you after I was suspended. But then you went and found my purse."

"I probably shouldn't have gone in your purse, but that ringtone . . ."

"I keep it annoying to make me answer it."

"It worked." His arms tightened around her briefly. "Go to sleep now. I have you, everything else can wait for a few hours."

Brent drove her to her house around ten. He told her numerous times that she could stay with him, but she refused. She told him she was not only an adult, but also a police officer and she could take care of herself. But that was only partially true. She needed time alone to think and to try to make sense out of the last few days.

Once she was home, she checked in with the department about picking her car up. Still on edge after the night before, she walked through her house, checking all the doors and windows, making sure the locks were working and secure. She double-checked her weapon and ammunition. And yet, she still jumped when her doorbell rang.

A quick glance at the clock told her it was time for Alyssa to stop by, but she verified it was her before opening the door.

Alyssa didn't look as if she'd gotten any more sleep than Janie had. At least Janie wasn't the only one.

Janie motioned to her living room, but Alyssa shook her head. "I won't be long. I just wanted to stop by to make sure you're okay and to tell you . . ." She bit her bottom lip.

"This is why you couldn't look at me last night?"

Alyssa nodded. "Yes, and there's no good way to tell you, so I'll just say it. Charlie was found stabbed to death at the shelter."

Janie grabbed the back of the chair in front of her so she wouldn't fall to the floor. An ache shot through her chest. "Charlie? Why? He didn't do anything." Another thought hit her. "Oh my god. It's my fault. I took him there. I told him he'd be safe."

Alyssa walked toward her. "It's not your fault, Janie. You didn't do this to him."

She reached out to touch her, but Janie jerked away. Her life was falling apart around her. She'd been suspended from work, Charlie had been killed, and Alyssa . . .

"I should have driven him straight to the office. If I'd done that, he'd still be alive."

Alyssa shook her head. "Don't play the *should have* game. Even if you had, he'd still have had a target on his back."

She appreciated Alyssa trying to make her feel better, but she knew the guilt would follow her for a long time. "I feel like we're getting close," she said, wanting to shift the conversation away from Charlie. "Damn it, we have to be." She couldn't stand it otherwise. Couldn't stand the thought of more death.

"He's escalating. He's going to slip and make a mistake. We'll get him," Alyssa said, when Janie finished.

"I'd like to get him *before* he has a chance to make a mistake." Maybe she'd ask around at the bar tonight, see if anyone had witnessed anything out of the ordinary after dark in the alleys and streets. Then it hit her.

No, she wouldn't. She'd been suspended. "Who's going to be working the bar?"

"I don't think anyone is. At least, not right now."

"Are you serious?" Janie couldn't believe it. "If the guy we're looking for is the same guy who killed Charlie"—damn, it hurt to say the words—"then the bar is the one place he's tied to."

"If the guy *I'm* looking for," Alyssa said gently. "You were suspended. It's no longer your case."

It pained Janie to hear those words, but she was right.

Yes, officially, she was off the case. Unofficially? That remained to be seen. This was her case. She'd been the one to put together the initial evidence. She was the one who worked the bar for hours, listening and watching. And she was going to be the one who solved it.

Brent met her for lunch later that afternoon and surprised her by bringing a picnic. He said they should eat by the waterfront and enjoy the light breeze. She appreciated the gesture, but it didn't take her mind off the fact that a killer was after her. She spent half of lunch looking over her shoulder.

Brent didn't appear to be in a hurry to get back to work after they finished. She knew he had to be busy with the potential move to Washington facing him.

"Heard anything new about the case?" he asked. "Or Charlie?"

She shook her head, trying to keep the tears for the kind old man at bay, but unable to do so. Brent scooted over and took her in his arms. She'd told him about Charlie when he called to ask her to lunch. She'd cried then, too.

"Did you have a chance to talk with your neighbors about security footage?" she asked when she'd stopped crying.

He frowned and traced her knuckles with his finger. "I did. One of them didn't have their cameras on and the other one didn't capture anything."

It was disappointing, but the truth was, she didn't expect there to be any footage of the guy. He was entirely too smart to be caught by a security camera.

"We're right back where we started," she said. "Except now I don't have a job."

"But now you have me," he replied softly.

It was surprising how much he'd come to mean to her in such a short amount of time. She should pinch herself to make sure she wasn't dreaming. To make sure she was really sitting with Brent Taylor.

She took her free hand and brushed back the long blond hair that had fallen in his eyes. "You're right, and that is no small thing. I can't imagine it any other way."

She tried not to think about him moving away or how they would work it once he did. Assuming he even wanted to try a long-distance relationship. Sitting here with him like this, it was hard to imagine him not being nearby. He lifted her hand to his lips and placed a gentle kiss on the top. The touch of his lips sent shivers of anticipation down her spine and she decided not to think about him leaving again. At least not when he was with her.

"I think I feel like going to a bar tonight. How about you?" he asked with just a hint of mischief.

"I don't know. If my boss finds out, he won't like it." *Won't like it* was an understatement. He would be furious that she'd disobeyed him.

"It's a public establishment, right?" Brent asked. "He

can't stop you from going there. All he can do is pull you from the case, and he's already done that."

She thought about it. "It'll depend on which manager is working. The one who doesn't like me may cause problems, but if it's the other one, it shouldn't be a big deal." She couldn't remember who was scheduled to work tonight. "It'll be nice to see Tilly, too. I never got to tell her good-bye."

"Is Tilly a waitress? I don't know her." He wrinkled his forehead in thought.

"Yes, and she's really sweet. She's goes to school during the day and works at night."

"I think what happened was a certain bartender caught my eye and blinded me to everyone else."

She leaned over and, much to his surprise, gave him a kiss.

"What was that for?" he asked.

"For being there that night when the creepy guy showed up. And for being here, now."

That night at eleven, Janie had Brent pull his car up to the entrance of the club. There was a line to get in, and the security guard working didn't like her. She turned him down when he asked her out the first week she worked at the bar. She wasn't sure if word would have trickled down to him that she no longer worked there.

She explained the situation to Brent, who just nodded in agreement. She told him he could go in, but he said there was no way in hell that he'd leave her alone in the car, gun or no gun. No matter how many times she told him she could take care of herself, he wouldn't change his mind.

"I'm going to send a quick text to Tilly. Let her know we're out here in case she has a free second."

She sent the text, not expecting an answer anytime soon. The club looked crowded tonight, so Tilly probably wouldn't get much of a break.

Brent pulled the car around to the side street she'd found Charlie on days before. It still hurt to think about him.

After he parked the car, Brent reached for her and she silently moved into the shelter of his arms. She didn't cry. She'd done enough of that lately, but she soaked up the warmth and comfort Brent offered. He'd known it'd be hard for her to be on this street and it meant the world that he wanted to ease that for her.

"Tell me what we're looking for," he said, pulling her mind away from Charlie and back to the reason they were there.

"In one of the early cases, we found grainy security footage of a man who appeared to be loitering around the area a woman was taken less than twenty-four hours later. We're thinking he's a Caucasian male, six feet two or three. Not sure of eye or hair color."

Nothing moved on the street. Even the wind was still. The streetlights dispelled some of the darkness, but there were still several places a person could hide. From her seat in the car, she tried to peer into them, uncover their secrets. The windows were up and the inside of the car was getting warm. Maybe it'd been stupid to come out tonight. What made tonight special anyway? Who was to say the man would strike tonight and not last night or tomorrow?

But, she told herself, if nothing else, maybe Tilly would be able to break free for a few minutes and she could tell her friend good-bye.

"Who's that?"

The alarm in Brent's voice took her by surprise. Her

head shot up and she looked to where he pointed. Her breath caught.

Someone was running down the street. She couldn't make out who it was, but she thought it was a woman. Whoever it was looked over her shoulder and fell forward, tripping over something.

Brent opened his door. "Stay in the car."

But her door was already open and she had her gun in her hand. "The hell I will."

He shook his head, but didn't say anything else about her staying behind. "Be careful, please."

She double-checked her gun and resisted the temptation to roll her eyes. "I don't mean any disrespect, but this is my job. Follow me and *you* be careful."

They inched their way toward the woman at the end of the street, who'd made it back to her feet. She wasn't running anymore, but stumbled toward them. Janie kept waiting for someone to jump out run around the corner. Her nerves were shot, but she fought it, forcing her body to do what it'd been trained to do, refusing to give into the fear.

"Janie!" the woman called out.

"Tilly!" Janie sprinted forward and motioned with her hand for Brent to hurry. "It's Tilly."

Janie made it to her friend and threw her arms around her. Tilly was still obviously frightened, her breathing was heavy and she kept looking around.

Janie took her face between her hands and forced her to look at her. "What happened? Tell me everything." A quick look at Brent confirmed he was keeping watch.

"Do we want to go back to the car?" he asked.

Tilly nodded, so Janie agreed. If it made Tilly feel better, she would do it. Besides, the car would give some semblance of cover. Tilly had twisted her ankle quite badly and couldn't walk fast, but she turned down Brent's offer to carry her to the car. Instead, they hobbled, baby step by baby step, back to the car.

They moved as quickly as possible. Janie kept her gun drawn and both she and Brent kept looking around to make sure they were alone.

Janie wasn't sure what time Tilly had left the club, but it was a given she would have been missed. Would they send someone to look for her? She offered Tilly her phone and asked if she needed to call the manager on duty, but she said she'd call later.

They made it to the car and settled Tilly in the backseat. Janie crawled in to sit beside her. Brent kept silent watch from the driver's seat.

Tilly took a deep breath and started talking. "I told the boss that I needed to step outside for a minute, that a friend was bringing me something I'd forgot and needed for my class tomorrow. He told me he'd give me ten minutes." She paused for a minute, struggling to compose herself.

Janie put her arm around her. "Take your time."

"I made it to the end of the street and someone came up beside me." She shivered. "Oh god. It was him, wasn't it?"

"I don't know." It didn't make sense. So far, all of the missing women had been Caucasian. Most of them didn't have close family members. "Did he say anything?"

"Not right away. He was just there, you know? I started walking faster and he did, too. I came to the corner and he laughed and said, 'Run, bitch. I'll give you a head start.' I looked over to him and . . . and . . ."

Janie put her hand on Tilly's knee and took a handful of tissues that Brent passed to the backseat. "It's okay. You're safe. Take your time."

Tilly blew her nose. "He had a knife. I didn't even think. I just ran. I knew you were this way."

"He didn't follow you around the corner, though," Janie said.

"Did you say anything about meeting us?" Brent asked.

Tilly shook her head. "No, I didn't say anything to him. I knew you were here and if I could just turn that corner"—she took a shuddering breath—"I'd be okay."

As far as Janie knew, no one so far had had known direct contact with the suspect and lived to tell about it. Why would he let Tilly go?

"He knew we were here," Janie said, sick with fear. "He wanted you to find us."

Tilly looked up in shock. "What? Why?"

"Fuck," Brent said, obviously coming to the same conclusion as Janie.

"What's wrong?" Tilly asked, looking from Janie to Brent.

"He was never going to do anything to you," Janie explained. "He just wanted to keep us occupied. Damn it."

She felt sick, knowing that tomorrow morning a new photo of a young woman would be flashed on the TV. A girl who had been snatched out from under their noses. Whoever was taking the girls was on to them, had studied them, knew their moves, and anticipated the ones they hadn't made yet. It was all a chess game to him and he'd just called "check."

But it wasn't checkmate. Not yet. Not by a long shot.

"Someone should probably go into the club and see

if anyone's missing. He may still be out there." Brent started the car up and inched toward the end of the street.

"I'll go in," Janie said. "The manager knows I'm a cop. Maybe he doesn't know I'm off the case. Then, I can find out if anyone's missing and let him know that Tilly was attacked and won't be back tonight."

Unfortunately, it wasn't that easy. Yes, the manager knew she was a cop, but someone, Martin, if she had to guess, had already informed the club that Janie was off the case. He refused to talk to her.

Janie punched his desk, hard enough to knock over a cup of pens. "Look. You're wasting time. Just tell me if anyone else left after Tilly. That's all I need to know and I'll get out of your office and your club forever. You don't ever have to see me again. But tell me. Please."

The manager crossed his arms over his chest. "I'm not telling you anything. I was told you're not on the case and I was to send any information I had to Officer Martin."

"One of your employees at this very moment could be in the hands of a serial kidnapper and killer. Are you just going to sit there and let her go?"

"No, he's not." Martin's voice came from the doorway.

Shit.

With a feeling of dread, she turned to find Martin and Alyssa standing just outside the half-closed office door. Martin looked angry as hell. Alyssa, on the other hand, appeared as if she wanted to crawl under the table.

"Officer Roberts, you're fired." Martin marched into the room. "Don't say another word to me and leave the premises or I'll arrest you for interfering in an active investigation."

Janie had always been told to pick her battles carefully. To know which mountains were worth dying on. She realized in that second, it was more than just that. Her job was a mountain she would die on, but the timing wasn't right.

She wasn't going to give up that easy, but she was smart enough to know that if someone was missing, that woman's life was more important than Janie's job. She walked past Martin and mouthed, *Call me,* to Alyssa. Her friend nodded and mouthed back, *Sorry.*

The smell hit her as she closed the door. Mint and cedar. She froze, looking around. She's smelled the same scent the night of the altercation between the stranger and Charlie.

The man they were looking for was here. Or had been recently. Her body pulsed with excitement. She was going to bring this bastard down.

She reached up to knock on the door, but stopped herself. Would anyone really listen to her now? Especially about a smell she *thought* might be related to the case? No, it'd only piss Martin off more, and he and Alyssa needed to get moving if they stood any chance of catching this guy.

She forced herself to leave the club and tried to ignore the feeling of defeat. Had she accomplished anything tonight, other than getting herself fired? She'd been played by a madman and all she had to show for it was a smell that probably didn't mean anything.

Brent waited for her in the car. He had wanted to come in with her, but Tilly had stayed behind and Janie knew she wasn't in the frame of mind to be alone just yet. She got into the car and said only, "Let's go. Tilly can stay with me tonight."

Later, she would tell Brent she'd been fired. Later, she would try to remember where she'd smelled that odd sent before. Later, she'd see if there was anything she could do to get her job back.

Right now, she wanted ice cream and bed. The rest of the world could wait.

But she found she couldn't relax enough to eat or enjoy the ice cream. Over and over, images of the missing girls filled her mind. Girls who would no longer eat ice cream.

The call came right at five in the afternoon, just like it did almost every Friday. His hands trembled as he answered.

"Hello?" He wondered if the new package had been received and accepted. He certainly hoped so. If it wasn't, he didn't know what he'd do. He thought it had been awfully smart of him to keep the cop and her lover busy while he waited for the real target. It made him giddy just thinking about it. Damn, when he was good, he was *good*.

"Nice job on the last delivery," The Gentleman said, and he let himself relax a tiny bit.

"Thank you, sir." He couldn't keep the smile from his voice. This last one had been nice and hearty. She should last for a long time.

"Unfortunately, that's the only good news I have for you."

His elation left. He closed his eyes and waited for the rest.

"In case you were unaware, the Charleston PD removed their plant from the club and placed her on suspension."

"Yes, sir." Of course he knew that. He'd found out it happened the night he took the shot at her. He'd wanted to laugh when he heard, but he hadn't been in a position to show how he felt. Besides, that's how he was able to concoct his brilliant plan to obtain the package.

"Officially, there's no one working the club, but you and I both know better, don't we?"

"Yes, sir." He knew exactly who was working the club now. Unofficially, of course.

"I made certain *Officer Roberts* was released from her duties."

"You got her fired?" He hadn't heard that.

"I can do anything I want."

He felt the sweat start to trickle down his back. He had a bad feeling about where this conversation was going. "Yes, sir. I know. I just didn't know you wanted her fired."

"I want more than for the plant to be fired."

He gripped the phone tighter, knowing what was coming and praying he was wrong.

"I want her for my collection and you're going to get her for me, aren't you?"

His whole body shook. Before, with the other girls, he could do what he had to because he was able to distance himself from the situation. They were a means to an end, that was all.

But he wouldn't be able to do that with Janie. There was no way and The Gentleman knew it, too. He should refuse. Take his passport and head out of the country. The dirt The Gentleman had on him wasn't worth this.

He wiped his hands on his pants. "Yes, sir. I'll get her for you." He spoke the words, but inside he thought,

There is no way in hell I'm doing that. In his mind he was already packed and on a plane.

"Good, that's what I want to hear." He paused for a second. "Oh, and just in case you're thinking about trying anything, I sent you a picture. Look at it."

Looking at a picture The Gentleman sent was the very last thing he wanted to do, but he opened the message anyway. It took him a few seconds before he realized what he was looking at. It was a candid picture of his girlfriend, walking down the street and talking on her phone.

"Call it insurance," the voice he hated more than anything said. "And just so you know, a sniper friend of mine took that picture. Someone's going to die. You get to decide if it's the ex-plant or your woman."

He swallowed, his body going clammy at his words. He was going to have to do it, he didn't have a choice.

"Do I make myself clear?" The Gentleman asked.

"Yes, sir," he whispered. "Very."

"Excellent. I'm feeling a bit generous. You have two weeks."

He wasn't able to answer before the phone went dead.

CHAPTER SEVEN

Janie scurried around the apartment, trying to get everything in order. Brent was bringing his sister over for dinner. She couldn't wait to meet the woman Brent cared so much about and shared so much of his life with. From the things he'd told her, she felt as if she already knew her.

Even better, Bea was apparently some sort of high-powered attorney and when Brent mentioned Janie getting fired, she indicated she'd like to have a chat with Janie to see if there was anything she could do. Janie didn't have the heart to tell Brent she couldn't afford his sister, so she'd gone along with it. The initial appointment was always free anyway, right?

At least at the end of the night she'd know if she had a case.

She tried not to think about how close they'd come to catching the guy. Maybe if they had, she would still have her job. But thinking that made her feel guilty and selfish because, as she'd feared, when she turned on the news the morning after they went to the club, it was there.

The headshot of the latest young girl who'd gone missing. Apparently, after Tilly didn't return, the manager had sent one of the waitresses, Robyn, out to look for her. She shook her head. What she wouldn't give to get her hands around the manager's throat or Martin's. Someone. What was he thinking letting Robyn go out by herself? Especially, when the first girl who left didn't come back.

The kidnapper had been hiding, waiting for her. No one knew if he had specifically wanted Robyn or if he just took her because she was the one who'd been sent after Tilly. Robyn fit most of the profile, but unlike the others, she had a family. A family who had already posted a substantial reward for Robyn's return. So far, they had no leads.

Alyssa had been by once. She'd hugged her and told her she was sorry and if there was anything she could do to let her know. Janie almost brought up the minty cedar smell, but talked herself out of it. They'd chit-chatted about men and insignificant things. While it felt good to talk about nothing specific, Janie was getting restless. If the talk with Bea didn't work out, she'd have to look into getting another job. Any job. She was going stir crazy in her apartment. She was a cop. It was who she was.

Brent had been a light in the darkness the last few days. Even dropping a few hints about her coming with him to Washington. She hadn't taken the bait just yet. But it was starting to sound better and better.

Her doorbell rang, interrupting her thoughts.

Ever since the knocker on Brent's door, she'd been obsessively careful. She peeked out the window and saw a deliveryman holding a long rectangular box.

Every horror movie she ever saw ran through her head.

Yeah, I'm stupid enough to fall for that one.

"What company are you with?" she asked through the door. He'd tell her and she'd call to make sure it was a legit delivery. Those chicks in the horror movies should follow her lead.

"Lady, please. I just want to deliver these flowers."

"Either tell me or leave them at the door."

She heard him say something about not having time for this and how no one told him he'd have to deal with wackos. But he eventually propped the box against a wall and left.

She was waiting for him to get in his van and leave so she could open the door, when her kitchen timer went off, alerting her the lasagna was ready.

After taking it from the oven to cool and putting a peach pie in to cook, she looked around. Everything was in place. The table was set. Food was ready. Brent was bringing the wine.

She stopped by her bathroom to check her hair and makeup. On a whim, she redid her lipstick and grinned at herself in the mirror to make sure there wasn't any on her teeth.

The doorbell rang again and a quick glance at the clock told her it was probably Brent and Bea.

"Be right there," she called.

After verifying it was them, she opened the door. Brent looked as good as ever. Today he was dressed casually in jeans and a tee. He gave her a quick kiss before turning to the stunning woman at his side. "Janie, this is my little sister, Beatrice."

His sister rolled her eyes. "I'm not going to kill you

for calling me that since this is the first time I'm meeting your girlfriend and I'm not sure how good she is at getting blood off of things." She held out her hand. "I'm Bea."

Bea didn't share her brother's golden looks. While he reminded her of sunshine and summer, Bea was a fiery fall, with long red hair, pale skin, and deep brown eyes.

"Janie." She shook her hand. "I've heard so much about you."

"Likewise."

"Looks like you got some flowers." Bea punched Brent on the arm.

"The deliveryman brought them about fifteen minutes ago. You didn't have to send me flowers, but it was awful sweet of you," she said with a smile. "And you didn't have to have them delivered. I'm sure the guy who brought them by thinks I'm crazy."

Brent picked the box up. "They aren't from me, and there's no florist listed on the box."

She forced herself to remain upright instead of crumpling to the floor like she wanted to. "Oh, god. It's not over, is it?"

"We should open it." Brent ran a finger along the edge.

"Inside," Janie said. "If it's him, he's watching."

Brent didn't say anything, but nodded in agreement and carried the box inside. He sat the box on her coffee table. Janie let herself collapse onto the couch.

"Want me to open it?" Brent asked.

Yes! she wanted to scream, but shook her head. "No. I'll do it."

She wasn't sure what she expected to be the box, but she was actually a little relieved as she took a deep breath and lifted the top off, revealing a dozen perfect red roses.

"Wow," Bea said. "Those are gorgeous. Is there a card?"

Brent reached into the box and pulled out a plain white card. He sat down on the couch beside her so she could read along with him.

Roses are red.
Violets are blue.
These flowers will die.
Just like you.

Read on for an excerpt from
the next novel in the *Sons of Broad* series

DEADLY
SECRET

Coming soon from St. Martin's Paperbacks

For a fleeting moment, she thought about asking him to come inside. He was already in her driveway, what were a few feet more? If she invited him in, she knew he'd sit as close to her as possible. He'd probably put his arm around her. It'd feel so good to be wrapped in his warmth.

But no, she couldn't risk it.

She was too wound up to go to bed and she wasn't in the mood to clean. She eyed the huge soaker tub in her bathroom. Now that sounded like a good idea. It had been way too long since she relaxed in the tub. At the moment, a hot and sudsy bath sounded like heaven on earth.

She started the water, poured in her favorite shower gel, and waited as the room filled with mist and the smell of lavender. Her fluffy bathrobe was in place for when she stepped out and her slippers waited beside. She hummed and swirled a finger in the water to test the temperature.

Perfect.

She pulled her hair up into a ponytail on top of her

head, grabbed her eye mask, and stepped into the tub. With a sigh, she allowed herself to sink shoulder deep and enjoy the warmth of the water.

She wasn't sure what first tipped her off that something wasn't right. One second she was enjoying her bath and the next, she had that prickly feeling she always got when someone was watching her. She told herself it was stupid, there was no one in the bathroom and no one could've got past Knox and made it into her house.

Unless they killed Knox.

Shit. Shit. Shit. Why hadn't she thought of that possibility?

She made it out of the tub with an ungraceful splash and threw her robe on. She didn't hear it until she stepped into the hallway.

Tick.

Tick.

Tick.

Her body shook with fear, her fingers so badly, she didn't think she could dial the police if she tried. *Someone was inside her house.*

Irvin L. Young Memorial Library
431 W. Center Street
Whitewater, WI 53190

Irvin L. Young Memorial Library
431 W. Center Street
Whitewater, WI 53190